SENTINELS of the DEEP

A Novel

J.S. Dunham

This is a work of fiction. Names, characters, places, events, and incidents are either products of the author's imagination or used in a fictitious manner. Any resemblance to actual persons, living or dead, or actual events is purely coincidental.

Tellwell Talent
www.tellwell.ca

ISBN
978-1-77370-582-8 (Hardcover)
978-1-77370-581-1 (Paperback)
978-1-77370-583-5 (eBook)

To Leah and Tessa

We ask you to clean
up your toys, yet
we've left you with an
impossible mess...

About the author...

Jason is a marine scientist who has been studying sea life in the North Pacific for more than 20 years. His research on whales and invertebrates has been published in scientific journals. Jason lives in British Columbia, Canada, with his wife and two children.

PROLOGUE

Andrea walked barefoot through ankle-deep water on the West Coast of central Vancouver Island. Stringy green algae mats covered much of the pebbles and sand. Sometimes a jagged piece of broken clam shell pricked the thickened soles of her feet. Countless green crabs the size of golf balls scuttled like cockroaches amongst shell fragments. Often she stopped and, crouching, pushed away bumpy green sheets of sea lettuce to find siphon shows of her favorite clams, cockles and butters. They were much harder to find now, ever since green crabs first appeared on the beach five years ago. Once again invaders from Europe were destroying Indigenous Peoples traditional food sources.

She reached behind her head and tugged two handfuls of long, black hair to tighten her ponytail. She often wore her hair this way to show her unusual green eyes, high cheekbones, and delicate features in a practical and professional manner. Andrea was Nuu-Chah-Nulth; the fiercely proud First Nation community had been living on the West Coast for thousands of years. She looked like her dad with her light brown skin and slender physique but, by the ninth grade, she had grown at least five centimeters taller than him.

She took a sip of mineral water from a thermos stored on the side of her knapsack. Sundrop scampered near the surf line searching for little treasures the ocean delivers to beaches on every high tide. As the low swell retreated, she ran down hard-packed sand flats after the receding foam only to be chased back to higher ground by a new wave sweeping across the bay. Andrea smiled, remembering her childhood, playing here during those long summer days with her sister, Laura, and an ever-changing pack of semi-feral dogs from the village. Together they chased flocks of plovers back and forth across the beach as the tiny birds scavenged for worms and insects living in the sand. Lunch was usually delicious homemade bannock cooked in the sand under an open fire.

Sundrop waved a stick over her head. "Mom, squid are everywhere."

Reluctantly Andrea walked down the slope of the beach. Biology had become the study of death, not life. Seaward, out in the bay, wisps of fog swirled around three rocky islets with scrubby vegetation that protected the bay and salmon farm from ocean swells. The distant hum of farm operations mixed with frequent 'caw caw' cries made by crows sitting amongst piles of splintered logs strewn haphazardly in the high intertidal by fierce winter storms.

Sundrop proudly stabbed a gelatinous blob with a slender piece of driftwood. Small for a seven-year-old and nicely pudgy, her straight black hair fell past her shoulders. Short cut bangs topped brown eyes and a kind, round face.

Hundreds, maybe thousands, of squid lay scattered at the water's edge—in places the relentless surf had piled them on top of one another. What would cause a mass mortality event like this? *Not another oil spill...please, Tiskin.* Thankfully no slick black ooze covered the brown sand. Andrea knelt over a decomposing squid, grasped two of its arms, and shook the sand off. The Humboldt squid was as long as her leg and mostly white and gray with blotches of red and brown. The mantle, tapered like a bullet, covered half the animal and terminated at two clear fins splayed open. Below the mantle, eight arms with rows of round suckers, and two longer tentacles, flopped on the wet sand. She habitually checked the ends of the fourth arms for the hectocotylus, a modified structure mature males develop to transfer sperm packages to females.

She stood and arched her shoulders and head backward, stretching. How different would the world be if human reproduction mimicked what squid do and guys simply handed globs of their sperm to lucky ladies? She snickered. Shaking hands would have a whole new meaning, that's for sure.

Ahead, a peculiar mound seemed out of place on the gently sloping beach. The mound was black and smooth, not brown and rugged like the rest of the beach.

"Sure you won't come with me to see it?"

Sundrop defiantly shook her head. "No, it's dead."

"So are the squid and most clams. This doesn't bother you?"

Sundrop dug her right foot toes into the sand and kicked the clump forward.

Andrea hugged her. "We'll only see live ones in the Galapagos, I promise."

Deliberately breathing through her mouth to not smell the awful stench, she continued walking alone. The sperm whale swam ashore three days ago according to her cousins. Four more whales had stranded to the north at Hesquiat Harbour. As long as a school bus, it lay partially on its side, the lower jaw, outlined in white, gaped open showing two rows of conical teeth. The large, square, barrel-shaped nose gave the whale's head a box-like shape. Seeing white streaks on the nose, she started jogging. The marks were long rows of circular scars made by suckers on tentacles of dying squid. Using her thumb and index finger, she measured several of the biggest scars and, from their size, concluded *Architeuthis* might have made them. She grinned at her discovery. Soon she will be the first person to capture video footage of epic deep sea battles between sperm whales and giant squid. Slender manicured fingers traced along crisscrossed deep permanent scratches where razor-sharp hooks at the end of tentacles had raked across the skin. How big were squid that made these? The largest *Architeuthis* she knew, pulled from the stomach in a fourteen meter sperm whale, was over ten meters long and weighed one hundred and eighty-five kilograms.

She walked past the unmoving eye and flipper and stood near the middle of the emaciated body. Kneeling, she pulled from her knapsack a red rubber disk the size of a dinner plate and pushed it firmly against the whale's side. To her dismay the flattened suction cup quickly regained its shape and dropped on the sand. She brushed it off and pushed it harder against the whale. Within minutes air seeped back into the suction cup and it fell off.

The whale's glossy, black skin was darker than a moonless night and thick like an elephant's hide. Dimpled irregular ridges snaked across the surface—escape paths for trapped air. The skin peeled in places suggesting the whale might have died from complications related to poor nourishment. Odd, considering countless Humboldt squid now jet through the North Pacific. A whale this big needs to eat hundreds of squid every day. If squid were dying en masse, most won't end up on beaches where someone can count them.

As she wiped the rubber material against her black hiking pants, she felt somewhat foolish. There was no one in sight yet—it was still early. They had deliberately arrived soon after first light to avoid tourists from Tofino who would eventually materialize to see the monster that had invaded the beach.

She climbed awkwardly up the slippery tail on top of the dead sperm whale. Behind the gaping S-shaped blowhole she dropped to her knees, pushed the suction cup against the skin, and started the stopwatch. Carefully she straightened and embraced the view from several meters above the beach. Sundrop was running wildly dragging a long piece of bull kelp. A German shepherd galloped toward the whale. This must be a dog's fantasy come true, all those smells, bones, and meat. A dark figure, probably the animal's owner, walked near the water in the distance. Sparse old growth Douglas-fir and cedar trees, intentionally left standing by logging companies to hide slash and burn clear cuts further inland, fringed the beach. In the distance beyond, like crosscut saw teeth, rugged gray peaks of the Coast Mountains cut a serrated swathe through the morning blue sky.

Legends she had learned growing up from watching dancers and listening to songs were never more vivid than now. Whaling was in her blood. Fondly she remembered resting in her grandfather's strong arms next to the crackling bonfire on the beach fronting the village, warm sand crumbling off her tiny toes. His colorful stories about their great whaling nation droned around her and joined smoke flowing into the night sky.

She paddled with ten brave warriors in a giant cedar whaling canoe whose bow flared to a sharp point with Thunderbird facing upward, wings spread out toward the hunters. Pointed paddle blades quietly pierced ocean waves as they cautiously approached a southward migrating gray whale swimming to warm calving lagoons in Baja after gorging all summer on amphipods living in the sand on the bottom of the Bering and Chukchi Seas. One of the muscular young men precariously stood and, aiming for the heart, thrust with all his strength a long harpoon deep into the whale's barnacle-encrusted side. The great beast thrashed its fluke from side to side and then dove, but could only struggle into shallow depths because of inflated seal skin floats attached to the harpoon rope. When the whale surfaced again, Andrea jumped out of the canoe onto the whale's back and dropped a rock in the blowhole. They cut its throat to let the blood out. When the whale rolled over dead at the surface, she plunged into the cold Pacific to sew its mouth closed and plug the throat so the carcass would remain full of air and not sink while they towed it to the village.

The flattened suction cup started hissing and swelling. The seal broke for good in nine minutes and thirty-two seconds. This wasn't nearly long enough; it had to stick for hours and hold the weight of a camera.

She flung the red disk like a Frisbee at the knapsack below. Precious time was swiftly running out. She needed to return immediately to Texas A&M University and talk to someone, perhaps students in the mechanical engineering department, and figure out a way to improve the adhesive capability of the suction cup.

ONE

"Over there!" Andrea shouted, pointing where a massive gray-colored head punched through the waves. Half the body lunged out of the water; white froth streamed off the giant's back. Fifteen tons then smashed down with a thundering splash. Squealing, Sundrop jumped up and down next to the guard rail. Stale air exploded from the sperm whale's lungs spraying water vapor out the blowhole three meters high. A nasal-sounding inhalation followed when the whale sucked a tremendous volume of fresh air into its nostril to feed oxygen-deprived tissues. Two more thunderous explosions erupted nearby where a pair of whales broke through the surface, one whale hurtling almost entirely out of the water. Massive heads, some black, others more gray or whitish, leapt up from the depths as remaining members in the group reached the surface. Cheers and clapping from the research ship acknowledged the arrivals.

The sperm whales respired in a cohesive group; exploding and sucking sounds shattered the afternoon's tranquil stillness. Breaths were short and rapid—each whale spouted about once every ten seconds to replenish oxygen reserves in its massive body. Panting continued for several minutes while the whales formed clusters of twos and threes swimming side-by-side a few meters apart. Gradually they settled and milled about, their breathing rates slowing until spouts blasted skyward every twelve seconds. They started swimming in a westerly direction away from the ship and its curious occupants gently rolling in the low South Pacific swell downwind hundreds of meters away.

Andrea stepped back from the rail. Such cautious animals, surprising considering their enormous size. She grudgingly respected their careful nature even though this inherent characteristic will probably wreck her research. No doubt it helps them survive. She disliked when people referred to sperm whales as shy. Nosy strangers who abruptly thrust their faces centimeters from Sundrop often called her shy when she recoiled from the intrusion. Like sperm whales, Sundrop wasn't shy, only cautious, and rightfully so. Andrea loved that about her.

A helicopter carrying two kayaks flew low over the R/V *M. Rubicola*, narrowly missing the deck's dangerous protrusions, the gantry crane arching mid ship and the telescoping boom crane mounted on the back corner near a zodiac. It landed gently on the white letter H painted in the center of the unfolded landing pad.

Eager to finally meet Josh, Andrea walked along the side of the deck through the swarming crowd as people congregated in the sunshine hoping to see glimpses of the leviathans. Leaning against the crane, she waited while the rotor blades gradually stopped spinning. A welcomed quietness replaced the noisy clatter. She had first spoken to Josh on the phone several days ago for about fifteen minutes. That's all she knew about the guy, and his sperm whale research. She worried he might be a quirky fuddy-duddy scientist who won't fit in with her research team.

The thin metal door swung open and a tall man stepped down onto the deck. Instinctively he lowered his head and walked briskly beyond the deadly arc of the rotor blades.

She waved and jogged over to her lost-looking guest. "Welcome to the Galapagos, Dr. Templeton." She ignored his outstretched hand and hugged him. His chest felt quite hard. He flinched so she let him go.

He grinned. "Thanks for the invitation...and reception. I'm really looking forward to the next few days."

Great smile. She had envisioned an older man, maybe because of his deep phone voice and impressive publication record. Instead, he looked more like a soccer player than a marine biologist—lean, with full lips perched above a square jaw, brown hair peeking out beneath a baseball cap. His blue tee shirt didn't match the khaki shorts, but it's probably just old boat clothes. Faint crow's feet pegged him to be an outdoors-kind-of-guy, probably in his early thirties, pretty young for a mad scientist. Not bad looking for an academic. Crew won't be happy.

"Your timing couldn't be better," she said. "The hydrophones picked up the whales an hour ago."

"We could see eight from the air. Let's get out to them before they dive."

The *Rubicola* powered forward, her bow thrusters fired, and she started turning.

Durant's voice boomed over the P.A. system. "Starboard side, folks."

Like a viscous liquid moving in a tilted container, people standing on the wrong side of the ship flowed to the right side. Josh jogged to the helicopter and wrestled a duffel bag, backpack, and laptop from the compartment in the fuselage. Crew, their blue uniforms emboldening them, chatted incessantly with the women researchers. Their endless generous offers to help were welcomed, but sometimes distracting. Andrea smiled. Poor me. And now sexy Josh.

She approached Naeco, a graduate student wearing a one piece orange bathing suit, her brown hair tightly packaged in beaded dreadlocks. Peach fuzz on her arms and legs glistened in the sunlight. Several homemade string bracelets slid around her wrists and ankles. "Naeco, can you and the crew please untie the kayaks and move them over to the side while I show Dr. Templeton his cabin."

She turned her attention back to Josh. "I certainly appreciate your efforts to get here so quickly. You must be exhausted."

He lowered the duffel bag to adjust his grip. "It's been a long couple days. Lots of waiting between flights..."

She led him across the main deck, the outdoor portion of the upper deck. Two thirds of the ship's length was designated the main deck, making her a capable support platform for a variety of marine science research experiments.

"...after you called, I left the next day for Vancouver," he said. "Then I waited about three hours for the flight to Dallas/Fort Worth International. I waited again almost six hours for the connecting flight to Guayaquil. I spent last night in a motel which was pretty comfortable except some rooster started cockadoodledooing early this morning. We left around nine for Puerto Baquerizo Moreno. That was a fun flight. The plane flew quite low so you could see lots of scenery."

The superstructure sat forward, decks and walls scrubbed shiny white by seamen working under the watchful eye of the Bosun. Stairs bottoming on the left side of the main deck led up to the fo'c'sle deck where two orange zodiacs sat ready to be launched at a moment's notice.

"Any luck attaching the crittercam?" he asked.

"No. The whales won't let us get close enough. It's been unbelievably frustrating."

"Engine noise probably scares them."

Stairs continued past the zodiacs up to the bridge deck. The bridge, encircled by broad square windows, provided the Captain and Officers of the Watch with a commanding view of the ship's exterior and surrounding waters.

"At first we used the workboat—I think it has a seventy-five horsepower engine. We've been trying one of the marshalling boats, but it hasn't worked much better."

They hurried into the superstructure and through the mudroom where crew removed deck gear and washed their dirty hands in two broad stainless steel sinks.

She paused at a room where several people sat in booths. "This is the mess. Lunch is over, but there's something waiting for you in that fridge there."

Two seamen walked past, one of whom unabashedly checked her out from head to toe. She winked at him.

They climbed down steep metal stairs to the second deck.

"I've found a steady noise that gradually gets louder doesn't seem to bug them as much as an abrupt change in sound," Josh said, as they walked past lockers and a public washroom. "The kayaks should do the trick."

"I hope so. They're our last chance."

They headed down a narrow hallway, stepped through a watertight door, and stopped at the first cabin on the right.

She knocked on the closed door, listened, and then opened it. "Your home away from home."

Brushing past her, he entered the small, clean room. On their left were two latched pine closets where guests could hang clothes. To the right of the entrance in the corner was a desk with an inexpensive chair tucked in close. Next to the desk a sink with a shaving mirror above it protruded from the wall. A gray blanket covered the bunk against the far wall.

She pointed at a neatly folded blue towel on the lower bunk. "The reason why I tracked you down."

Josh dropped his luggage by the sink. He unraveled the towel; inside was a stained satellite-linked tag covered with white barnacles.

"Naeco found it floating in the water."

He wiped the casing and found the serial number. "This is definitely the tag we attached to the bull. Have you seen him?"

"Not yet...sorry." She nodded in the opposite direction from where they had just come. "You need to get signed in on the bridge—"

"Right now?"

"Captain's orders. Head down here and go up the stairs to the bridge. Get your butt on deck whenever they let you go. We'll have the kayaks ready and waiting."

"I'm still amazed the bull travelled here from Hawaii. I sure hope he gets a chance to breed. There are so few males around anymore. Their numbers keep declining, now more than ever."

"How come?"

"Don't know. The bull's behavior was bizarre. I think something's happening in the ocean."

She smiled to hide her fear and touched his arm. "It's wonderful you're here, Josh. With your experience tagging sperm whales, I know we'll finally be able to attach the crittercam."

"Your research program is brilliant, Andrea. You know better than anyone squid are a critical part of oceanic food webs. Hopefully the whales will show us what's happening in the deep."

Encouraged by his kind words, she jogged back the same way they came. Emerging on deck, she squinted from the bright sun, it being such a contrast to the ship's dim interior. She snaked through the crowd to sneak up behind Sundrop who was sandwiched between Randi and several adults.

Sundrop was standing on her toes peering over the side at a cluster of whales hundreds of meters away. She wore purple shorts and a white tee shirt with pink horizontal stripes. A blue beaded necklace matched her earrings.

Using the crane, the Bosun lowered the workboat into the water.

Randi gently held Sundrop's hand when she started chewing her fingernails. Randi's green wide-brimmed hat didn't completely hide luxurious coils of red hair bouncing along freckled porcelain cheeks. Her yellow hoody and gray yoga pants seemed out of place on the ship—she could've stepped straight out of a television commercial.

"Please stay close to Randi while I'm kayaking," Andrea said to Sundrop. "Keep out of the crew's way and always watch out above you."

Sundrop rolled her eyes. "Mom, you say that every day."

Two seamen flung a ladder over the side and climbed down into the zodiac. They unhooked the boat and drove it around to the left side where they tied it against the ship. Naeco and a couple guys lowered the kayaks, one at a time, in a sling to the workboat. They lifted the kayaks by hand into the water and tied them against the blue pontoons. The Officers of the Watch kept the *Rubicola* positioned so the ship would provide an effective barrier to the wind allowing the three small craft tied alongside to float relatively undisturbed in a protected calm patch of water.

Wearing a snug black wetsuit, a red lifejacket, and a neoprene spray skirt around her waist, Andrea hung suspended high above the water against the side of the *Rubicola,* her left foot searching aimlessly for the next step below. Small hands held on white-knuckle tight to the two ropes that passed through the series of wooden treads. She never would have dreamed her fear of heights would be tested while working at sea level. When the *Rubicola* rolled to one side, nails dug into her palms as the side ladder swung away from the ship. Her foot eventually found the next step and lower she climbed, gingerly, toward the zodiac below.

Thrilled to have something solid beneath her feet once again, she inspected the components of the crittercam, all wrapped in a titanium cylinder perched at one end of a telescoping pole. Attached to a red suction cup were a video camera, sound and depth sensors, data logger, computer, and radio beacon. Hopefully the newly designed barbed suction cup would do its job; her research program depended on it. She ran her hand over the fiberglass kayaks' smooth curves. Both boats were canary yellow on top and white underneath.

Naeco and Rene, a petit boyish-looking blonde, leaned over the workboat's pontoon and held the kayak steady while Andrea squeezed into the front cockpit. She stretched the spray skirt over the cockpit to seal it watertight. Strapped to the kayak in front of her was the standard safety equipment: a hand pump, paddle float, and floating heaving line, and an extra paddle should she need it. Josh handed her the crittercam pole which she held firmly above her lap with arms bent at ninety degrees. He climbed into the cockpit behind her, untied the lines, and pushed the tipsy boat away from the safety of the *Rubicola.*

Gentle gusts buffeted the kayak. A surprisingly sturdy wave broke against the side. Her entire body tensed. She felt unbalanced from the weight of the crittercam at one end of the pole. Choppy waves broken by the kayak's sleek bow soaked her bare arms. Thankfully Josh seemed like a strong paddler and soon they were travelling straight as an arrow toward the whales a kilometer away. Warm wind at their backs pushed them along. Plenty of open water now separated them from the ship. Hard to believe her great grandfather routinely paddled in a canoe eighty kilometers offshore to spear migrating northern fur seals. Soon her left shoulder started aching, an unpleasant reminder of the time when she cracked her collar bone playing field hockey in college.

She rested the pole across the spray skirt. Beads of sweat rolled down her temples. "Where did you do your PhD, Josh?"

"In Montreal at McGill."

"Why did you study sperm whales?"

"I was doing my Masters tagging gray seals at their rookery on Sable Island when four sperm whales stranded basically in front of my tent. One survived for three days so we got to know each other pretty well." He paused. "For my PhD I switched species and tagged Atlantic sperm whales to better understand their social dynamics. Their social structure isn't very common in the animal kingdom. Long-finned pilot whales and orcas show similarities. Elephants are the most similar."

"What do you like to do when you're not harassing whales?"

He kept paddling. "I, uh, teach at the university, supervise grad students, work on data collected during field seasons, globe trot all over the world on a whim to assist other researchers. Typical prof stuff."

"What do you do in your free time? You know, for fun." She took several sips of water from a bottle.

"I used to do outdoor activities like camping and climbing, but not so much anymore. I SCUBA dive fairly often."

She wiggled her lower body to get more comfortable.

"What do you do when you're not harassing squid?" he asked.

"Oh, hang out with my daughter."

There was a long pause. "Sounds nice, you're lucky."

Soon the two women caught up. Rene was paddling furiously while Naeco filmed them and the whales. The kayaks, one shadowing the other, moved slowly into the group because only one paddle propelled each boat.

The lethargic whales resembled logs with their rounded dorsal fins and backs just out of the water. Some whales swam alone, others clustered in twos or threes oriented in the same direction spaced about two hundred meters apart. The group moved in rank formation steadily westward at three kilometers per hour. Josh needed to keep paddling to stay with the herd. One whale sidefluked showing only a portion of its tail. Two others performed shallow dives; they didn't fluke-up and disappeared for only a minute or two.

"It's nerve-wracking being so low on the water near such large animals." Andrea had felt much safer in the workboat. One whack from a well-placed fluke.... She glanced anxiously around the kayak for whales surfacing under them.

"I count eleven whales," Josh said. "We probably have two, maybe one, social unit here."

"What's a social unit?"

"It's a group of females and immatures that are constant companions and live together for many years. There could be more than one matriline which is a grandmother, mother, and an immature."

They glided within forty meters of three sperm whales swimming side by side. Small waves washed over the backs of their immense black bodies.

She felt a wonderful burst of energy. "It's working, Josh. We could never get this close in the workboat. They don't seem to notice we're here."

"Oh, they know. They just don't perceive us as threatening."

She peeled away the spray skirt to access a video camera. With the pole precariously balanced across her lap, she panned the camera around zooming in and out on the backs of the three whales. The cluster didn't exhibit any avoidance behavior. Josh was bang-on about the kayaks. In a low voice she said, "Our mission now, Dr. Templeton, if you choose to accept it, is to move closer to these whales."

"Hey, that's my kind of mission. I accept, ma'am."

He nudged the kayak ahead. Two whales swam side by side, the third slightly behind. Their breathing rates had synchronized; three consecutive violent exhalations blasted moist droplets skyward, some of which settled on her and, unfortunately, the camera lens.

Grinning, she lowered the camera. "Yay, we're too close!" Reaching behind the seat, she felt around for a square plastic container. From it she pulled out a soft cloth to wipe the lens clean. This was the best footage she had gotten so far.

Josh carefully back-paddled them away from the whales. A loud splashing sound startled her. A sperm whale, its head pointed downward, raised its tail in the air and then swung it down slapping the water's surface.

"That's called lobtailing," he said.

The whale repeated the movement, slapping its tail again and again.

She knew the term for the behavior. "I've seen that before. Why does it do that?"

"She."

The whale stopped after making seven loud splashes.

"How do you know it's...she's a she?"

"Females are smaller and slimmer than males. You often see this in polygamous mammals. Mature females sometimes have a whitish callus on the dorsal fin. It's a secondary sexual characteristic." He pointed with the paddle blade. "You can see it on that whale over there."

"That one has it too."

"Yep, she's a female. The callus isn't a foolproof indicator though. Not all females have them and sometimes immature males do. They aren't born with them so their growth might be stimulated by estrogen or some female hormone."

"These are all females."

"I know," he said, sounding disappointed. "I don't see the bull. Have you seen any spouts windward from the group? Sometimes bulls withdraw a short distance away."

She turned to face the ocean breeze. Only a ship far away interrupted the thin horizon line.

"Whalers have killed about seventy percent of sperm whales, especially bulls."

Numerous white specks hovered behind the *Rubicola* indicating crew were cleaning the trawl net. "Were sperm whales hunted for food?" she asked.

"Not really, more for oil in their heads. That's what started the open boat hunt in the seventeen-hundreds. They were hunted in the Atlantic first, then the Pacific, and then the Indian Ocean. Between eighteen-twenty and eighteen-sixty tens of thousands were killed. In nineteen-sixty-five the Russians and Japanese killed twenty-three thousand in the North Pacific alone."

Andrea sat perfectly still, elbows resting against her sides, holding the pole parallel above the waves. Droplets trickled down the smooth shaft and dribbled off the crittercam into the ocean. She had yet to hear a story about non-Indigenous people hunting only what they needed for survival. They always slaughtered their quarry until an irrelevant few remained. They were exterminators.

"Actually sperm whales have fared better than other whales," Josh said.

"Now that's looking at the bright side."

"They were generally left alone while whalers targeted baleen whales. By the nineteen-fifties most baleen whales had become scarce, many populations reduced by ninety percent or more. Whalers have killed a biomass of whales equivalent to one and a half billion people."

A sudden sense of urgency took hold. She pointed at an adult female milling about sixty meters away. "Can we put the crittercam on that one?"

Dipping the paddle in the water, he steered them around the resting whale so the sun was behind them. She took several photographs of the female floating lazily near them.

A young sperm whale suddenly appeared alongside and bumped the kayak with its pectoral fin. Startled, Andrea automatically pressed her knees against the inside of the cockpit for stability and unconsciously lowered her hand to steady the rocking motion. Inadvertently she touched the wrinkled gray back of the whale. Her hand jerked out of the water. The whale's eye rolled upward and held her gaze.

Its curiosity apparently satisfied, the young sperm whale sank deeper under the kayak and, with an easy flick of its tail, vanished for a few seconds until its head popped out of the water several meters away, as if to take one last look. Before she could aim her camera the curious animal slid back under the waves and disappeared.

She twisted around. "That was amazing! Did you see it wink at me? You could tell there was something going on behind that eye. What a cutie."

"You made a new friend today."

Clusters were even bigger now with three to five whales in each. It was a good sign; the herd was starting to socialize.

"Check out that dive puddle, thirty degrees on the starboard bow," Josh said. A soupy brown patch floated at the surface. "That whale's been feeding."

"They're definitely not moving as much anymore. If they're doubling back there's probably prey here."

Quite a racket echoed across the tropical ocean. Staccato sounds of air being pushed with great force through large pipes punctuated the afternoon stillness. The giant beasts splashed about more vigorously. Several raised their tails high in the air and then smacked them against the surface. On occasion a whale leapt above the waves. Unusual sounds generated by the whales, like whistles and chirps, and occasionally a dull knocking, penetrated the fiberglass kayak.

Josh steered them toward a nearby cluster, in particular a solitary individual with no other whales close by. "I like the way this one's behaving."

The whale was logging—lying still at the surface—her tail hanging down. Only portions of her black head and dorsal hump were visible. They approached the whale from behind out of her line of sight. The whale remained motionless as if daring them to try and place the crittercam on.

"Ready, Andrea?" he said, quietly.

"I'll apologize now in case I throw up." She raised the pole up high holding the crittercam steady three meters off to the side.

The kayak moved parallel to the whale, remaining about one meter from its leathery side. The rank smell of whale breath filled their nostrils. The crittercam at the end of the pole dangled precariously over the whale's back. The sperm whale, four times longer than the kayak, barely moved, seemingly unaware of the commotion around it.

With arms straight out, Andrea leaned over to lower the crittercam. At that moment the whale started rolling.

An unseen force lifted the front of the kayak. Suspended in the air, she let out a muffled shriek and dropped the pole. Josh shouted something behind her. The kayak fell hard to one side.

Warm seawater smashed the side of her face and flooded her wetsuit. Groggy, struggling to remain calm, she groped blindly with her left hand for the pull tab sticking up on the spray skirt. She wrestled the skirt off the cockpit and pushed and kicked until her legs slipped free from inside the kayak. The blurry shape of Josh's body floated above. She shot to the surface next to him. He was treading water vigorously, anxiously looking down.

"Where's the whale?" she sputtered.

"Behind you."

She spun around. Then she remembered. "Oh, no! The crittercam!?" Splashing, she rotated again and started feeling dizzy.

He chortled. "I got it. I'm alright, too, thanks for asking." He pushed the pole through the water in her direction. "Hold on to it." He swam over to the upside down kayak and raised the bow above the surface which allowed much of the water inside to drain away.

The sperm whale that had flipped their kayak drifted to within five meters and remained broadside to the swimmers.

Watching the whale with trepidation, she moved closer to Josh. *Does it think we're juicy squid?*

"I've never seen a sperm whale from this perspective," he said.

"This would make an amazing photograph."

He gently tugged her arm. "I don't think she can see us now. They're a bit far-sighted."

Suddenly the whale broadcast a creak-like sound into the water. Andrea grunted and doubled over, her arms instinctively wrapping around her midsection for protection. The whale seemed to have mysteriously reached out and somehow punched her.

The sperm whale silently faced them and then flipped its right pectoral fin and moved slightly to the side, its round eye following them. Andrea held her breath when it glided past several meters away.

Still clutching her chest, she turned to Josh. "Please tell me what happened."

"Are you hurt?"

"Not really. It felt like something hit me in the chest. It just surprised me, that's all."

"I think you were nailed by sound waves generated by that whale. That's incredible! She looked right at you using sound waves instead of light waves."

"Why me? Why not you too?" Any other time she would have loved his youthful enthusiasm.

"Andrea, this is fantastic. Their vocalizations truly are highly directional." He spun around searching for the whale. "I wish it did happen to me. Maybe I can catch up to her." He started swimming away.

She laughed. "Get back here! Don't you leave me."

He dog-paddled over to her. "I'm joking, I'd never leave you."

"You're so sweet." She couldn't take her eyes off the whale. "It's amazing because I felt something go right through me."

He met her eyes. "No one really understands how sperm whales see with sound, but they wouldn't see you like I do—"

"How do you see me, Josh?" She smiled when he ignored the question.

"They'd see all your insides, like your internal organs, your bones, your beating heart. It's hard to keep any secrets from them."

She placed her right hand flat across the left side of her chest. "I think my heart skipped a few beats." She took a deep breath. "I don't think I want the whole group checking me out like that."

He reached between the cockpits and flipped the kayak right side up. Using the hand pump, he started pumping water out.

Up and down she bobbed in the smooth wavelets. The combination of wet suit and lifejacket made floating effortless. The peaceful whales seemed happy to ignore them. Gradually she started feeling more relaxed. They were simply lounging in an enormous warm bath... with gigantic tub toys. Tilting her head back, she wet her hair and pulled it away from her face. She licked drops of seawater off her lips. Definitely more salty than back home.

Several whales milled about fifty meters away. The odd whale lay motionless at the surface alone, whereas most interacted in clusters comprised of several individuals.

"There seems to be a lot of physical contact," she said. "They're constantly touching each another."

"Sperm whales are very social." Josh stopped pumping and rested, one arm draped over the kayak. "They're incredible animals. Do you know they have the largest brain on Earth?"

"Bigger than yours?"

He smirked. "Barely. They also probably have the most powerful natural sonar."

"That I believe." She placed her hands over her stomach.

"They have the greatest geographical separation of the sexes. They can dive deeper than most animals. They live a long time too, roughly the same age as us. And to top it off they have an incredibly unique social system. Sperm whales are truly…." His voice trailed off.

She carefully studied his handsome face. He was certainly easy on the eyes. "You love them, don't you?" Men who can love something besides themselves were incredibly sexy.

"They're on the brink of extinction. I believe they're canaries in the coal mine, telling us something about the health of the deep ocean. If they don't survive, somehow I doubt we will either."

"Orcas!" Rene screamed.

Andrea twirled around. Both shouting, Naeco and Rene were madly paddling toward them. Rene repeatedly stabbed the air with her paddle frantically gesturing behind them.

Four slender, black dorsal fins sliced through the waves, black and white shimmering beneath the surface. Like a pack of hungry wolves, the carnivores swam toward them at an astonishing speed.

"Get in the kayak!" Josh hissed.

Andrea yanked the paddle from the cockpit and jammed the paddle float over the blade. Naeco and Rene held the empty kayak firmly against their boat for increased stability. Rene grabbed under her arms as Josh pushed her up out of the water. Buoyancy the foam block provided to the paddle gave her additional leverage and she quickly wrestled herself into the cockpit.

Loud, sharp blows blasted skyward as sperm whales swam feverishly to one another, bow waves forming in front of their heads. The orcas narrowly swam past them. His chest heaving, Josh remained in the water, both arms draped over the kayak.

Andrea watched the orcas closely. If they were in the workboat she wouldn't hesitate to move closer. It would take at least fifteen minutes to travel to the *Rubicola* and get the zodiac. By then it might all be over. "Do you think this is dangerous, Josh?"

"Honestly, I don't know. I suspect they're more interested in the sperm whales than us though."

Two orcas changed course to cut off a lone sperm whale swimming toward the ever-growing cluster of whales. Their sleek fins disappeared like submarine periscopes when they dove to attack. One savagely bit the sperm whale's tail. Rolling and shaking its head, it tore away a piece of tough flesh. Oil and blood oozing from the wound pooled at the surface.

The cluster of sperm whales maneuvered at the surface into a defense formation similar to what musk oxen do. They swam into a circle with their tails at the center and heads facing outward. Strong, hot breaths blew constantly above the formation.

One sperm whale suddenly broke away, swimming to aid her injured daughter struggling toward the group. This selfless action caused the pair of orcas to temporarily cease their attack allowing the two sperm whales to join the safety of the formation.

Circling the round cluster, the four orcas swam purposefully, occasionally diving at a particular sperm whale. But they would always end up retreating. After only a few minutes the orcas seemingly lost interest and abruptly swam off.

The confrontation ended as quickly as it started. Many mammalian eyes nervously followed the black fins as they glided toward the islands. Tails slapping the water and a series of breaches served to help dissipate a collective nervous energy pent up in the group of sperm whales.

"I'm glad that's over." Naeco took several photographs of one sperm whale breaching for the fifth time.

The slender dorsal fins shrank in the distance. "I've never seen this before," Josh said. "That was scary…and I'm not a sperm whale."

Slowly the tight group of sperm whales broke into smaller clusters and carefully dispersed.

"So this doesn't happen often?" Andrea asked.

"I don't think so," he said. "Their biggest enemies are people, orcas, pilot whales, and sharks. They can generally fight them off, except people. But predation must be significant because sperm whales have obviously evolved a strategy to fight off predators. I don't think predators normally can kill adults, but calves are certainly vulnerable.

That's probably why females live in groups. They have low reproductive rates and need to protect their young."

"That would be a horrible death," Andrea murmured, trying not to think of a calf being viciously torn apart while still alive. She had struggled with this paradox before—in one instance nature could be so beautiful then, suddenly, so horrific. There had been several occasions when she could have interfered to save a wild animal from a natural death by predation, but she deliberately chose to remain a passive observer and not interfere with the natural processes she researched. It wasn't an easy decision though. Every time she watched a young animal die it broke her heart.

They paddled together, the two kayaks side-by-side. Like sperm whales they knew there was an undeniable sense of safety in numbers.

Andrea was relieved to still see spouts pluming above the waves. "I hope the attack doesn't scare them away." So far the whales seemed content to mill about at the surface, but how many times had she seen that before when, without warning, the whales would vanish into the depths.

Josh paddled faster. "The timing was bad. Let's get the crittercam on. If there are two social units here their association will only be temporary and the group could split anytime."

Into the herd they paddled once again. They approached one whale which immediately dove. The next one lazily rolled onto one side, almost upside down, then righted itself. It sank under the waves and then surfaced.

"I think she's sleeping." Josh paddled the kayak ahead and they quickly moved alongside the whale.

Andrea strained to hold up the pole; it seemed much heavier than before. Pain radiated from her shoulder. Her arms started shaking.

The sperm whale remained upright, floating motionless, the pectoral fin beneath the kayak barely moving.

"Maybe she's not dreaming anymore," he whispered.

She reached out with the pole and pushed the crittercam down, squeezing air out of the suction cup through a one-way valve. She tugged gently on the pole. The crittercam seemed to be firmly attached. She pulled the trigger and released it.

He furiously back-paddled the kayak a safe distance away.

She couldn't believe it! She thrust both arms and the pole high above her head and breathed a heavy sigh of relief. So much planning and hard work had gone into achieving this moment.

Josh patted her back. "You did it, Andrea! You're the first person to attach a crittercam on a sperm whale. Congratulations!"

Beaming, she turned to look at him. "We did it. I couldn't have done it without you. Your kayaking skills are fantastic. I was in perfect position."

"Well, this time."

"That's true. Everything works well when your subject cooperates."

They sat quietly staring at the crittercam stuck on the whale's back. It seemed rather anticlimactic. The whale could've pretended to care, at least a little. Fortunately the contraption remained in place and didn't slide off.

The kayaks came together and floated as one, paddlers watching the crittercam suctioned to the sleeping whale's back.

"Did you put batteries in it?" Josh asked.

Andrea turned, her eyes wide with a look of mock horror on her face. "Is it facing the right way?"

"How long will it stay on?" Rene asked.

"Who knows? Hopefully eight hours and not eight minutes. The suction cup has a wire release mechanism. Salt water will corrode the wire. When it disappears a valve should open and allow seawater to flood the cup, which will break the seal. The crittercam should then release and float to the surface."

"How about you two heroes paddle around the whale," Naeco said. "I'll take some pictures."

"Can I climb on her back?" Josh asked.

"I've done that. It wasn't alive though. Does that count?" Andrea slid the crittercam pole under bungee cords which held it firmly against the kayak. She grabbed the spare paddle and they paddled around the sperm whale for the photo shoot, hamming it up with the whale lying in the midst of the excited humans playing around it. The whale floated at the surface, relatively still, unaware or completely disinterested in the significance of the moment.

Andrea waved at the pair in the other kayak to signal the long paddle back. Heading toward the *Rubicola,* they practiced maneuvering the kayak among choppy waves. By paddling with the rudder out of the water, they learned to balance their paddle strokes to each other more efficiently. They increased their stroke rate and sprinted several hundred meters.

Sweating and winded, she rested the paddle across her lap. Her left shoulder was now quite stiff. The sleek boat continued slicing through the waves.

Huffing, Josh said, "You found two good kayaks. This boat moves true through the water."

She rocked her hips gently from side to side. "Josh, do you recommend gathering any information about the herd?"

"It couldn't hurt to record group behavior. I wonder whether attaching the crittercam affects the whale or causes changes in group behavior."

"What should we be looking for?"

"I would record group number, direction of movement, are they socializing, cluster sizes, these sorts of things."

Squirming in the seat, she flexed her left leg to prevent her foot from falling completely asleep. "Is this something Durant can do from the bridge?"

"Who's that?"

"He's a shipboard technician. Jamaican, I believe. About my height, dark, pretty buff, did Naeco's hair. Really nice guy, very helpful."

"I know who you're talking about. Sure, get him to record observations every fifteen minutes."

The other kayak raced past. Naeco and Rene smacked the water with their paddles, splashing them. With a playful cry Andrea dug her blade deep into the water and they chased after the fleeing yellow boat, paddling with all their energy straight for the *Rubicola*. Before the two women could get out of their kayak and climb to safety, they caught up. Andrea squirted streams of water at them using the hand pump. Josh slapped the surface with his paddle spraying seawater over the kayak into the zodiac. Then she turned the hand pump on Josh and it became a free-for-all, every woman and man for themselves. Their shouting and splashing continued until a lanky seaman climbed hesitantly down into the workboat.

Andrea struggled out of the kayak and sat exhausted, thoroughly soaked, on the pontoons at the workboat's bow trying to catch her breath.

"Captain wants to see you pronto, Dr. Megin." The seaman flicked a toggle switch on the steering console to activate the bilge pump. A stream of water poured out behind the zodiac. He climbed up the side of the ship pausing several times to glance down at the group basking in the tropical sun like marine iguanas warming themselves on rocks after a cool foraging dive.

TWO

Four months earlier...

Pale moonlight spilled through the open escape hatch into the boat's sleeping compartment. Stagnant air smelled of men's sweat and soiled clothes. Occasionally a lonely voice chattered on a radio in the wheelhouse. Josh, wearing only white boxers, lay on his back on top of the sleeping bag, his feet dangling over the end of the cot. Water gurgled around his head as waves lapped against the steel hull. He vigorously rubbed his tanned, whiskered face. Sleeping on the *Go For Broke* used to be easier than breathing. He contemplated closing the escape hatch on the deckhead in case it rained, but ocean air flowing into the musty compartment smelled fresh and clean.

He groped for the flashlight and book on a shelf near his head. From between the pages he pulled out a picture of Diane who was soaking wet, posing among sand dunes like a Parisian runway model. Straight blonde hair framed numerous freckles—angel kisses he had called them—sprinkled across her nose and cheeks. An unexpected and intense sun shower from a single dark cloud had plastered her green knit pullover against her small breasts. Tight blue jeans rolled up to her knees revealed firm legs shaped by fifteen hours of cycling each week. In one hand she carried a pair of white sneakers.

Delicately he placed the picture and book back on the shelf, the flashlight next to it. He had taken the picture at Nesika Beach when they traveled by car down highway 101 along the Oregon coast for their honeymoon. For five days they had hugged the coast starting with a gorgeous sunrise on the needles at Cannon Beach and ending in the rain at Brookings near the California border.

He closed his eyes. Her radiant, happy smile still took his breath away. *Where are we?* Probably about two hundred kilometers offshore. Today they had been cruising over deep water beyond the Hawaiian Ridge where the shelf drops away, evident not only by the marine chart in the wheelhouse, but also by the rich blue color the water had turned yesterday.

He sat up in semi-darkness. Lono's wheezy snoring occasionally interrupted the constant drumming of the generator. He held his breath. *There!* Something regular—vague and unobtrusive—mixed in with the irregular. He pressed an ear against the cool hull. Ever slight vibrations tickled his scalp. Faint clicking sounds popped through the metal.

Adrenaline crackled through his body like a million pinpricks. He madly groped at the duffel bag under the cot. Lying down, he squirmed into gray sweats and a blue tee shirt and pulled a tattered ball cap over messy, thinning brown hair.

He stumbled over to the bunk and shook the soft shoulder of a heavyset young man with dyed blonde hair who was part Hawaiian and Japanese. "Lono, get up! We found one."

Lono moaned. He absently scratched the green palm tree splayed across the crotch of his tacky brown tourist shorts. A tattooed Celtic dragon climbed up his left calf.

"Meet me on deck," Josh said, loudly, as he climbed up the ladder into the wheelhouse.

Colorful lights danced across the wheelhouse windows, reflections from active electronic equipment surrounding him. A pocket of cool air flowed through an open window and door. The air smelled foul, not just salty. He hurried outside onto the foredeck and deeply inhaled through his nose. How he missed this smell. The Bamberg rose garden couldn't even compare. Winds gusting from the southeast rattled cables climbing the boom and mast. The sun's fingers clawed at the eastern horizon lightening the dark morning sky. Swirling clouds extinguished what could have been a spectacular sunrise.

"Where are you?" he whispered to the foreboding ocean.

He jogged along the narrow walkway next to the house past the trawl winches, still wrapped tightly with trawl net cable, and a cluster of fifty-five gallon fuel drums. A powerful lamp on the boom illuminated the rusting deck. He lifted a heavy red hatch near the aluminum sorting table and climbed down into the hold. Straining his back, he struggled up the ladder carrying a wooden crate and pushed it through the opening onto the deck.

A light turned off in the head. *Take your time, Lono.* Captains. He never liked any of them, except Peter, who treated him like a son. Even though growing up Josh had spent most of his spare time around boats of all sorts, he had never been a commercial fisherman or in the Navy or Coast Guard and most Captains, Commanding Officers, or whatever they liked to call themselves punished him for that.

Lono eventually sauntered outside with a handful of cookies. Crumbs sprinkled his chest as he crammed several into his mouth; ones that didn't fit he flung overboard.

His chubby hand plunged inside the crate through a thick ball of coiled black cable. "Sure you brought enough, Dr. T?"

"It's only eighty meters. I nearly brought two hundred when I found out a strong young fella was coming this trip."

Josh carried the power supply—a small, but surprisingly heavy metal box—through the galley to the wheelhouse. Lono followed dragging the cable and speaker.

A wooden wheel with six knobby handles centered the small, rectangular wheelhouse. Two stained, white swivel chairs faced the row of windows. Three VHF radios, occasionally sputtering voices received on different channels, hung from the deckhead in front of the windows. Radar was bolted to the counter; a green line swept around the screen in a clockwise motion indicating no reflective surfaces within range. A depth sounder, monitored infrequently here where depths were generally in the hundreds of meters, hung near the starboard corner.

Josh pushed several charts off the counter and set the electronic equipment down. He stepped outside through the port side door. "We're gonna have to hang the hydrophones away from the boat because of the racket from waves hitting the hull. We need a float."

"Where is it?"

"In the hold. Grab the earphones too. Thanks."

As Lono wandered through the galley, Josh called out, "Bring two floats just in case."

He assembled the electronic listening equipment connecting all pieces to a heavy duty laptop. Lono returned with earphones and an orange float tucked under each arm.

"Put one float around twenty meters."

With outstretched arms Lono counted off twenty meters of cable and tied the float in place. Josh gently lowered the hydrophones over the side playing out more cable as the boat drifted. When the float hit the surface, he loosely tied the end of the cable to a cleat on the bulwarks and tossed the remaining cable overboard. The orange float, barely visible in the early morning light, bobbed twenty meters from the *Go For Broke*. The vertical array of three hydrophones hung down from the float to a depth of sixty meters.

He slipped earphones over his head. When strong ringing clicks, regularly spaced, filled the headset, he grinned widely. "We finally won the lottery, Lono." He clicked a button on the computer to record the sounds.

The hydrophones converted sound energy to electrical energy. Sound pulses were hitting the forty meter hydrophone first and then the other two a fraction of a second later. This indicated the middle hydrophone was closest to the whale. A software program on the computer measured the time delay between the various pairs of hydrophones for the click recordings. From time-of-arrival differences it calculated the whale to be forty-six meters below the surface.

Josh started timing intervals between sound pulses. The time between each click was long, about five seconds, instead of every second. "Listen to this." He passed the earphones to Lono. "These are slow clicks, not usual clicks—the sound pulses normally used for echolocation. Only males make slow clicks."

"Why's that?"

"No one really knows. They could be some type of honest signal showing off their size and fighting ability. Females might be choosy who they mate with and pick males based on characteristics of the slow clicks they hear."

"Maybe it's telling us to get lost."

"I thought we are lost."

He squeezed behind Lono and twisted several dials on the echo-sounder. On the sounder's screen, a thick solid trace formed around thirty-one hundred feet where the seafloor reflected most of the sound waves. Two other dark bands, one around fourteen hundred feet and the other more shallow between six hundred and seven hundred and fifty feet, indicated the presence of deep scattering layers.

Josh pointed at a single blip near the surface. "There's our visitor."

Lono read off the depth scale. "Hundred and twenty-three feet."

Josh tapped the scattering layers on screen. "Wonder what these are?" Normally there was only one, usually congregations of schooling fish or zooplankton.

The arched-shaped image rose and fell between seventy-five and one hundred and twenty feet below.

"It's messed up," Lono said. "Just sitting there under my boat."

"It is bizarre. I've never seen anything like it." Josh unplugged the earphones and plugged in the speaker. "Sure hope he's not a rogue whale."

Bubbling noises from the ocean filled the wheelhouse. Absent now were the predictable sharp pulses.

Lono licked his lips. "What's a rogue whale?"

"It's a sperm whale that doesn't fit into any particular social group. They're solitary and aggressive. Sometimes whalers encountered them—big males that would smash boats and kill people with little provocation."

"Kanaloa," Lono whispered.

They huddled around the sounder. Indeed, the device showed something immense, almost motionless at a depth of ninety feet, directly beneath the research boat.

THREE

Using the boom, several burly seamen lifted the trawl net and maneuvered the bulging cod end over a cordoned off opening in the deck. On the mesh clear globs stretched by gravity resembled glistening stalactites. A deckhand untied the cod end; the catch tumbled into the hole down a chute to the wet lab below.

Andrea grabbed Josh's hand. "Let's peek in the lab and see what the trawl caught."

On the way to the lab they stopped at his cabin to look at a schematic of the ship hanging on the wall next to the door. The *Rubicola* had five levels or decks: one deck below the cabin, the lower deck, and three decks above, the upper, fo'c'sle, and bridge decks. The engine room, laundry facilities, and a recreation lounge were located on the lower deck. Down the hallway from where they stood were the wet and dry labs, workshops for the ship's crew, and more cabins for visiting scientists. There were also cabins on the upper deck next to the mess. One could go outside on the main deck near the mess. The highest level on the ship was the bridge deck, the command center of the *Rubicola*.

They strolled past a row of lockers and through two sets of heavy doors. The rank smell of dead fish permeated the air in the bleak white room. Five people wearing yellow rubber overalls and gloves up to their elbows stood along a black conveyer belt that snaked across the lab. The 'gate keeper' controlled the flow from the chute onto the conveyor belt by lifting and lowering a stainless steel door like a guillotine. He seized the biggest fish—several with bulbous heads, large eyes, and slender bodies with silvery scales, likely a type of lanternfish—and dropped them in their own designated basket. In a steady trickle the rest of the catch—mostly invertebrates—moved past him along the belt; the other biologists pounced with wooden-handled picks and sorted the remaining species. The last person in the line, probably some poor student, had the envious task of sorting the smallest species, in this case mostly clear lumps of squished jellyfish.

A seaman with black-smudged hands entered the lab and walked past the conveyor belt system to a door. He punched a button on the wall; a siren buzzed and a red light flashed in concert while the door automatically slid open. Loud banging noises from the engine room filled the lab. The Engineer disappeared down a ladder as the door automatically closed.

Andrea preferred kayaking to being in the lab. The fishy stench, no windows, and noise, combined with the slow roll of the ship, were making her feel crappy. And today was calm. She couldn't imagine working down here in heavy seas.

They wandered among rows of baskets. In one basket was non-living debris scooped up by the net like rocks, chunks of wood, and two stone-like, rounded discs about forty centimeters in diameter.

Squatting, Josh bear-hugged one and struggled to lift it. "These are whale bones—vertebrae near the tail. The net was definitely fishing on the bottom."

Andrea picked through several invertebrates in another basket and held up a squid-like critter; it weighed about a kilogram, but was heavily damaged and hard to identify. "This is the problem trawling for squid."

Josh stepped over a row of white pails. "How long was the tow?"

"Probably thirty minutes. This might be a *Histioteuthid*, it's hard to tell."

He poked the gelatinous creature. "Sperm whales eat these around Hawaii."

She dropped it in the basket. "I doubt they're very tasty. They're full of ammonium ions."

Two men carried and pushed several baskets over to a large scale. A short woman with a clipboard stood next to the scale; when she nodded they placed a basket on the scale and she wrote down the species, number, and weight. The pair then dumped the contents on the belt which moved the slimy pile to the hopper, a vertical system of stainless steel buckets that continually lifted in revolving fashion discarded materials to the deck above and overboard.

"We should go," Andrea said. "I hear the Captain waits for no one."

"Is this everything caught in the tow?" Josh asked the woman with the clipboard.

She nodded while using the top of the pencil to erase something.

"Where's all the fish? Did the net fish properly?"

"The Fishing Master said there were no problems."

Andrea playfully chased Josh up two flights of stairs to the bridge, a dimly-lit, cluttered room where computers, depth sounders, plotters, and radar, all in duplicate or triplicate, covered the counters. A row of radios sputtering on different channels hung from the ceiling. The Officer of the Watch plotted the ship's progress on marine charts spread out on a broad, square table at the center of the bridge. Shelving held numerous books and binders about navigation, meteorology, and seamanship. A series of massive windows wrapped around the bridge and offered an excellent view of decks and surrounding water. The Chief Mate and Captain stood silently facing the windows, their backs to the scientists.

Only the Chief Mate turned when they appeared in the windows' reflections. He was tanned and solid like a rugby player, weathered by ocean winds for almost fifty years. He eagerly stepped toward her.

"Your research moving along, Andrea?" He ran a strong, chunky hand through short salt and peppered coarse hair.

"Hey, Curt, yah we finally attached the crittercam."

Captain Matthews turned. "We know that. We know everything that happens aboard this ship."

A man in his early sixties, gray gelled hair parted to one side topped an angular, almost gaunt face—not chubby like many of the crew—suggesting he was disciplined about what he put into his body. Spotless, pressed white slacks and a short-sleeve shirt covered his slender frame.

"I'm curious what happened earlier." Matthews fiddled with reading glasses dangling around his skinny neck. "Were you having trouble with the kayak?"

Andrea swallowed, her mouth suddenly dry.

"I saw people in the water. What happened?"

She shrugged nonchalantly. "We were trying to put the crittercam on a whale, sir, and it flipped our kayak."

"You were in the water a long time."

She hesitated, surprised Matthews had been watching their every move. People weren't kidding when they said he ran a tight ship. "It won't happen again, sir."

"It wasn't anyone's fault, Captain," Josh said. "We certainly didn't want it to happen."

Matthews stepped forward, his steely gaze still on her. "You are the scientist in charge of your little group. They are your responsibility." His breathing seemed labored.

Oh, God, here comes a speech.

"Seagoing operations are inherently hazardous. But this ship has an impeccable safety record, one we're very proud of. I expect strict compliance with safety-at-sea precautions so no one gets hurt or the ship damaged. From now on the bridge is to be informed of all activities relating to your project and permission must be obtained to do them."

"I've been doing that, sir."

"Is that understood, Dr. Megin?"

She nodded slightly. "Sure."

"I wasn't happy not having the workboat accompany the kayaks, but I consented because you said it interfered with your research. But I never would have agreed if I had known people would be frolicking with those animals." He glared at her and then Josh. "You're not going to pull any more stunts like you did today. The next time I see someone in the water there will be a man," he looked at her again, "or woman overboard drill and it will embarrass all of us." He wiped his lower lip. "That'll be all." He walked over to some electronic gizmo and, muttering, pushed several buttons.

Head down, Andrea moved past Curt to a counter where, with trembling hands, she sorted through a stack of papers to find some field data sheets. She carried a clipboard and binoculars outside on the bridge deck. A light breeze blew in her face, the late afternoon winds struggling to maintain their gusto. She took a deep breath of salty air.

"What a jerk," Josh whispered in her ear.

"Could you give me a couple minutes, please?"

"I'll get you something to drink."

"Make it a double." She forced a slight smile.

She leaned against the rail and absorbed the wonderful view. Sperm whales peppered the ocean off the right side. Why would he humiliate her like that? Beads of sunlight sparkled off waves rolling past the ship. It's always a fight. She used to believe one day she would reach that safe place where everything would be easy, but that day never comes. Through binoculars, blows shooting above waves vaporized in the breeze. Buffy was still there, the red suction cup visible on her back. Ten whales? No eleven. For the first time she envied sperm whales, their nomadic existence, roaming the globe for soul sustenance.

Josh wandered up the stairs carrying two mugs. She took one mug in exchange for the clipboard and binoculars; he continued climbing to the monkey island, the platform above the bridge where the ship's compass lived, protected from all the steel.

She waved at Sundrop and Randi who were jumping to the rhythm of an imaginary game of hopscotch two decks below. Times like this, what she wanted to do most of all was curl up with Sundrop on the couch; they would share a bowl of ice cream and Sundrop would talk endlessly about her school day and friends.

After several minutes she joined Josh on the platform above. She wrapped her hands around the warm cup of green tea. It was comforting to hold on to something—anything—when so high up.

"What's your Captain like?" she asked.

"He's a drug addict."

"Oh?" She waved again at Sundrop.

Josh snickered. "He's just a kid. I used to go out with his father."

"What a cute couple you two must've been."

He laughed. "Peter—the father—owns the boat I use for research. I've hired him every summer for, oh, many years. He's a real friend, but recently he developed health problems so this year his son, Lono, ran the *Go For Broke*." He passed the binoculars to her. "You can see the camera on the whale."

"Buffy."

"What?"

"Sarah named the crittercam whale Buffy." Grinning, Andrea started humming a tune vaguely familiar to Josh.

He sighed. People always anthropomorphize whales. They simply cannot help themselves. After a brief pause he asked, "So Sarah is her…legal name?"

"Yes, but to me she'll always be Sundrop. She's a wonderful drop of sunshine in my life, every day."

"She looks like you."

Andrea smiled. "Not really." From day one Sundrop had always looked so much like Roy, even her toes and earlobes.

"She acts like you is what I meant to say."

"Oh, how so?"

"She seems to like it here. She has a certain, I don't know, zest for life."

"That's very kind, thank you." Josh was definitely saying all the right things. "Sarah sure loves the outdoors. She never stepped foot in a mall until she was at least four."

"She's lucky. Most kids watch TV all the time."

Seeing the magnified whales made her feel closer to them, almost part of their group. "It helped growing up in a beautiful place away from the city. Whatever chance I got I took Sarah to my favorite spots."

"Where's that?"

"I love the intertidal and estuaries. It's sacred where ocean meets land. There are so many unique habitats and the biodiversity is amazing. I'd really like to see mangrove trees sometime."

"Better hurry, they're disappearing fast."

She lowered the binoculars. "Have you always been a professor?"

"After I graduated I worked for oil companies studying effects of seismic activities on marine mammals."

A guy like Josh worked for the oil industry? "Were you involved with the Barnathean spill?"

His hands shot up, palms facing outward. "I had nothing to do with it."

"My brother helped with the clean-up."

"I'm sorry, Andrea. That was a massive spill. It should never have happened."

"His health is ruined. The oil dispersants they sprayed damaged his lungs. Nobody warned them about the dangers or gave them respirators." She paused, looking homeward across the ocean. "We didn't want pipelines or tankers in our territory and yet we've been the most impacted."

"So you're from around Tofino?"

"My people are the Ahousaht."

He leaned back against the guard rail. "The North Coast hasn't fared much better."

"I know, a friend of mine studies *Didemnum*."

"It's the same old, sad story. Corporations and governments convince the public some kind of industrial activity is in their best interest; it will create jobs, pay for social programs, blah, blah, blah. But we don't have a clue how ecosystems function and now tanker traffic has introduced an invasive colonial tunicate to the North Coast where it has spread like greased lightning and covers Hecate Strait, completely changing the ecology of the area, wrecking a bunch of fisheries, and decimating communities." He snorted sarcastically into his cup. "Hardworking taxpayers always end up holding the bag."

She sipped her tea. "Do you like your job now?"

He hesitated. "Yah, I do."

"You don't sound very convinced."

"I get to do my own thing, which is good. But, truthfully, most of us who study threatened species just aren't effective at stopping, or even slowing, the demise of our own research subjects. We conduct all sorts of elaborate projects, we publish our results, but...all we do is whine about needing more money to do more research. And the system rewards us because we bring in funding, not because we actually do something meaningful like protect species or habitats. So what you have is an endless progression of grad students, new wings on university buildings popping up all over the place, yet species continue to disappear in record numbers. Most of us know what's happening, but we don't speak up. We're the experts yet we hide in our ivory towers while the world crumbles around us."

"What does your wife do?" She figured he must be married even though he wasn't wearing a ring. Somehow he acted like a man in a committed relationship.

His hand dug under the collar of his tee shirt.

Maybe he's gay. Sometimes it's hard to tell. "Sorry, I should say partner, not wife."

"My wife's a teacher."

"Oh, good for her. What grade does she teach?"

He closed his eyes and paused before answering. "Elementary school."

"Do you have children?"

"No." He handed her the clipboard. "I need a refill." He walked over to the ladder.

"Thanks for the drink," she called out.

"See you later." Head bowed, he climbed down to the deck below and disappeared inside the bridge.

He seemed put-off by my questions. She stretched her arms straight above her head. *Don't be so nosy, girl. Keep it professional.* She inhaled deeply. The ocean smelled like home. Funny how home seemed closer on a ship in the middle of the South Pacific than at Birch Creek.

FOUR

Four months earlier...

Josh stood at the *Go For Broke's* stern between the three-meter-high A-frame trawl davits where the deck can be raised and lowered like a ramp to support the weight of a bursting trawl net. Heaving on a thick orange tow rope, he pulled the *Catchalot,* a gray six-meter-long zodiac, toward the fishing boat. The Def Leppard song, *Pour Some Sugar On Me,* boomed through loudspeakers mounted near the door.

"Dr. T!"

He spun around.

Lono shouted out the door to the house, "The whale's at twenty-five feet right under us. I'm gonna fire up the engine."

Josh vigorously shook his head and waved his hands. "No, don't. You'll spook it. They're skittish and will flee at the faintest sound. We're fine drifting."

"Sure hope you're right." Lono disappeared inside headed back to the wheelhouse.

Josh leaned over the bulwarks. Even with good visibility the choppy water made it difficult to see beneath the surface. But after several seconds the dark outline of a massive animal whose length was similar to the *Go For Broke* materialized.

Lono stepped out on deck again. "It's making those crazy clicking sounds really fast."

"He's producing codas." *Funny, males don't usually make those.* "They're thought to be for social communication purposes. He's alone, right?"

"Hope so."

Grinning, Josh pointed over the side. "Check it out."

Lono strolled over to him. Just then a mound of water swelled beneath the *Go For Broke* causing the surface surrounding the boat to boil. The dome of water lifted the seventy-ton vessel; she listed dangerously from side to side.

"What the...?" Lono hollered, his eyes wide.

The two men steadied themselves by grabbing on to each other.

"That's a bubble burst. Lono, get the camera. This whale's about to surface."

Lono reappeared on deck with a camera sporting a three hundred-millimeter telephoto lens. "Kanaloa!"

They could easily see the outline of the whale. The head was under the stern, the fluke over by the bow. A paddle-shaped pectoral fin sculled slowly back and forth. With a gentle flick of the fluke, the whale swam beyond the stern of the *Go For Broke.*

Surface waters around the zodiac started churning.

"It's coming up!" Lono shouted.

They jogged to the stern. The zodiac bucked in the turmoil as if she wanted desperately to escape, but the rope tied to the bridle constrained her. A long pole lying on deck nearly bounced overboard.

Josh grabbed the towrope. "Let's get the *Catchalot* out of the way!"

But it was too late. A massive barrel-shaped head, like the hull of a shiny, black submarine, broke through the surface, white foam streaming off deep folds in the animal's leathery skin.

"He's huge!" Josh cried out.

A low rounded dorsal fin, two-thirds the way down the whale's back, poked above the waves. An explosive blast erupted from the nose at an angle, the geyser of sea spray and water vapor spewed skyward many meters. They scrunched their faces as the whale's fetid breath filled their nostrils. Lono pulled his tee shirt over his nose.

Swimming slowly, the whale seemed indifferent to the research boat drifting nearby, although the zodiac did attract some attention. Each time the forty-five ton animal bumped its head against the pontoons, Josh cringed. Comparing the whale's log-like back to the *Catchalot,* he figured the bull might be sixteen meters long, large enough to breed.

"So that's a sperm whale?" Lono asked. "Is it gonna shoot its big wad at us?" His laugh, wrapped in yellowing teeth, sounded like a throbbing, high-pitched wheeze.

"See his square head? It's shaped that way because of the spermaceti organ which is full of oil. Whalers first believed the oil was the seminal fluid of the whale. Spermaceti means the seed of the whale."

"That noggin's full of oil? We're rich!"

"Tens of thousands were killed for their spermaceti oil to make lamp oil and candles."

The bull spouted fifty meters off the stern.

"That's one big candle over there," Lono said.

"Now we know spermaceti oil has amazing sound transmitting qualities. The spermaceti organ is probably a sound-focusing chamber used for underwater echolocation. Sperm whales produce powerful low frequency sounds that can be transmitted long distances. They can echolocate hundreds of meters or communicate with one another over tens of kilometers. You heard the clicks earlier."

Nasal-sounding inhalations followed each exhalation. The old whaler's rule is sperm whales blow once for every minute they had dived. Moreover, a fifty-foot animal such as this one should dive for fifty minutes. But the twenty-sixth spout was particularly forceful; the whale rounded his back into an arch, the dorsal hump rising above the waves.

"He's diving! Make sure you photograph the fluke."

Lono hurried to turn on the camera and remove the lens cap as the whale sharply bent his body, exposing the dorsal fin and four knobby knuckles where the trunk narrowed to the caudal peduncle. The triangular fluke rose majestically into the air. Lono fired off several photos. Instead of two overlapping lobes, there was only one and a ragged portion of another. Nearly half the fluke was missing; it seemed a massive chunk had somehow been ripped away.

Lono laughed. "It probably just swims in circles."

A partial semi-ovoid scar on the intact left lobe suggested a cookie-cutter shark had sunk its teeth into the fluke and then spun and twisted off a piece of flesh.

With much less fanfare and commotion than when it arrived, the bull sperm whale disappeared beneath the waves. He had been at the surface for six minutes.

Josh ran across the deck. The wheelhouse was quiet when he entered. He started the graphic recorder. The stylus coupled to it automatically began drawing images from the sounder on scrolling paper.

The crescentic echo image on the sounder moved steadily deeper. The speaker remained silent until the whale reached a depth of one hundred and fourteen feet. Then, suddenly, regular click-like sounds spaced about one second apart pulsed through the wheelhouse. After one minute the whale was about two hundred and fifty-five feet below and continued to produce a steady click pattern.

"Usual clicks," Josh murmured. "The whale's echolocating to the bottom."

He watched the echo-sounder screen with the kind of intensity most men save for game seven of the Stanley Cup with the score tied at one and two minutes remained. At times the constant click pattern stopped briefly and then started again. The sperm whale swam deeper at a rate of two hundred and forty feet each minute. After three and a half minutes, when the bull reached a depth of seven hundred and seventy-eight feet, his descent rate slowed.

"Here we go," Josh whispered.

Faint clicks escaped the ocean's grasp. The whale remained steady around eight hundred feet. Abruptly the click rate increased to about two hundred per second. Creaking noises, like a rusty hinge opening and closing, could faintly be heard in the wheelhouse.

"He's chasing something." Josh made sure the laptop and graphic recorder were still recording. "I'd give my life to see what's going on down there." He visualized the whale closing in on a squid swimming frantically for its life.

After ten seconds the strange sounds stopped. Not hearing anything, even regular clicks, he closed his eyes, concentrating on the speaker. "I'll bet he's eating the squid he just caught."

"Nope, it's coming up," Lono said.

"Already? That's a shallow dive." Maximum depth on the hydrographic chart was three thousand two hundred and sixty-five feet.

The crescentic image passed the seven hundred, then the six hundred foot mark.

"Stay with this whale, Lono, whatever you do."

Josh jogged on deck. Waves splashed against the *Catchalot's* bow as he struggled to pull her toward the *Go For Broke.* Finally the starboard pontoon brushed against the tilt stern. Standing at the edge, he hesitated to jump while the zodiac lurched on swells below. Then the wind started pushing the zodiac under the *Go For Broke's* stern.

There wasn't much time. He sat down on the roller, waited until a wave lifted the boat, then dropped clumsily onto her deck narrowly missing the fuel tank mounted in front of the steering console and seat. He scrambled around the console and pushed a switch on the throttle to tilt the ninety-horsepower engine into the water. The outboard sputtered and died. He turned the key again and, at the same time, pushed it in to activate the choke. The engine roared to life. The stiff midday breeze dissipated smoky exhaust while he fished the towing bridle out of the water in front of the zodiac and slipped the G-hook off the metal ring. Standing at the stern, Lono hauled the tow rope onboard the *Go For Broke.*

Josh steered the *Catchalot* along the port side of the twenty-meter-long fishing boat. Lono had elegantly compared her peeling black hull and dirty white house to a giant bird turd. Bright, clean white lettering spelled 'Go For Broke' on both sides of the bow. Many years ago Lono's father, Peter Tanaka, had purchased the *Ocean Storm* from an albacore fisherman and renamed his new boat *Go For Broke* to honor his father who was killed in action in Italy in 1943. Many Hawaiians of Japanese ancestry fought bravely for America in Italy and France and adopted 'go for broke' as their battle cry.

Josh grabbed the handheld radio in the protective sleeve secured against the low Plexiglas spray guard poking above the steering wheel. "*Go For Broke,* this is *Catchalot,* over."

"I figured it was probably you," crackled Lono's voice.

"Radio check channel two four alpha, over."

"Loud and clear, you're good."

"I'll stay in sight and hopefully get a tag on fast. Please stand by on two four." He waited for a reply. "Do you copy?"

"I heard ya."

"*Catchalot* out."

He jammed the radio back in the sleeve. He steered the *Catchalot* at slow speed up and down over low swells away from the *Go For Broke.* Too often floating garbage—pieces of plastic, Styrofoam, and remnants of fishing gear—momentarily distracted his gaze.

Whump

He pulled back on the throttle. Something hard had struck the hull at the waterline. He stepped across the deck and sprawled across the bow pontoon. No debris floated in front of the boat. Several meters behind a green object bobbed almost under the surface. He put the boat in gear and turned her by making a wide circle. As the zodiac slowly motored past, he leaned over the pontoon and grabbed a coconut and tossed it on deck.

The boat dipped into the trough between two green waves. Something brown churned under in the frothy wake behind and disappeared. The engine coughed and stopped.

"What now?" he muttered.

He raised the engine leg out of the water. Fishing net smothered the propeller. He leaned over the transom and grabbed handfuls of nylon mesh and struggled to pull several meters of thin, nearly invisible strings over the pontoon. Entangled was a partially decomposed broadbill. The driftnet had snared the swordfish's upper jaw, elongated into a bill, and rigid dorsal fin. No longer a metallic color the cylindrical body, nearly a meter long, had turned an ugly dark brown. Scavenging worms and crabs nibbled at glassy eyes. The slimy carcass was a small adult because it had no teeth, scales, and lateral line. The smell of rotting flesh made him feel nauseous.

"Blow off the bow, ten o'clock!" Lono shouted out the wheelhouse door. Several hundred meters from the *Go For Broke* a spout blasted skyward.

Josh nearly tore the door on the steering console off its hinges to get a knife from the toolbox inside.

Another exhalation erupted, this time closer. Leaning precariously over the engine, he hacked madly at the mesh wrapped around the propeller. Thin strands cut into his skin as he uncoiled pieces twisted around the shaft.

"Dr. T!" Lono hollered, barely audible above the wind. He pointed at his feet. "It's under the boat!"

Leaving the motor partially tilted, Josh stepped around the tagging gear and leaned over the bow just as the sperm whale surfaced between the two boats. The bull glided straight at the zodiac like a battering ram. Josh instinctively stepped backward and nearly tripped over a plastic tub. Moist breath exploded from the blowhole at the front of the huge head. He leapt behind the steering console and grabbed the wheel just as the whale's nose butted into the pontoon. As the *Catchalot* bounced violently away, his stomach slammed into the steering wheel and, with a loud grunt, he collapsed heavily onto the deck. He rolled painfully on one side and wedged himself between the console and transom in case the whale should get even friendlier with his new rubber play toy. His gut and ribs throbbed. Thunderous exhalations erupting beyond the pontoon drowned out his wheezy breaths.

Slowly he raised his head above the pontoon. Three meters away the magnificent nose of the giant mammal pointed toward him. Queasy sensations in his stomach faded. On the flattened front of the whale's head was a light patch of skin. Whalers had written about head whorls in their journals, but he had never seen one. For the first time in his life he was face-to-face with a gray-haired old Cachalot.

Using the steering wheel for support, he pulled himself up on his knees and crawled around the console to the tagging equipment.

"Need a hand?" Lono yelled from the *Go For Broke.*

"Shaddap!" Josh hissed, waving at him. He placed his index finger against his lips.

Fumbling fingers opened the canvas bag. The satellite-linked tag consisted of a Global Positioning System (GPS) and other complicated electronics sealed in a clear, watertight, plastic container. On one end were two long barbs, on the other a short antenna. He hated the intrusiveness of penetrating tags, but suction-cup tags never stayed attached for more than thirty hours and he needed tags to stick for days or weeks to be able to track sperm whales' long range movements.

"Six four five six...six four five six," he murmured, memorizing the identification number stenciled on a plastic plate on the front of the tag. His contact information was also printed there in case someone, such as a fisherman, should find it.

Gingerly he lifted one end of the telescoping pole and dropped the tag in the dispenser. Kneeling, he extended the pole over the pontoon and the whale's head, which remained remarkably still at the surface. But the sweet spot remained just out of reach because the bull lay almost perpendicular to the boat. He edged closer by sitting on the pontoon.

"Come on, come on." He leaned out stretching his arms as far as he could. So close, yet so far!

Reluctantly he withdrew the pole and placed it across the pontoons. He grabbed a wooden paddle strapped along the inside of one pontoon, thrust the blade straight out, and pulled it inward to the boat. This action repeated swung the stern toward the motionless whale. He then turned and, facing the stern, paddled the *Catchalot* backward beside the enormous body. Waves hitting the zodiac pushed her closer to the sperm whale. Paddling furiously off the opposite pontoon barely prevented the boat from touching the bull.

Almost in position, he dropped the paddle and grabbed the pole and surrendered the boat to the waves, which promptly picked it up and slammed it against the whale. The giant stirred, hot breath exploded out the blowhole. Josh sunk the satellite tag firmly into the blubber layer sending a violent flinch rippling across the whale's back. The whale swam ahead with a slow undulating movement of its fluke and instantly was out of reach.

Drops of perspiration stung his eyes; he wiped his forehead with the back of his hand. He remembered his unbridled excitement when he tagged his first gray seal. The boat load of graduate students went berserk and the party started right there.

A spout blew high near the stern of the *Go For Broke*. Josh considered starting *Catchalot's* engine, but decided to wait until the whale dove. The *Go For Broke*...she's such a workhorse. But they were always pushing her limits; she can only carry so much fuel and handle waves only so big. With nineteen hundred gallons of diesel on board, they could remain at sea for fourteen days running twelve hours a day at seven knots. Her range was about twelve hundred nautical miles. Hopefully the *Blue Wanderer*, a fourteen-meter ocean-going sloop for sale on Maui, would be his next research boat. Sailing would save money on fuel, they could remain at sea longer and, best of all, no engine noise would allow them to tow the hydrophones all day.

He leaned against the warm cowling, steadying himself as the zodiac pitched in the swell, and pulled down his pants and started urinating. The wind continued blowing the fishing boat away to the northeast. A Laysan albatross, its long, blackish-brown wings nearly touching tips of waves, swooped near the *Catchalot*. The bird's white head tilted toward the strange floating object, its eye, hidden by a dark patch, watching him. The albatross followed the flow of the ocean, gracefully flying low over waves that playfully hid it from view periodically. He wished it was the endangered Short-Tailed albatross; it will probably go extinct before he sees one. The albatross changed course and flew toward the *Go For Broke* when Lono tossed some garbage overboard. Josh tied his pants and, crouching, splashed his hands next to the engine leg. The beauty of being so far from shore—out here were the real fliers, oceanic species like albatross, frigate birds, terns, and petrels that can soar for days without landing.

One side of the boat suddenly lurched out of the water.

"What the...!" he cried out. He jumped into the middle of the zodiac. A thunderous blast of foul air plumed off the bow. The whale had shoved his pectoral fin under the pontoon; Josh could now almost reach the tag with his hand. The bull gradually settled under the surface. Firmly holding the pontoons, Josh glanced around nervously. Seconds later the bull surfaced, the hump emerging first, then the top of the head. Waves washed over the black leathery back of the motionless leviathan. Minute particles of lung moisture wafted over the ocean's surface. Josh moved behind the steering console and placed his hand on the ignition. Based on size, the whale was probably about thirty years old, similar in age to him. He could only guess—he would never know for sure unless he examined the annual layers of dentine in one of the whale's upper teeth.

The abrupt fluke-up caught him off guard. It happened without the usual build-up—there was no increase in swimming speed and the whale didn't raise his head. Only a swirling puddle remained where the whale had vanished.

Grinning, Josh pumped his fist in the air. The tag will already be collecting location and dive data. Every time the whale surfaces and the tag is exposed to air, a saltwater switch inside will be activated allowing stored data to be transmitted to orbiting satellites which will, in turn, conveniently relay them to his computer at the university.

Suddenly, with incredible agility for such a large animal, the sperm whale lunged almost entirely out of the water.

"Nooo!" Josh screamed.

Rotating in the air the whale's underside became visible—white pigment speckled the rich, black skin under the jaw and around the single long genital slit and anal regions. The enormous body fell back with a tremendous splash. Sea water rushed to fill the temporary hole in the ocean.

Josh stepped around the steering console and kicked a plastic tub. His clenched fists could've crushed diamonds. Why breach now? He had seen sperm whales breach countless times, but normally socializing females and immatures did it, not large males.

The bull spouted and rolled on his side. Up and down his fluke slowly beat, propelling the immense body further astern from the *Catchalot.*

Hands clasped behind his head, Josh watched the sperm whale glide through waves away from him. The tag had disappeared; it wasn't on the whale's back or floating in the water. Was the whale playing or did he simply want the irritant off his back? Or did such behavior have a deeper purpose like an attempt to communicate? Breaching is energetically expensive to do. Could it be an honest signal in which only a strong, fit animal can communicate in such a manner?

"Please come back."

Blows became progressively more forceful and climaxed with the body bending in half, exposing the dorsal hump first and then a series of knuckles. At last the ragged fluke sprang forth, flared open and, smoothly without a splash, vanished into the blue.

FIVE

Outside on the bridge deck, Andrea and Sundrop documented behaviors of the group and, in particular, Buffy. They recorded her behavior for five minutes every fifteen minutes and described any unusual behaviors like breaching or lobtailing whenever they happened.

Generally not much had changed; the whales were behaving normally although Buffy seemed to be moving around more, acting more social. They expected this considering she probably had been sleeping when they attached the crittercam. Andrea still counted eleven whales so none had dove yet on a foraging expedition.

Sundrop watched the whales through binoculars. "Mom, I saw a fluke."

Andrea scribbled the time on the datasheet. "Where?"

"Over there." Sundrop passed the binoculars to her.

Josh picked up another pair and scanned the group. "Their activity level is up. They're moving with more purpose. Anyone see the crittercam?"

"Two more just dove," Andrea said.

Josh handed binoculars to Durant. "They're more active now. They're charging their bodies and storing—"

"I see Buffy," she cried out. "She's diving! You go girl!"

Buffy was swimming faster and raising her rostrum during breaths. After inhaling for the last time, her snout dipped into the water, body bent in the middle, and head plunged straight down. Up in the air whipped her tail as if to wave goodbye to observers on the *Rubicola.*

"Elvis has left the building." Durant searched the dive puddle for the crittercam.

Andrea jotted down the time when the dive began. By now only a couple of whales remained at the surface; they didn't matter, the majority of the group had dived into the ocean depths. For the first time the researchers celebrated there being no sperm whales around. The slapping of high-fives reverberated throughout the bridge deck.

"Now all we can do is wait," she said.

"And pray," Durant said. He clapped his hands together and dropped to his knees. "Please turn on."

Everyone laughed.

"Please stay on," Andrea whispered.

A pressure sensor would turn the crittercam on at ten meters and it would continue to operate until the memory space filled. By now it should already be spying on Buffy's every move as she descended into abyssal depths where oceanic squid live.

Buffy dove at precisely the right time; supper was served minutes later. The mess held four booths, two on each side. Officers sat on one side, science personnel on the other; in total twenty-four people could eat at the same time. A broad window linked the mess to the galley food preparation area. On the left side of the window, a tray of cutlery, coffee maker, and microwave sat on a slate gray counter. A fridge stood on the other side. The steward, a short man with a handle-bar mustache, scrawled meal menu choices on a whiteboard hanging on the wall. He never took someone's meal order without cracking a joke.

Squeezed in the booth under a wide-screen television, the research team, especially the kayakers, hungrily devoured their meals prepared by the four cooks.

Most were gorging on their second helping of dessert when Durant walked into the mess and approached the booth. He hesitated, standing at the table's edge, looking intently at Andrea. "I think the crittercam popped off."

Instantly all conversation stopped. She and Josh simultaneously looked at their watches.

"It's only been twenty-five minutes." She didn't even try to hide her disappointment. New optimism about her crittercam research deflated like a punctured balloon. Her greatest fear had come true. The suction cup can't seal properly to the skin. Her research was finished. She had dragged Josh half way around the world for nothing.

"The indicator light is blinking on the bridge," Durant said, "meaning the ship is picking up a radio signal from somewhere on the water. Most whales are still at depth according to the hydrophone. I couldn't see any at the surface. So, unless the crittercam's beacon is on the fritz, it's out there, not on any whale though."

Andrea massaged the back of her neck. "Well, we need to find it." She lay her fork next to a half-eaten wedge of bumble berry pie and stood, holding the plate. She glanced out a porthole. "We should leave soon before the sun sets." She dumped the pie in the garbage and piled her dishes in the wash tub by the window. She led the procession of people filing out of the mess.

Crew lifted the kayaks and stored them to one side on the working deck. Several seamen gathered on the fo'c'sle deck and pivoted the davit, swinging one of the orange zodiacs over the side. A crew member piloted the boat around the *Rubicola* and moored it against the workboat. Josh assisted Durant with loading the receiver antenna and a shoulder pack into the larger zodiac.

The orange and blue zodiacs motored away from the ship and stopped a short distance away and drifted. No one spoke while Durant donned earphones and adjusted several dials on the unit. Holding the antenna over the water, he swept it in a broad circle. The antenna received radio signals from the crittercam's beacon and relayed sounds to the earphones. Signals came in stronger when the antenna was closer to the beacon. After several revolutions, he gestured in a northwesterly direction to which Andrea steered the zodiac. The orange boat followed, to the side and slightly behind, with Naeco filming Durant at work. The two zodiacs zigzagged several kilometers away from the *Rubicola*.

"We're close." Durant set the heavy antenna down and moved the earphones around his neck.

The zodiacs puttered in random directions, everyone searching the surface in earnest for the suction cup.

"There it is!" Durant shouted.

Upon closer inspection the 'crittercam' turned out to be an empty oil can. Josh fished it out of the water and tossed it at his feet. Eyes strained to find the crittercam. Floating pieces of Styrofoam and plastic bags often resembled it and garbage soon littered the deck.

For a moment Andrea turned her attention skyward to acknowledge the sun setting low on the horizon. She pulled a knob on the console turning on white, green, and red navigation lights. Soon she would have to call off the search. Left overnight to currents, the crittercam might drift many kilometers by morning. If they had to resume searching at daybreak they probably would never find her precious scientific equipment and any images captured would be lost forever. It was now or never. She shouted at the boat shadowing them to spread out and cover more area.

Durant put the earphones on and waved the magic wand around. "We're practically on top of it according to this gizmo."

"These waves aren't helping," Josh muttered.

"I see it!" Sundrop cried out, pointing to a dark object bobbing in the chop.

"Don't take your eyes off it." Andrea turned the zodiac and steered straight to where Sundrop was pointing. The crittercam, partially submerged, fast approached the right side.

Durant leaned over the pontoon and scooped it out of the water. "Awesome, film's still rolling!"

"We have video!" Josh said.

What did Buffy see? Andrea wondered. How deep did she go in twenty minutes?

Durant turned the crittercam off and held it up over his head for people in the other boat to see. "We found it!"

Andrea pushed the throttle forward, eager to get the boats off the water before it got too dark. The blue zodiac gradually picked up speed and soon they were bouncing along wave tops at twenty-five knots toward the *Rubicola* looming in the fading evening light.

SIX

Drinks in hand, people gathered in the conference room and clustered in comfortable office chairs at one end of the long oak table near the television. Andrea helped Naeco connect the laptop to the television. Josh leaned against the wall behind the group next to a flimsy desk barely capable of supporting a general-purpose computer and printer.

With a dramatic flourish, Durant lifted the crittercam from a rubber tote in the corner. "Speech?" he said to Andrea.

She vigorously shook her head. "I'm shy."

Everyone joined Durant and chanted, "Speech, speech."

She stood next to Sundrop and faced her research comrades. "We know a tiny bit about the first hundred meters, but virtually nothing about the deep ocean. Every time a sperm whale dives it probably meets a species never before seen by people. Okay roll it, Durant."

Durant used the mouse to start playing the video software. "A sperm whale dive starring Buffy the sleepy whale." He switched off the lights and sat down.

The crittercam faced forward on Buffy's back. The grainy image showed the top of her head and five meters or so in front as she descended into blackness. As her giant square head swayed from side to side, leathery grooved skin rippled in front of the crittercam when various muscles flexed as she swam. In the lower right corner of the screen white digital numbers indicating depth continually increased.

A constant rain of plankton glimmering from light produced by the crittercam drifted past. Dots of light occasionally winked on and off as bioluminescent creatures swam by. A squid, its large, round left eye looking up at surface light, the smaller right eye looking down for bioluminescence, jetted into view and followed the crittercam. Light-producing organs around the right eye occasionally blinked to illuminate potential prey below it.

Andrea grinned widely. "That's beautiful *Histioteuthis.* A perfect living specimen." The technology works!

Seemingly uninterested in the small squid, Buffy continued echo-locating toward the bottom, her sonar clicking repetitively. In addition to drumming sonar, squelches and squawks could also be heard.

"I need to get the sound track for this movie, it's awesome," Durant said.

The dark shape of another sperm whale swam into view some distance away. Then another whale suddenly appeared and began rubbing its head near the crittercam. Portions of a third whale became visible and she, too, bumped and rubbed against the two whales. At times Buffy initiated the nuzzling and approached others in the group.

"I can't believe how much contact there is," Andrea said.

"Me neither," Josh said. "I thought they would spread out more."

The rubbing, bumping, and touching became more aggressive. One whale rubbed its lower jaw vigorously on top of Buffy's head. For a brief period the third whale disappeared from view and then reappeared beneath Buffy, slightly in front. The other whale swam almost out of sight, then back again, and rubbed against Buffy's side close to the crittercam.

The whales separated. Now Buffy seemed to descend alone. Deeper and deeper she swam, at one point passing a translucent creature, bioluminescent photophores speckling its football-shaped body, relaxed arms and tentacles swept backward in a tuft over its head. It vanished when the crittercam's lights hit it squarely.

"I think that's some kind of bizarre squid," Andrea said.

A jellyfish shaped like a ballet tutu, dark red in the center and the size of a human fist, drifted across Buffy's head and nearly bumped the crittercam. Several more jellyfish, pulsating in effortless synchrony, lazily floated past her eye and blowhole.

Buffy's sonar clicks increased in intensity sounding like machine gun fire.

Andrea wiped her hands on her thighs and leaned forward searching the television screen for fleeing squid.

A shadow army of discrete dark shapes suddenly materialized and ambushed the lens. At first she thought the crittercam's lights had burnt out because the top of Buffy's head faded to black. They were so numerous they blocked most of the artificial light produced by the crittercam.

Josh walked briskly toward the television screen. "Durant, can you pause it?"

For a moment life stood still. Pale light pierced translucent bells, cone-shaped on top and crown-shaped with soft scalloped edges on the bottom. Twelve thin, short tentacles curled upright just higher than tops of bells.

"Does anyone know what species of jellyfish this is?" he asked.

Andrea shook her head.

"Would anyone on board know?"

"Didn't they catch jellyfish in the trawl?" she asked.

"Who did I talk to, the woman recording data?"

Naeco stood. "It's probably Susan Faulkner. I'll see if I can find her."

After Naeco left, Durant clicked the play button again. Josh knelt beside the television. Buffy struggled into the jellyfish layer; the depth counter on screen continued to increase, albeit at a much slower rate. Mindless dark shapes indiscriminately battered the crittercam lens.

The view field jerked upward.

"The crittercam's coming off." Andrea glanced wistfully at Josh.

The depth counter stalled at one thousand three hundred and forty-eight feet. The same type of jellyfish with short tentacles swirled across the lens.

"Is it still attached?" he asked.

"I don't think so. It's actually stuck there."

Jellyfish jostled the crittercam spastically shaking their view. The white numbers gradually changed from one thousand three hundred and forty-five to one thousand three hundred and forty-two. Jellyfish started drifting from top to bottom of the screen.

"It's moving now," Josh said.

The crittercam gradually picked up speed as the jellyfish swarm thinned into clumps and then the odd individual. Free at last, the crittercam rose steadily toward glowing surface waters, white particles streaming past.

Only the low throbbing of the ship's engines could be heard in the room.

Occasionally a fish attracted to the lights passed through the viewfinder. At the surface the remaining footage showed similar images of waves lapping against the lens while the crittercam floated in the swell.

Durant flicked the lights on and stopped the video—there was no point watching forty-five minutes of South Pacific sea surface conditions while the crittercam continued to record until the search party found it.

Andrea turned in her chair to face the group. "I don't know what to say. This isn't what I expected. But the crittercam works. We saw two squid…I think. One of them I have no idea what it is."

Josh stood and leaned against the wall. "That's quite a jellyfish bloom."

"Do sperm whales eat jellyfish?" Durant asked.

"Not if they have a choice. Buffy was probably passing through."

Naeco entered followed by a thin woman with sharp features and spiky, dirty blond hair.

Andrea recognized her from the lab. She offered Susan her seat.

"Naeco's been telling me you have some fascinating deep sea footage," Susan said.

Durant started the video where the jellyfish appeared. Susan seemed mesmerized. Andrea carefully watched her reaction to the images.

"Stop here, please." Susan leaned forward, her fingers drumming on thin lips covered by a wispy moustache. "Rewind it a tad?" Eventually she straightened and, with subtle trepidation in her eyes, asked Andrea, "Can you tell me the precise location where you filmed this?"

"Sure, I'll check my notes."

"We could trawl there, but the mesh is too coarse to effectively catch jellies," Susan said.

"What are they?" Josh asked.

"I believe they're a type of *Periphylla*. It's a common deep sea jellyfish. They're normally found deeper than this though. They migrate vertically, but always remain fairly deep because they're sensitive to light. The numbers here are fantastic. I'll confirm with our trawl samples." She studied the images on the television screen. "It goes to show our knowledge about jellyfish...and the deep is quite rudimentary. There are likely millions of species down there. So far we've only catalogued a couple hundred thousand."

"The ocean's a big place," Josh said. "It covers seventy-one percent of the Earth's surface and is deeper than Mount Everest is high."

"So why would jellyfish bloom?" Andrea asked.

"Normally it happens when environmental conditions are just right," Susan said. "Jellyfish will take advantage and reproduce rapidly. Almost all observations of jellyfish blooms occur at the surface because this is where plankton blooms occur and where people are looking. I'm sure similar conditions arise at depth that will encourage a particular species to bloom. Maybe there's plenty of food or few predators."

"We were lucky to get the crittercam back in one piece." Josh walked closer to the television. "It sure produces decent images though. You know, Andrea, we should try attaching it to a bull; they aren't as social as females and eat bigger squid."

"My dream—if the crittercam works—is to take it to Antarctica and film the colossal squid, the king of cephalopods."

"How big do they get?" Durant asked.

"Possibly twenty meters. A trawler in Antarctica recently caught an eight-meter-long juvenile at twenty-five hundred meters."

"Let's watch it again." Durant dragged the laptop closer.

Everyone chattered at once and many refilled their drinks.

Andrea raised her mug to her colleagues. "A toast…to the mysteries and wonders of the deep. Thanks for all your help. Cheers."

Cups and glasses clinked in unison and beverages warmed the throats of weary researchers.

SEVEN

When Josh woke he couldn't tell for several seconds whether his eyes were open or closed. Disoriented, he searched the blackness for clues as to his whereabouts and how he got there. His head throbbed. The *Rubicola's* powerful engine drummed in the background. As all those horses turned the giant propeller, everything on board vibrated including the metal rod that raised and lowered the drain plug in the sink. The motion of the ship felt different compared to the *Go For Broke.* In the low South Pacific swell she rolled slower and longer from side to side. She was probably less stable because of the towering superstructure. He didn't like the feel of this modern ship, especially this morning. He had never felt this way on the *Go For Broke.*

Fragments of last night's activities flickered in his consciousness. After watching the crittercam video at least five times, a party spontaneously erupted in the conference room. When the noise increased, Andrea convinced everyone to move below to the dry lab away from the captain and chief scientist staterooms. It turned out to be a good idea because the partying went late into the night, or rather early in the morning. For a supposedly dry ship there seemed to be no shortage of alcohol. Then out came the game Pictionary which soon escalated into a full contact sporting event. He couldn't remember having so much fun. Andrea had assembled a terrific group of people who accepted him as an integral part of their team.

He rolled on his side and winced from a dull ache in his back, probably caused by Andrea jumping on it. She was definitely not a delicate creature. Playing Pictionary, she had wrestled him into submission several times. She had the body of a rock climber. And her eyes—so green, so piercing, like dewy West Coast moss.

He foolishly switched on the reading light and surrendered to the glare by burying his face in the pillow.

Why am I awake?

Although Andrea threatened everyone with a wake-up call at first light, she was still playing Pictionary around eleven, at one point forcing Durant to say 'uncle' by putting him in a vicious headlock. The last game ended sometime after midnight, but no one went straight to bed; rather, they raided the mess for ice cream and leftover desserts. He contemplated waking Andrea now just for fun, but decided against it for fear she might put him in a headlock too.

The book lying beside the bunk caught his roaming eyes. He pulled out the picture stuck between the pages. "Hey, baby," he whispered. "Miss you."

Diane danced toward him across the beach.

He loved everything about her—the smell of her skin after a bubble bath, her sultry bedroom voice, the particular way she chopped tomatoes. She would've been so proud yesterday when they attached the crittercam on the sperm whale. He wished she had kayaked with him among the whales. He wished she had swum with him among the whales. For one year and one hundred and sixty-three days all he did was wish for a life that could never be.

He wished the pounding in his temples would stop. At least the night shift crew made few sounds as they roamed passageways fixing and polishing items to ship-shape standards. He slipped the photograph between the pages and dropped the book on the mattress. He struggled out of bed and placed a towel over the fixture in the sink to stop the incessant buzzing.

Piles of manuscripts and photographs covered the wobbly desk. Perched to one side was his laptop computer. He sat down and looked again at pictures in his photo identification catalogue Lono had taken of the bull's ravaged fluke and compared them to one particular photograph of mediocre quality taken six years ago near the Aleutian Islands in Alaska. The whales in the pictures appeared similar except the one in the Alaskan photo wasn't missing a chunk of its fluke. The wound, probably from a ship strike, might have happened recently but, unfortunately, he couldn't make a three-point match and, therefore, a positive identification.

The computer screen displayed a map of the Pacific Ocean. A trail of red dots started two hundred and thirty-four kilometers from Hawaii and speckled the Pacific Ocean in a remarkably straight line in a southeasterly direction for nearly fifteen hundred kilometers. Some dots clustered close together, others were spaced further apart. They represented locations where the bull surfaced and the tag had successfully transmitted data to several satellites. Three transmissions were needed to triangulate the whale's position to within one kilometer. Only one or two successful transmissions meant the whale's location could not be determined but, from these signals, he still received information collected by the tag such as time, date, dive depth, dive duration, and time at the surface. Sometimes the tag didn't transmit any data even though the bull would have surfaced. If no satellites were passing over the exposed tag, then any signals sent would not have been received. Transmissions ended on day twenty-eight indicating the tag's electronics had finally stopped functioning.

The sperm whale rarely meandered and his constant hurried pace suggested some primal sense of urgency. Only when the bull reached the Clarion Fracture Zone, a deep oceanic trench that runs in an east-west direction off the Mexican coast, did dots on the map cluster, but only for three days.

Josh roughly measured the distance between Hawaii and their location in the Galapagos. It wasn't clearly understood how much male sperm whales moved around. Males seeking breeding opportunities generally came from Antarctic feeding grounds and not more northern areas, or so people believed. The bull may have undertaken a long migration. One sperm whale had traveled from North to South Africa, about seven thousand four hundred kilometers, in four and a half years, a significant achievement because the whale had crossed over the equator.

Did the bull breed? Where is he now? Maybe a fisherman found the tag, took it for a ride, and tossed it overboard. It's probably been drifting for two months. Impossible. The tag must have remained attached for Andrea to find it. Why didn't it keep transmitting? What dumb luck. To finally stick a tag on real solidly and then have the electronics crap out.

He chugged several glasses of stale ship water. Everyone and his dog knew female sperm whales congregated around the Galapagos. Higher productivity in the region, a consequence from upwelling that occurred when the Equatorial Undercurrent hit the islands and was forced to the surface, meant abundant food. So why are they producing fewer calves? Not enough males? What's happening to them? Has the Undercurrent weakened and fewer nutrients in the area mean less food available for whales?

He wondered about the bull swimming far below the agitated surface where light is virtually absent, temperature very cold, and pressure unimaginable. How do sperm whales even catch squid, sharks, and rays? Do they use vision to zero in on bioluminescent prey? Perhaps squid are lured to white markings around their mouths and then sucked into the gullet when they get too close. More likely sperm whales rely mostly on their sonar capabilities to detect organisms in the darkness. What the whale did to Andrea suggests they have evolved the ability to focus sound waves that can stun or kill swift-moving creatures.

He tilted his head back and wiped his eyes. Too many unanswered questions. Hopefully coming here won't be a waste of time. Should be good fun though. The cool water felt good, but was missing one important ingredient. The next crucial step on the road to recovery, he decided, involved an infusion of caffeine.

Wearing jeans, a gray fleece, and a ball cap, he walked stiffly to the mess, filled a mug from the cupboard with coffee, grabbed a crusty day-old bran muffin from a basket on the counter, and sauntered up to the bridge.

Curt swiveled around in a chair. "Have a good day at school, sport." After a pause, he started laughing. "You're right, today should be a holiday. Listen, I'll call you again tonight. Happy birthday, Jeff, love you. Remember, thirteen is good luck." He gently placed the phone on the table.

"Morning, sir." Josh gazed out one of the large windows at relatively dark water. It was too early to see whales. "How did the night shift go?"

Curt leaned back, stretched his arms out, and yawned. "Pretty uneventful. Did a bunch of grid transects to collect water samples for Granger's group."

"How are the whales?"

"Don't know." He yawned again. "I haven't heard a squawk from the hydrophone all night."

Josh strolled around the bridge in front of the broad windows. The deck below seemed deserted. "How long have you been working on this ship, Curt?"

"Four years. Best decision I made."

"Why's that?"

"It's rewarding being at sea helping you science folk. I spent five years on the Great Lakes, but that was seasonal work and barely paid the bills. I worked on cargo ships—good pay while it lasted—but pretty soon they started flying foreign flags and hiring only cheap grunts from poor countries instead of Americans. And I did time on a cruise ship after my wife left."

"I suppose it's tough always being away."

"She was a housekeeper. She kept the house." He laughed.

Several seamen wandered outside to huddle around the boom crane and drink coffee and smoke.

"Oh, I nearly forgot." He gestured at the radar. "Two ships showed up a few hours ago."

Josh walked over to the electronic device. On the black screen two green blobs almost touched each other. "How big are they?"

"Definitely bigger than this tub."

"Have you contacted them?"

"Negative. I tried, but didn't receive a response."

"When?"

"About an hour ago."

"What do you think they are? Navy? Bulk carriers? Cruise ships?"

Curt folded his arms and shrugged. "It could be any of those…or research vessels. I doubt they're cruise ships; they normally travel at night unless they're having engine trouble."

Josh tugged the brim of his cap. "Seems odd they're dead in the water and not answering their radios. Would you mind trying to hail them now? Maybe they need help."

As Curt began working the radio, Josh calculated the ships to be about twenty-five nautical miles away.

For five minutes Curt tried hailing the mystery vessels on several of the common marine radio channels. Josh paced around the bridge straining to see the mystery ships beyond the horizon. The Chief Mate has the authority to move the *Rubicola,* but it would take at least two hours to get there. What if the whales show up while we're gone? We could be back in five hours, maybe. A couple zodiacs could wait here. The helicopter?

He descended the ladder two steps at a time and jogged down the upper deck passageway. Peering inside the mess, he was relieved to see Andrea sitting in one of the booths eating breakfast with Sarah and several science personnel. He motioned to her; she excused herself and followed him into the passageway.

Her black hair, beautifully disheveled, fell gracefully across her cheeks. Her lips glistened from a touch of moisturizer. "Looking for a Pictionary rematch tough guy?" She wore tight red yoga pants and a white tee shirt with a colorful cartoon on the front.

The cartoon provided the perfect excuse to stare at her chest. Several whales, covering their giggling mouths with their pectoral fins, held strings attached to plastic flukes floating at the surface. People in a boat photographed the flukes while the whales below tugged their strings creating quite a show for the gullible human spectators.

"Sorry to bother you..." Maintaining eye contact required all his concentration. "There are two ships nearby that won't respond to our attempts to contact them. They've been dead in the water for several hours according to the officer on the night shift. It's probably nothing, but I wonder if we should check them out just in case. They may require assistance and I'm worried about the whales. We could fly over in the helicopter. We wouldn't be gone long, maybe an hour."

"What are you worried about?"

He shrugged.

"There's no whaling, is there?"

"Not for sperm whales. Not since eighty-five. People don't really like sperm whale meat...except the Japanese and Indonesians. It's supposed to taste pretty bad. The flesh is greasy and has a high myoglobin content. But that doesn't mean whaling never happens."

"Who would do it?"

"Could be several countries. Japan, Russia, and Norway don't agree with the International Whaling Commission's whaling ban and set their own quotas. Iceland and Korea kill whales under the guise of doing scientific research."

She paused, thinking. "Okay, I'll inform the bridge and find the pilot. I assume you want to go?"

He nodded. "You bet."

"We should get pictures if there's something fishy going on."

He exhaled heavily. "Great, thanks, Andrea." It felt good to do something proactive. "Can we leave in fifteen minutes?"

She pretended to pout. "I'll try, but I need to curl my hair and get a facial."

Definitely no work was needed on such a perfect face. "I'll see you on deck whenever you're ready," he said.

EIGHT

Josh paced near the helicopter parked idle at the stern. The air seemed cooler than yesterday, but it was still early. Sloppy waves broke against the side of the ship. Kayaking today will be tough. Do waves bother whales? Are they annoyed when seawater splashes in their blowholes when they breathe?

The noticeably stronger wind stretched skittish gray clouds in front of the sun. A solitary bird with a white head circled above the ship. Without binoculars he couldn't tell whether yellow marked the back of the head and neck. He hoped to see the Waved Albatross; it lives only around the Galapagos, specifically on one island, Española. Unfortunately the seabird seemed too small; the Waved Albatross has a wingspan of nearly two and a half meters.

For fifteen more minutes he wandered around the outer deck until Andrea approached. She pushed the last piece of a bagel into her mouth. "Are we ready to go?"

"Pilot's not here yet."

No sooner had he spoken when an older man strolled out of the mudroom.

"Speak of the devil." He hadn't seen Dan since his flight to the *Rubicola* two days ago.

Dan unlocked the doors on the helicopter. "I hear there's a couple of ships up to no good?"

"Don't know, they won't tell us," Josh said.

"How far we going?"

"Round trip is roughly fifty nautical miles."

"Our fuel's low, but enough for a short trip. I can pump some in now if you wanna wait."

"If you're confident we won't run out we'd like to leave as soon as possible, as long as it's safe. Your call," Josh said.

"We're good. We're not flying to South America."

Andrea stepped up to the front seat where the view would be more conducive for taking photographs. Josh sat behind her. They adjusted their radio headsets while Dan spent several minutes walking bowlegged in cowboy boots around the helicopter inspecting the rotor blades and exterior thoroughly. Frequently he paused to stuff tails of his plaid shirt into his blue jeans which hung loosely around skinny legs. The wind kept messing his carefully combed gray hair.

He finally climbed in and started the engine. The blades began turning, slowly at first, then faster and faster. He double-checked readings on various panel instruments. The flimsy metal shell vibrated and rattled under the spinning blades.

Josh instinctively tugged on his seatbelt to make sure it was firmly locked. He silently berated himself for not bringing earplugs. The noise from the helicopter was aggravating his headache.

"Hang on to yer shorts!" Dan hollered.

The helicopter lifted vertically off the stern. Dan wrestled for control as gusts of wind shook the aircraft. Upward they flew in ever-widening circles, the research vessel shrinking beneath them. At an altitude of three hundred meters, a height where they could effectively search a wide swath of ocean, Dan pushed the control stick forward. The helicopter's nose angled downward propelling them in the direction of the mystery ships.

The vast expanse of the South Pacific Ocean unraveled as they flew high above the rippled blue membrane. Faintly visible in the distance were islands in the Galapagos chain blanketed in a cream-colored haze. Occasionally a fishing boat passed beneath, the skipper searching for urchins or lobsters. Flocks of unrecognizable birds glided in cohesive groups. At one point they tried counting dolphins in a pod, their streaked bodies shimmering under the surface.

Concentrating on fighting off waves of nausea, Josh remained silent during much of the flight. The motion of the helicopter being bucked around by the wind and unidentified ships operating in the same sector of the ocean where their research whales foraged made him feel sick. To keep his mind off his queasy stomach, he gazed out the window at the horizon. Warmer and then hotter he felt. It helped somewhat when he unzipped his fleece. Nauseous feelings subsided even more when he opened an air vent on the window and his lungs filled with fresh morning air.

After twenty minutes Dan pointed at a dark speck on the horizon. Two ships were moving at three knots on a southeasterly course. They approached from their sterns all the while gradually decreasing altitude.

Single stacks near the sterns indicated powerful diesel engines propelled the ships. The bridges, located amidships, were relatively small compared to the large command center sitting forward on the *Rubicola*. A tall mast towered in front of each bridge. The ship closest to the helicopter was approximately seventy-five meters long, her hull generally black except for red rust patches eating through metal in numerous places. Her sister ship seemed even less seaworthy.

The ships disappeared from view behind them. The helicopter banked for another pass. They flew closer off the port side of the smaller vessel. The sick feeling in Josh's stomach intensified and it had nothing to do with the motion of the helicopter. A whispered prayer, barely audible, escaped his lips. He knew what these ships were designed for. The mast topped with a crow's nest in front of the bridge gave it away. A catwalk extended from the bridge, above the narrow hull, to an elevated platform at the bow where a harpoon cannon was mounted. A slipway, a ramp-like modification to the stern commonly found on whaling vessels, made it easier to haul whales out of the water onto the deck for butchering.

"These are whaling ships," he said. "There's a gun at the bow and a stern slipway. They're pirates." He hated everything about these ships—their existence and the people who built and operated them. "These are trawlers that have been converted into killer-factory ships." Vessels like these terrified him because if they proliferated in use they could be the straw that breaks the camel's back in terms of whale conservation. They roamed international waters unregulated, circumventing quotas set out by the International Whaling Commission.

Andrea looked back at him. "What's a killer-factory ship?"

"Whaling fleets are no longer economical since there are so few whales left, so smaller ships like these are used." He adjusted the uncomfortable headset. "They're essentially a whaling fleet-in-one. They have the capability to kill, butcher, and freeze whales. It's a cost effective way to hunt small populations."

She turned to Dan. "Can you fly closer so I can take pictures?"

"Closer the better."

The helicopter circled around to the other side of the vessels. The name *MV Runto* was painted on one of the bows. At least that's what Josh thought it said—it was hard to tell with the last two letters partially missing.

"I wonder where their port of call is," Dan said.

"It doesn't matter," Josh said. "Where ever these boats are registered, it's meaningless. It's all smoke and mirrors. Pirate whalers never want their true identity known. These ships continually change names, ownership, and their base of operations. Ultimately, though, they're somehow connected to the Japanese black market. That's where the whale meat eventually winds up."

Face pressed against the window, he mumbled incoherently occasionally to himself. Activity levels seemed to be increasing on decks of both pirate whalers. Tiny people scurried about unified with some great purpose. Black plumes belched from the stack on the smaller vessel when her diesel engine kicked into high gear. The killer-factory ship moved away from her sister. Suddenly, a kilometer off her bow, a great exhalation wafted misty particles into the air.

"There's a whale!" he cried out.

Two more whales surfaced and exhaled in synchrony, their slender black bodies easily identifiable from the air. The ship picked up speed and raced at eighteen knots toward the three whales.

"Those are sperm whales!" Panic crawled under his skin. This could easily be their research group.

One of the whales raised its head out of the water and slowly milled around in a circle.

"Dive, dive!" he shouted, his breath fogging the window. He grabbed the radio microphone between Dan and Andrea. "*MV Runto,* this is the *Rubicola,* over...*MV Runto, MV Runto,* this is the American scientific research vessel *M. Rubicola. MV Runto,* the sperm whales you're attacking are currently being studied by an international team of researchers and are not available for harvest. Acknowledge." Deep down he knew it was futile. Pirate vessels didn't care which whales they killed. They hunted endangered whales, undersized, nursing, calves, at any time during the year and in protected areas. No whales were off limits to them.

Receiving no response on one channel, he called the ships on other channels, but still heard nothing. He tuned the radio back to channel seventy-three and begged, "*Rubicola, Rubicola,* how do you read, *Rubicola,* over."

"Go ahead," Curt said.

"The two ships are illegal pirate whalers attacking sperm whales as we speak. Please come here and on route contact the Ecuadorian Navy and request they send a warship, over."

"Roger, we're already in transit. We heard your previous transmissions. Our ETA is thirty-five minutes, over."

"Can you land on that ship?" he asked Dan.

Dan surveyed the scene below. "Nah, no can do. Too much crap on deck." He cocked his head sideways, his lips forming into a gleeful smile. "Ya wanna help those whales, huh? It'll mean flying this bird in a way I'm not supposed to. Are you kosher with that? You're my customers—I need to get yer permission."

Josh and Andrea glanced at one another not entirely sure what he meant.

"You're in good hands," Dan said. "I'm Navy, retired. I've flown over two hundred combat missions."

The pirate whaler was rapidly closing the distance to the three sperm whales. Reluctantly Josh nodded, convinced he might regret this decision someday.

"Do what you can," Andrea said. "Save the whales."

"Roger, ma'am." Knuckle joints popped when Dan squeezed his fists together. "Let's see what this ol' bird can do."

He shouted "hang on!" a second too late. Wind screamed through the rotor blades when the helicopter banked hard and dove. Two pairs of hands shot forward grasping for support. The feeling of his stomach sliding up into his mouth almost made Josh vomit as they raced toward the hulking ship.

The helicopter roared over men on deck. Although a powerful ship, the whaler could not match the helicopter's speed and soon fell behind. Expertly Dan brought the helicopter to a standstill hovering only meters above the whales. The deafening clatter from the rotor blades frightened them; flukes sprang forth from swirling spray indicating the whales were headed for deep water.

Josh patted Dan on the shoulder. "You're the man."

The pirate whaler slowed and veered from what would be a collision course with the helicopter hovering off her bow.

Andrea let go of the handle above the door. "I recognize the smaller one from yesterday. She has a serrated scar on her tail."

"I hope we scared the crap out of them," Josh said, for the first time in his life. In the distance the second pirate whaler turned and seemed to be heading in their direction. "Time to harass those guys."

The helicopter climbed to eighty meters and banked to the east. They saw no whales as they quickly covered ground to the *MV Runto.*

"Let's pay a visit to the harpoon gunner," he said, knowing captains often fired the harpoons on whaling ships.

They flew low across the ship's bow. The gunner waved his arms at the helicopter skimming over his head.

"I don't think El Capitan is too happy," Josh said. "Buzz the bridge." He really didn't know what he was saying. Desperately he wanted to wake up so this crazy nightmare would end.

They flew over the ship's working deck and hovered close to the command center, rotor blades spinning dangerously near the mast in front of the bridge. The lookout in the crow's nest at the top of the mast shrank in the container where he stood. Josh could almost see the men's eyes widen in the bridge when the helicopter suddenly appeared out of nowhere in front of them.

He held up the microphone to encourage crew to talk to him on the radio. Andrea took several photographs of the bridge and crow's nest and then waved her camera to show their actions were being documented. But the men in the bridge just flailed their hands like they were shooing away a pesky fly at a picnic.

The helicopter banked away from the ship and dropped some distance off her starboard side fifty meters above the water's surface.

Dan spoke to them like they were having a casual conversation over lattes in a coffee shop. "Don't worry, I'm good at ditching these things. It's an art, really. You have to hit the water just right so when the prop's ripped off it don't come spinning through the cockpit. You want it to spin away from the fuselage. I had to bring one of these babies down in a lake in South Africa. Notta problem."

Neither one replied; Andrea's response said it perfectly for both of them. She nonchalantly aimed her camera at Dan and took his picture.

"Oh, no, there are two whales!" She pointed in several directions. "There's a blow over there too."

The group of sperm whales surfaced around the killer-factory ships. Two whales blew close to the *MV Runto,* which immediately gave chase. Dan pushed the control stick forward sending them skimming above waves in pursuit. The gunner kicked the stop on the mounting and swiveled the cannon at the closest whale, all the while shouting orders to the bridge through a microphone beside him.

But the sperm whales were out of range and, when they sounded, cheers rang out from the helicopter. The whales didn't fluke-up, however, so their dives would probably be shallow and of short duration. Not wanting to overrun them, the ship slowed, as did the helicopter, which continued to circle above, watching.

Minutes later one whale surfaced, this time close to the pirate vessel. Spreading his legs wide, the gunner stooped over the weapon and aimed it at the whale's mid-section.

Crack

A seventy-five-kilogram barbed steel shaft shot from the bow trailing steel cable behind it. The harpoon arced over the waves and plunged just shy of the target spraying seawater into the air. There was an eerie silence—like time had abruptly stopped—and then a low thud erupted when the grenade screwed to the leading end of the missile exploded, its metal casing shattering inside the whale. Thirty-centimeter-long barbs flared open and lodged the steel shaft deep in its flesh.

The sperm whale lunged and rolled, the immense fluke churning the sea surface into a frothy soup. Instinctively it dove to the safety of the deep. Dark blood pouring from the gaping wound turned the dive puddle black.

Cable attached to the harpoon spun from a hydraulic winch below the ship's deck as the whale struggled downward. At first the engineer allowed cable to play out unfettered, then he applied the brake to put resistance on and slow the whale's descent. Life seeped from the mortally wounded animal. The winch rattled as it took up slack in the cable when the whale swam to the surface to breathe.

While the gunner talked to his compadre standing in the crow's nest, another fellow ran down the catwalk and reloaded the gun with a killer harpoon. Two sperm whales surfaced this time, the other whale had joined its wounded companion underwater. Before the dying whale could dive again, the gunner shot it from close range behind the head.

The ship's bow nudged close to the motionless animal. The gunner leaned over the bulwarks and repeatedly thrust a long, thin lance into the body.

In death, the sperm whale rolled over exposing its cream-colored underbelly and ventral grooves behind the jaw. It, rather she, was a female—white patches of pigmentation revealed the genital slits, the mammaries on either side of the urogenital opening.

A lifelong companion porpoised near the dead family member. *Get out of there,* Josh pleaded silently to her. Groups have been wiped out by whalers because of this trait in members of a social unit.

The whaling crew wrapped cables around the fluke and floated the whale's body to the stern. A massive claw-like pair of tongs descended into the slipway, clamped on the fluke, and dragged the carcass up the ramp. Four men climbed on top and thrust long flensing blades deep into the skin and through the thick, yellow mantle of blubber. Black blood poured from the incisions over rubber boots of grizzled onlookers waiting on deck.

At first no one in the helicopter said a word while whalers peeled strips of blubber off the dead whale.

With no emotion in his voice, Josh said quietly, "It's our life mission to stop this from happening to another whale. Andrea, take plenty of photographs. The world needs to know what's happening on the high seas. Dan, do whatever you need to do. I don't care."

With a vengeance, Dan steered the helicopter toward the first sperm whale he saw. Swooping down, they hovered above the frightened whale, the helicopter's skis nearly scraping its back until it dove. Spying two other whales swimming three hundred meters away, they raced toward the pair and Dan performed the same maneuver because it seemed to work. Like a flat rock skipping across the smooth surface of a pond, the helicopter leapt from one whale to the next, hovering only as long as it took for them to disappear.

But not all sperm whales could be saved. The second killer-factory ship, in hot pursuit of a frightened young whale, chased it to exhaustion. The gun fired and the harpoon struck its mark. When the whale surfaced a minute later, beads of blood in the purple spout splattered the ocean. The harpoon had pierced the lungs and death came swiftly. The gunner didn't need to fire a second kill shot.

"Let me get some pictures," Andrea said, grimly.

The upside-down whale floated against the ship's starboard side, a milky cloud of regurgitated stomach contents dissipating around the head. By now only a few squid remained at the surface; the larger pieces had already sunk out of sight.

Dan's flying style became increasingly bolder—lower and faster they raced toward whales and ships. The hair on Josh's neck stood erect as the side of the whaler loomed directly in front of them. At the last second the helicopter rose up over the deck narrowly clearing higher structures. Back and forth they buzzed above men clamoring over the slain sperm whale. The tiny helicopter near such large ships and whales resembled a lone honeybee defending its hive against two marauding bears.

While Andrea was taking photographs a crew member stepped outside the superstructure and pointed something in their direction.

Josh stiffened when yellow flashed below. "They're shooting at us! Go up, up!"

Dan yanked the control stick back. "Yee haa." The helicopter climbed steeply above the whaling ship beyond the range of the small caliber weapon.

Josh exhaled heavily. "Everyone alright?"

Dan seemed to be having the time of his life. Andrea didn't answer.

Josh leaned forward and squeezed her arm. The limb fell limply down by her side as her head slipped forward.

"Diane!" Pure terror grabbed hold. He struggled to release the belt that restrained him.

She turned slightly, the limp arm now functioning perfectly. "Sorry." She wiped her eyes.

Hand over his racing heart, he slumped back in his seat. Lifeless Diane lay crumpled in his arms.

"Here comes the *Rubicola*," Andrea whispered, looking to the north-east. Running at full throttle, the research ship plowed through waves that were increasing in height as the morning winds strengthened.

"Good timing," Dan said. "We're nearly outta fuel."

The *Rubicola* slowed several hundred meters off the port side of the *MV Runto.* Surprisingly the killer whaler didn't really respond to the presence of the American vessel except deliberately keep some distance away. Behaving almost indifferent to the chaos surrounding her, the *Rubicola* moved ahead at two knots, not approaching any ships or whales. The deck remained deserted.

"What are they waiting for?" Josh asked.

Two seamen eventually emerged from the superstructure and congregated around the port side davit.

"They're launching the zodiac," Andrea said.

He nodded. "Good. I was hoping they'd send a party over."

Crew lowered the zodiac and tied it alongside. Any second a group wearing red life jackets would appear. But the working deck remained strangely empty of blue uniforms. Every minute that went by with pirate whalers operating unconstrained meant fewer living sperm whales inhabiting the ocean.

Josh grabbed the microphone. "*Rubicola*, come in."

"Go ahead."

"Hey, Curt. Sure good to see you guys. So what's your plan of attack?"

Curt didn't immediately respond, the silence coming in loudly over the airwaves.

"I assume you're sending a boarding party to the whaling ships. Proceed with caution because they already shot at us."

"Uh, thanks for that. We're going to monitor the situation for now. Stand by."

Josh dropped the microphone. "Monitor? What's there to monitor?"

One of the whaling vessels gradually moved away from the *Rubicola.* Their strategy seemed obvious—one ship would distract the research vessel enabling the other to continue hunting. Soon a sperm whale was swimming for its life.

"They're making fools out of us," Josh said. "Let's harass that ship while the *Rubicola* deals with this one."

"Tank's practically empty," Dan said. "We gotta land."

"How can we be out of gas?!"

Dan half-turned in his seat. "I told you we didn't have much fuel. This"—his right hand waved in the air—"wasn't in the regular flight plan. We'll make one more pass, that's an order."

The violent scene below continued to unravel. The gun on the bow fired saving countless squid.

Whalers secured cables around the dead sperm whale's fluke. Instead of dragging it up the slipway, they hoisted the body vertically above the bulwarks and hacked the tail off. The mutilated carcass fell into the ocean. Floating behind the pirate whaler, the whale moved eerily as if it were alive. When the stump began to sink, the head rose out of the water and did a partial pirouette, pitchpoling in death as in life, but now the eyes registered nothing and did not move. There was no forceful spout when it slipped beneath the surface, the body soon to nourish sharks and abyssal scavengers.

The speed and efficiency with which the pirate whaler reduced a once vibrant living whale to a few steaks stunned everyone in the helicopter.

"If only I had some missiles," Dan murmured.

Nothing Josh had heard about this type of whaling came close to the truth. It was far worse. Before the end of the day all the tails from this special group of sperm whales would be frozen in holds on these two ships. "Please land," he said, bitterly.

Expertly Dan guided the helicopter in its descent toward the *Rubicola*. As they approached the pad, he turned to them. "Generally I fly workers to oil rigs—it pays the bills, but it's boring, routine crapola. I had more fun today than I've had in years. I remember why I always wanted to be a pilot."

"You're a terrific pilot," Josh said.

Andrea touched his arm. "You saved many whales today, thank you."

Dan picked up the microphone. "*Rubicola*, request permission to land and refuel."

"Permission granted. The landing pad is clear, over."

In gusty winds Dan brought the helicopter down gently on the rolling deck.

Josh immediately unlatched the door. Violent, swirling air filled the cockpit. He struggled down to the deck and ran, head bent low, under the spinning blades. He sprinted across the main deck and up the ladder to the bridge.

Out of breath he hurried past Durant and Curt and approached Matthews who was watching the *MV Runto* through binoculars and dictating intermittently to a crew member, "...heading two four eight degrees, speed three knots."

Breathing heavily, Josh asked, "Have you made radio contact?"

Matthews didn't look at him. He continued watching the ships through binoculars. "Negative. We've tried hailing them on all channels. They're deliberately not contacting us."

"Captain, we don't have time to be diplomatic. They're slaughtering the group. At least three whales have already been killed. Why don't you move the *Rubicola* alongside so I can go aboard?"

Matthews lowered the binoculars. "Those vessels are moving too erratically."

"Let's send a party over in the zodiac."

"I want to talk to them first."

Josh threw up his hands. "About what?" Durant and Curt remained silent and pretended to be doing something important. In a cooler voice, he spoke more slowly. "Captain, these are pirate whalers engaged in highly illegal activities. We have every right to engage them."

"I understand, Jerry—"

"Josh."

"Josh, yes, we have contacted the Ecuadorian Navy. This is their jurisdiction. For now we will stand by and monitor events as they unfold. Am I making myself clear?"

"Is the Navy sending a ship?"

"I...believe so."

"When?"

Matthews didn't immediately answer. Josh knew the pirates would be long gone before the Navy arrived, if they ever did. The Navy's warship was probably tied up, literally, or chasing drug smugglers up and down the coast. Saving a few sperm whales wasn't likely a high priority for the military.

"We can't wait for the Navy. Let's cut them off, harass them, get in their faces, do something."

"Those ships can out-maneuver the *Rubicola*." Matthews jabbed his reading glasses at him. "We're not going to argue and you're not going to question my authority again. Who do you think you're talking to? This is my ship and my decisions are final, so be careful, son."

Josh's jaw tightened and breathing quickened.

Someone gently grabbed his arm. "Josh, please," Andrea said, softly.

He pulled away and stepped dangerously close to the Commanding Officer of the *Rubicola*. "Why don't we just sit here and watch those butchers slaughter the group?!"

Matthews' lower lip quivered. "There's nothing I can do as Captain of this United States Navy vessel to stop them from whaling in these waters. I have followed correct protocols and contacted the proper authorities. What do you want me to do?" He had now lost it. Coffee-tainted breath puffed in Josh's face. "Ram those ships? Jeopardize everyone's safety on my ship because of a goddamn whale?"

They glared at each other for a long second.

"Now get off the bridge!" Matthews shouted. "I have a job to do!"

"What job? You're not doing anything!" His face flushed, Josh stormed past Andrea, Curt, and Durant. Passing through the door, he smashed his hand against the bulkhead between two windows. He ran down the ladder.

"Josh, where are you going?" Andrea called out behind him.

"To get some coffee," he hollered without looking back. He cut across the rear of the bridge and hurried down the ladder to the upper deck. Instead of going inside to the mess he jogged across the main deck and climbed down the ladder into the zodiac.

NINE

Frantically Josh untied the bow and stern lines and pushed the zodiac away from the *Rubicola*. Choppy waves rocked the boat and splashed over the pontoons. The zodiac raced away from the ship, sea spray lashing his face. The hand-held radio rattled around in the waterproof box tucked under the driver's seat.

Hundreds of meters away a blow vaporized in the wind. As he struggled to put on a lifejacket and steer, the zodiac, her bow hammering into swells, careened wildly toward the whale. Seconds before impact he yanked the throttle back into neutral and allowed the boat's momentum to carry her forward.

I'm going too fast!

He slammed the throttle in reverse and braced himself against the wheel. The bow plowed into the side of the sperm whale.

Stumbling around the steering console, he shouted, "You think that hurt? It's nothing compared to a harpoon. Dive, dive, you stupid whale!"

The fluke thrashed from side to side. The sperm whale rolled away from the boat, buckled at the midsection, and dove.

Josh jumped behind the console and turned the wheel hard to port, steering the zodiac in tight circles around the dive puddle. At times the boat lurched forward when he revved the engine in attempts to frighten the whale into deep water.

Two spouts blasted skyward near one of the whaling ships. The zodiac turned sharply and bounced toward the whales. The shiny back of one whale seemed unusually large, like its exhalation.

His heart sank. "No, no, no…don't show up now," he cried out to the wind.

The hunter-whaler gathered speed and bore down on the whales while they spouted. No way could he beat the diesel-powered ship to the whales. A dark figure hunched over the harpoon.

The spouts separated. The bull sperm whale, its head raised out of the water by powerful undulating strokes from its fluke, swam directly at the oncoming ship which turned sharply to avoid a collision. Out of control the steel hull rammed into the smaller whale.

The ship shuddered and rapidly came to a standstill, her engine powered down. Two men ran down the catwalk to help the gunner who had been injured when he was thrown against the harpoon. One man carried him up the catwalk, the other took his position at the bow.

Black exhaust belched from the stack when engineers re-engaged the whaler's engine. Superficial structural damage to the reinforced hull wouldn't stop this sturdy ship for long. Built to be able to maintain full speed in heavy seas, her hull was specially designed to not crumple under stress. The whaler turned to position the harpoon for firing.

The gunner viewed the struggling whale through the sight on the weapon. Pectoral fins rapidly beat the water for propulsion to compensate for the limp, useless tail.

The zodiac darted between the pirate vessel's bow and ailing sperm whale and dropped in a trough of a swell.

Crack

The harpoon screamed overhead. Josh instinctively ducked. The steel cable attached to the harpoon fell into the ocean and sliced through the front of the boat, shredding the bow pontoon. He slammed into the steering console, his head careening into the metal pipe that reinforced the windshield. Stunned, he collapsed on the pontoon, jarring his diaphragm and knocking the wind out of him. The engine sputtered and died when he tripped the kill switch.

He squirmed on the wet deck desperately gasping for air. Gradually regular, but shallow breaths returned. He lay on his back propped against the pontoon, his body numb and unmovable. Blood flowing from a deep gash on his forehead pooled into his eyes and trickled down his face. A salty mixture of blood and seawater coated his lips and found its way into his pasty mouth. A hollow quietness embraced him. In a daze, stinging eyes traced outlines of clouds in the sky, ringing ears listened to waves slapping under pontoons at the waterline.

Her bow flattened, the zodiac drifted silently with the plankton, steered no longer by a propeller, but now by the whims of the wind and currents. She wouldn't sink thanks to compartmentalized pontoons that allowed only air in the ruptured portion to escape.

The rust-pocked whaling ship loomed menacingly in his field of vision. Cables securing her fluke, crew floated the gored female to the slipway and dragged her aboard. They walked their flensing knives along the twisted, swollen body, slitting it open from the throat grooves behind the jaw to the genitals. A three-meter-long wrinkled black calf spilled from the uterus onto the bloodstained deck. After a giant blade severed the curled fluke and umbilical cord, they pushed the near-term fetal carcass down the ramp back into the ocean.

The lifeless body floated upside down near the zodiac. Tears moistened globs of dried blood plastered on Josh's cheeks. Abruptly the baby sperm whale vanished, as did the whaling ship, the zodiac, the wind and waves. Instead Josh saw with absolute clarity a red hatchback racing along a winding country road. He saw himself behind the wheel peering intently while wipers worked feverously to sweep torrential rains off the windshield. Diane, gasping, struggling to breathe, sat beside him, her hands massaging her pregnant belly.

He convulsed as the car sped into a deserted intersection. His mind screamed for the vehicle to stop, but the driver paid no attention to the warning. Suddenly a black pick-up truck appeared out of nowhere and crashed into the passenger side pushing the car through the intersection until both vehicles came to rest against a telephone pole in the ditch. His eyes were wide open and wild as he viewed the smoldering wreckage that remained of his life.

As he stood alone in the waiting room, a doctor approached, her green smock splattered with blood. The surgeon removed her mask and placed a sympathetic hand on his shoulder. While he watched himself slump into a chair and bury his face in his hands, consciousness mercifully slipped from his troubled mind.

TEN

Josh vaguely could hear a boat approaching. Someone called his name several times.

"He's in the zodiac," someone shouted.

A boat bumped the damaged zodiac. She then rocked when people stepped on the pontoons and jumped in.

Durant knelt next to him. "Don't move." He leaned close and listened to his breathing.

"Where's the whaling ships?" Josh asked.

Half the bow had been shredded and collapsed. "Everything's fine." Durant grasped his right foot. "Wiggle your toes…more…good. Tell me if it hurts anywhere." Maintaining eye contact, he felt around his head and neck and examined his ears. "Can you take a deep breath? Easy now."

Josh sucked in a chest full of air and held it for a second before exhaling.

"Good." Durant placed a hand on his abdomen. "Push your stomach out." Still watching his facial expressions, he pressed on both sides of his hips and squeezed down each leg.

Josh flinched when Durant touched his left knee.

"That hurt?" Durant peered closer. "We'll check that later. I'm going to stabilize your head in case you have a spinal injury." He positioned himself behind him and pressed firmly against the sides of his head to immobilize the neck joint. With arms wedged in place, he called to a seaman in the other zodiac, "Radio the *Rubicola* and have them come here. Tell them we need to lift a zodiac on deck because we have a suspected spinal injury. And we need someone with first-aid training standing by with a spine board." While the seaman relayed instructions, Durant said to Josh, "I'm sure you're fine, but we should be careful."

The two zodiacs drifted tied together. Josh lay on his back across the wet deck with Durant forcefully squeezing his head. Sharp pain pulsed through his upper body. He found it difficult to concentrate. Once in a while he moved his toes just to make sure.

Soon a portion of the *Rubicola's* fo'c'sle and bridge decks interrupted his view of the drab gray sky. Engines started and a seaman steered the damaged zodiac alongside the ship under the port side davit where a lifting bridle dangled near the water. They secured the crumpled boat to the fall and then scrambled into the other zodiac to minimize the weight of the load being lifted. With only he and Durant aboard, crew hoisted the boat four meters up onto a moveable platform jutting out from the fo'c'sle deck. Several men carefully lifted him onto a spine board and securely strapped down his head and neck.

"You're going to be fine, Josh," Andrea called out from somewhere behind the wall of onlookers.

"Andrea, come here," he said, hoarsely.

Breathless, she tried to squeeze past a particularly heavy fellow. "Josh, are you okay?"

"Listen, sperm whales often flee danger to windward. And they can move sixty kilometers in a day."

"Oh, Josh."

"Save it for later, you two," said the Second Mate, a tall gangly kid with a messy crop of reddish brown hair.

Durant and the Second Mate carried Josh on the spine board down a passageway to sick bay, a modified supernumerary stateroom. They lowered the board on a padded table. Square white tiles covered the deckhead. The table was positioned against one bulkhead. Near his feet was a sink and next to it a standing cabinet about two meters high stocked full of bandages and drugs. A stainless steel oxygen tank with plastic hoses sprouting out the top leaned against the cabinet. An unsettled feeling swept through him.

"Hey, Durant, tell Andrea and the bridge that I'm alright. I don't want us to return to port."

"It'll depend on your injuries," the Second Mate said. "If you need x-rays we'll have to get you to a hospital cause I can't do them here."

Durant walked toward the door.

"Hey, thanks for your help," Josh said. "I could tell I was in good hands."

Durant forced a thin smile. "My dad's an ambulance attendant and my mom's a nurse. We're always practicing first-aid. I actually haven't used my skills for a while."

"Now you tell me."

Durant chuckled. "I hoped your heart had stopped so I could practice CPR."

"Sorry to disappoint you."

Durant paused in the passageway. "I'll tell everybody you're in good shape and to leave you alone so you can rest."

The Second Mate approached. "My name's Trevor. I'd like to check your back. I need to slide you on the table."

He peeled the straps apart. Josh inched sideways off the board. With Trevor's support he stiffly rolled onto his side facing away from him.

"Let me know if it hurts when I push down." Starting at his neck, Trevor gently pressed on each vertebra all the way down his spine. "How's that feel?"

"Alright." *Probably a bad sign.*

"Can you sit up?"

Josh rolled onto his back and, with Trevor's help, raised himself into a sitting position.

"Swing your legs over the side here." Trevor bent down and examined his knee. "It's swollen. Did you bang or twist it?"

"I don't know."

"You don't remember?"

Josh shook his head. "No."

"Can you bend it? Only go as far as it feels comfortable."

He slowly bent and flexed his knee throughout half its range of motion. He strained to move it further. Shooting pain radiated from the knee into his thigh. He tried not to show any discomfort. "Feels pretty good."

"It's probably sprained. Stay off it for a day or two." Trevor looked closely at the deep gash on his forehead. "How'd you do this?"

"I got a real close look at the windshield."

"That'll need a few stitches." He opened the cabinet and gathered several sterile pads. He cleaned the wound and surrounding skin, first with water, then alcohol. He inserted a frightfully long needle containing a local anesthetic several times into Josh's forehead. He tapped several spots around the wound. "Feel that?"

"What?"

"Never mind." He positioned himself at the edge of the spine board. Josh had no choice but to lie still like a wax statue while Trevor pushed the needle back and forth through the wound. He tied knots in the thread and clipped the excess off with scissors.

"Like mending nets," Trevor said. "You'll have a scar, but it'll fade eventually."

"How many stitches?"

"Thirty-two."

"What!"

"Just kidding. Nine."

Josh sighed. "Call me Joshenstein."

"Relax, you look like a hockey player." Trevor handed him a bottle of prescription painkillers. "Take two every four hours for the next twenty-four hours. Let me know if your headache doesn't go away after two days." He threw up his hands. "That about does it. Get plenty of rest and avoid the Captain like he has the Ebola virus or he'll toss you in the brig and throw away the key."

Josh politely refused any more help and limped down the passageway. Somehow he survived the ladders between decks and, by deliberately avoiding high traffic areas like the mess, managed to arrive at his stateroom without meeting anyone he really knew.

Once inside he locked the door. Reluctantly he inspected his face in the mirror. In an instant he had aged ten years. A reddish lump protruded from his forehead. Dried blood caked his thinning hair and streaked his face and neck. He really wanted a shower, but that meant leaving his stateroom and out there he might bump into Andrea. No way can she see me so messed up. She probably wants nothing to do with me anyway. He filled the sink with warm water and soaked a wash cloth and scrubbed away blood on his face, being careful not to get the stitches wet. He rubbed the damp cloth along the back of his neck. Although he had no desire to brush and floss his teeth, he did anyway, having not missed a day since his braces came off when he was sixteen years old.

He slumped on the lower bunk and buried his face in his hands. How many whales died today? It's only a matter of time before they're wiped out if those few that do grow up get slaughtered by pirate whalers. Maybe sperm whales are disappearing simply because of wide-scale unregulated whaling? He massaged his temples. Andrea's research was finished. Whoever remained of the group, if any, would be long gone and finding them would require a miracle. Why is their time at depth so brief? For some reason they're not diving as deep as they used to. He remembered the oxygen tank in sick bay.

He switched off the reading lamp and slipped under the cool sheet. Footsteps and voices echoed in the passageway. The engine throbbed relentlessly. Nature was becoming less predictable, more disorderly, and chaotic. He finally had accepted this conclusion after more than a decade of fieldwork—subtle, nearly unperceivable, changes were taking place in the ocean but he, like everyone else, chose to ignore the warning signs.

Exhausted yet restless, he tried several positions to get comfortable. Eventually he drifted off, waking intermittently during the next few hours with a mind-numbing headache even powerful painkillers could not extinguish.

ELEVEN

Balancing a tray piled high with breakfast foods, Andrea tapped on the cabin door. Hearing nothing, she knocked again, this time louder. "Good morning, Josh." She tried sounding as cheery as possible.

The room remained quiet.

"Josh, it's me, Andrea." She waited. "Please say something so I know you're okay."

A muffled voice seeped through the door. "Morning, Andrea. I was sleeping."

She pressed her cheek against the door. "We're all worried about you. You didn't show up for breakfast."

"Nearly getting decapitated tired me out, sorry."

"I brought breakfast. Would you like to eat together?" She listened to him move around inside the room. *At least he can get out of bed.*

"How about a rain check?"

Is he hurt badly? She placed the tray on the ground. "I'll leave some porridge outside the door in case you get your appetite back. I'll check back this afternoon." She stomped not too far down the hall and then, grinning slyly, slipped off her shoes and tip-toed back and stood beside the door against the wall.

The cabin door opened very deliberately. Dressed in sweat pants, a tee shirt, and a ball cap, Josh bent down stiffly like an old man to pick up the tray.

"Boo!"

He snapped to attention. "Geez, I nearly had a heart attack."

She snickered. "Just making sure the ol' ticker's still working." She picked the breakfast tray off the floor.

He let out an exaggerated sigh. "You might as well come in since you're still here."

She patted his shoulder as she brushed past. "I always get my way." She stopped in the middle of the room. "How about we sit on the floor and pretend we're having a picnic?"

Josh vigorously swung the door back and forth to fan stale air out of the stuffy room. "It actually might be good to be in another position instead of lying down."

"Trying different positions can be a lot of fun." Like usual no obvious reaction. Such a serious guy. She pushed the chair under the desk.

He grabbed a gray wool blanket from the closet and spread it over the floor. He eased himself down and leaned against the bunk. Not quite comfortable, he wedged a pillow behind his back. She placed the tray on the blanket and then sat cross-legged facing him.

Both surveyed the breakfast goodies: porridge, toast with jam, orange juice, tea, milk, two single boxes of cold cereal, and a couple of jam busters.

Andrea laughed. "I didn't know what you liked so I loaded up with everything."

"It looks great, I'm starving." He surrounded himself with items off the tray.

She poured milk into a cereal box. "Durant thinks your injuries aren't too bad. How are you, really? Please tell me the truth."

"Um, so-so. I had a brutal headache, but it's a bit better today. My leg's pretty sore."

He seemed subtly agitated, more stressed than usual. "Durant mentioned you needed stitches."

"Yah, I sliced open my forehead."

"Ooo, can I see?"

"I'll bet you were one of those kids who tortured bugs, like pulled the legs off spiders or wings off flies."

Her eyelids fluttered long lashes at him. "A woman can't divulge all her secrets."

He shrugged. "It's just a few stitches, it's nothing." He spooned some porridge into his mouth.

They ate quietly, sampling different foods. He tended to look down at the floor rather than at her.

"Andrea, I want to apologize for what happened. I acted without thinking."

She found his soft gray eyes mesmerizing. "If you didn't do something all the whales might have been killed. You acted courageously... albeit stupidly." Her grin vanished. "But I would never have forgiven myself if you were seriously hurt."

"I jeopardized your research project. I'm sure the Captain's royally pissed off."

"You saved my research, Josh. We attached the crittercam because of your expertise."

"It's always too little, too late," he murmured.

"Hey." She sat up straighter. "I wanted to tell you, feel free to make as many long distance calls as you want. Have you told your wife about your little adventure?"

He shifted uncomfortably. "No."

She bit into a jam buster and took her time licking icing sugar off her lips. With difficulty he pulled himself up by the bed frame and washed his hands in the sink. He lay down on the bunk with his hands behind his head and gazed at her for an uncomfortably long time. At last he rolled part way over and grabbed a book on the shelf. From between the pages he pulled out a photograph and passed it to her.

"She's beautiful." Andrea carefully passed the photograph back. "You don't look anything like your sister."

He meticulously replaced the picture among pages in the book. "We should've been married four and a half years by now. Diane died two years ago."

A deathly quiet smothered the room. Andrea couldn't help it—she tried to stop them—but tears trickled over her cheeks. "I'm so sorry for your incredible loss," she whispered.

"Me too."

Sitting cross-legged, she wiped her cheeks and brushed loose strands of hair away from her face. Sheepishly they studied each other for what seemed like an eternity. Josh's shoulders gradually drooped as muscles loosened. Tension evaporated from his body erasing years off his face. He seemed to want—probably needed—to talk about it.

"Will you tell me what happened?"

"What version do you want to hear? The newspaper's or mine?"

She looked at him quizzically.

"Some kid high on drugs T-boned us. Half the car was crushed… where Diane was sitting."

Andrea covered her mouth with her hand. "I'm so sorry, Josh. That's horrific."

"A changing climate is what really killed her though."

Her brow furrowed. "How do you know…is that possible?" She wondered if grief had poisoned his perspective on things.

"A friend of mine works at the Pacific Climate Center in Vancouver. Generally over the past few decades the weather where I live has become warmer and wetter and El Nino more frequent. Their climate models have accurately predicted the last four El Nino events. Two years ago we had an unusually wet winter which caused the deer mice population to explode. Our community had five cases of Hantavirus that year—an unprecedented number. You get it from deer mice crap. Diane probably got it poking around in the barn." His watery eyes stared beyond the bunk into another time and life. "We figured she had the flu. The night of the accident Diane was already dying. She could barely breathe—" He suddenly froze. Slowly he turned. "What other research is happening on this ship?"

"Um…" The unexpected question yanked her back to the world of work. "Let's see…one group is doing substrate mapping, there's microplankton research, trawling, Allison is studying how persuasive small pieces of plastics are in the marine environment, and there's water sampling and oceanographic studies. Why?"

"Who's doing water sampling?"

"Sullivan Granger's team."

"We need to find out if they've analyzed any samples."

"Okay, why?"

"Sperm whales are behaving weird, it's bugging me. Something is...very wrong."

Suddenly feeling exhausted, she leaned back against the desk. Her plan had been to cheer him up. Now he only looked unbearably sad.

An awkward silence followed.

"Well, I should be going." She stood and lifted the tray off the desk. "Thank you for sharing breakfast with me."

He snapped out of a trance and tossed the book near his feet. "I haven't been on a picnic for ages."

"And just think, no ants."

He grinned. "Or uncles or any family for that matter, just the two of us."

"Ha, ha. I'm glad you're feeling better." She opened the door with one hand while balancing the tray with the other. "I'll track down Sullivan. You should get some rest." She flashed him a quick smile and walked down the hall. The first thing she would do is find Sundrop and hold her tight. For some reason she felt strangely frightened, not for herself, but for Sundrop and all the children back home.

TWELVE

The clatter grew louder. Andrea strolled outside on the bridge deck and joined Sundrop and Randi who were standing next to the life rafts—two white canisters resting on metal cradles near the rail. The helicopter banked in a wide circle above the *Rubicola*. Its blotchy green and brown color, broad shape, and open side door screamed military, but it wasn't always obvious what poor, small countries used old helicopters for. After circling the ship twice it continued north, nose angled downward, flying low over the water.

Andrea stepped back inside the bridge.

"The Brazilians are playing war." Curt clipped the microphone on the radio. "At least that's what I think he said."

Hands behind his back, Matthews watched the crane deploy a red and white buoy over the side. Trevor sauntered into the bridge and approached the Captain.

Matthews turned. "What's the status of the workboat, Schneider?"

Curt stopped writing in the ship's log. "Compartments one and two are badly damaged, but they might be fixed with materials on board. Tommy's looking at it and will let you know."

"And the outboard?"

"Ship-shape, sir."

Matthews huffed. "So what's the verdict, son?"

Trevor cleared his throat. "He's fine as far as I can tell. The spinal stuff was just a precaution. He gashed his head pretty good. I stitched that up. Oh, and he hurt one knee."

"Should he go to a hospital as a precautionary measure?" Matthews asked the question like he really hoped it would happen.

"I doubt it. I told him to rest in his stateroom for a couple days."

Gently stroking his pointy Adams apple, King Matthews looked down at his subjects. "Is he fit to fly?"

"Oh, definitely."

His head cocked sideways. "Dr. Megin?"

She perked up pretending she hadn't been listening. "Sir?"

"How much time remains for your project?"

"Uh, only two more days."

Matthews mulled the information over. "Dr. Templeton is to be flown off my ship by seventeen hundred hours. I want to talk to the pilot."

Curt grabbed a hand-held radio lying on the chart table. "Deck, bridge. Sven, find the helicopter pilot and send him up pronto. Captain wants a word."

Andrea approached Matthews. "Captain, I wonder if you would reconsider and allow Dr. Templeton to stay for two more days."

"He's a danger to this ship and himself," Matthews said, bitterly.

Dan strolled into the bridge. "Reporting for duty, sir." He gave an exaggerated salute.

"Good afternoon." Matthews suddenly became more pleasant and offered to shake Dan's hand. "Captain Brad Matthews. We have a scientist who must leave this afternoon and I'd like you to fly him to the airport."

"Nuthin I'd like to do more, but I need to fix the chopper first."

"What's the problem?"

"Looks like a bullet hit the fuselage near the fuel tank and clipped a couple hoses. Those nervy whale killers shot at us."

Matthews said to Curt, "Why wasn't I informed of this? Get an oiler out there asap. Find someone off duty, I don't care. I want that helicopter flying by eleven hundred hours tomorrow."

Dan turned to leave. He winked at Andrea.

Matthews put glasses on and read from a long scroll of paper. "Until he's escorted off my ship Dr. Templeton is to remain in his stateroom. Is that understood?"

Trevor straightened and grew several centimeters. "Yes, sir."

"Keep me informed of his progress."

"Yes, sir."

"I want you to check on him at least twice daily."

"Yes, sir."

Matthews shuffled toward the stairs and motioned for Trevor to follow. "Come on, son, I'll buy you a coffee."

It didn't sound like an invitation to be declined without good reason. Trevor seemed pleased and fell in line behind the Captain.

"I'll return in one hour," Matthews said to no one in particular as they left the bridge. Tinny footsteps gradually faded on metal stairs.

"So what's the Captain like to work with?" Andrea asked.

"You mean work under. Oh…not bad." Curt picked his words carefully. "Matthews is a real man of the sea. He probably should've been in the military—I don't know why he didn't have a career there. He's retiring next month. This is his last trip."

"Is that good for you?"

Curt watched the helicopter several kilometers away through binoculars. "Can't hurt. Looks like they're hovering."

"I don't see any ships," she said.

"Let's find out what they're up to." He adjusted the *Rubicola's* course and increased her speed to nine knots.

As the research vessel approached, the helicopter abruptly gained altitude and flew off.

"Something is there," Andrea said. Waves were breaking over a massive cream-colored object.

Curt maneuvered the *Rubicola* near the floating mass, but not so close it could come into contact with the hull. They walked outside to the bridge deck's rail.

A tapered flipper stuck straight up from the whale's gray body. Waves shattered against the white belly on which long pleats stretched from the underside of the jaw to the navel. Sharp, brown triangular fins periodically broke the surface around it.

"Don't fall overboard," Curt said. "It's a feeding frenzy." He strolled inside the bridge and promptly returned with a camera.

Andrea gently grasped Sundrop by the shoulders and turned her from the rail. She subtly gestured to Randi.

"I just adore your long eyelashes and cheekbones," Randi said.

Grinning, Sundrop bowed her head. Sometimes her cuteness was simply overwhelming.

"Is that a fin whale?"

Andrea glanced over her shoulder. "Hi, Durant. I think so. It would help to see the coloration on the jaw."

Bending over, Randi gently lifted Sundrop's chin with her finger. "Let's go to my room. I have make-up you can try. It'll be fun."

Sundrop's face lit up and her eyes widened. "Really! I'm not allowed to wear any at school."

"For sure you wear moisturizer?" Randi asked, genuinely mortified.

Andrea smiled. "You're not in school right now. I think it's a good idea."

"I'll show you how to put make-up on so all the cute boys in high school will chase after—" Randi seemed distracted by something seaward. "Us princesses need to stick together, you know," she murmured.

The *Rubicola* vibrated and water around her bow frothed white as bow thrusters fired to move her away from the dead fin whale.

"The head's a bloody mess," Durant whispered to Andrea.

"Oh?" Red and black patches covered much of the side of the head and jaw. "You're right. Josh should see this."

"It's dead as a doorknob. What's he gonna do?"

She didn't reply. Yes, what would Josh do? A deep heaviness pressed on her heart. Why can't anyone stop those whaling ships? Ravenous sharks tore apart the lifeless lump. She had promised Sundrop they would see only living whales in the Galapagos. At least this whale will nourish other creatures. We waste so much, but nature wastes nothing.

Andrea leaned against the rail. How should she advise her people? Council was seriously entertaining the possibility of returning to whaling to generate money for their poor community. They needed to create jobs and revive their culture and get young people excited about the future. Her people historically hunted gray whales and the north-east Pacific gray whale population had recovered to historic levels; thousands migrated through their traditional territory twice a year. Japan and Norway already expressed interest in buying whale meat from them should they be able to provide it. Although the U.S. Endangered Species Act protected gray whales from commercial whaling, this could change in the near future. Representatives from her community were actively lobbying governments to stop classifying gray whales as endangered. Soon her people could be killing them just as they had been doing for thousands of years. But will this solve their social problems? Even with a small quota, how many whales will be injured and escape only to die later and not be counted toward the annual harvest? Some whales return to the same places year after year. Are we going to wipe out resident groups?

Randi gestured at the horizon. "Did anyone see that?"

Keenly all eyes followed the thin line where ocean meets sky.

"I thought I saw something...I don't know." She waved her hand to dismiss it. "It was probably nothing."

"I'll check the hydrophone," Durant said. "How far away was it?"

Randi took a deep breath. "I don't know. It was pretty tiny."

"They might be out of range," Durant said.

They followed him inside the bridge. He put headphones on. Soon he offered them to Randi. "You wanna listen?"

"Do you hear a whale?"

"Nope."

Randi delicately placed the headphones on trying not to mess her hair. "What do they sound like?"

"Radio static if there are lots of them. If there are only one or two you'll hear single clicks."

"Like this?"

"What?"

She passed the headphones back to him. He cupped one over his ear.

"Hear them?" she asked.

He motioned for her to be quiet. Suddenly his eyes widened and his frown turned into a broad smile. "Right on, Randi." He held his hand up to high-five her. "There's definitely sperm whales out there."

A second chance! Andrea walked around the chart table and approached Curt. "Have you seen Sullivan Granger?"

"Not for a while. Maybe check the lab."

She headed to the door. "Durant, show Curt where the whales are and get us close." She hurried down to the deck below, past the mess, down the stairs to the second deck, and turned right by the washroom. She stepped through a narrow door into the dry lab.

The lab was the size of a typical office. A row of microscopes sat on a stainless steel counter opposite the door. Two students were huddled around one microscope, their backs to her.

The guy pushed his chair away from the counter to allow the young woman to look through the eyepiece. He seemed agitated and kept rubbing his eyes. "Every single one looks deformed."

The woman hunched over the microscope and began replacing one slide after another. "I see mostly coccolithophores and a few foraminiferans." She spun the nosepiece trying different objectives. "I think you're right. The coccolith structures are malformed."

"What are you looking at?" Andrea asked.

Startled, cute guy turned. "Plankton." He stood. "I'm going to find Sullivan." He walked past her out the door.

"Can I see?" Andrea asked.

The young woman straightened and gestured at the microscope. "Be my guest." With eyes partially closed, she rolled her head from side to side stretching her neck. "These are mostly coccolithophorids—single-celled algae with calcareous structures. They're very common. The irregular dark shapes are tiny pieces of plastic."

Andrea looked through the eyepiece and adjusted the focus by turning a knob on the microscope's arm. The highly magnified field of view contained several distinct spheres each covered with overlapping circular striped disks that resembled bicycle wheels. She had on several occasions seen plankton under magnification before and those specimens were beautifully symmetrical and intricate. In contrast, the spheres here appeared to have been beaten with the ugly stick; they weren't smooth and elegant, but quite misshapen, the circular disks warped.

"Are they alive?" she asked.

"Hard to believe, isn't it. I doubt they'll reproduce."

"These were collected around here?"

The woman nodded. "Two days ago, I think."

"Why are they like this?"

A heavy, bearded man with tinted glasses marched into the lab followed by the student. "This is a restricted area," he said sternly to her.

Andrea stood and casually pushed the chair under the counter. "I didn't realize that." *Poor man probably had terrible acne in high school.* If he were a woman she would've thought he was carrying twins. She smiled sweetly. "Dr. Granger, I presume?"

"Uh, huh."

"Can we go outside for a minute? I'm really interested in your research."

Sullivan murmured something unintelligible and nodded.

With him huffing behind, she strode briskly down the hallway to Josh's room and knocked on the door. "I have Dr. Granger here with me."

The door flew open. Josh shook Sullivan's pudgy hand. "You're the expert chemist, I hear. Have you been collecting water samples in this area?"

"Yes, we've done quite a few vertical CTD casts."

"What data are you collecting?"

"The usual—salinity and temperature at depth."

"Do you sample for dissolved oxygen?"

"That too."

"How do the numbers look?"

Sullivan shrugged. "I'd say fine."

"Good to hear." Josh glanced at her. "I assume your CTD continually samples while in the water?"

"For certain things. We also collect water samples at particular depths of interest."

A woman walked around the corner so they moved against the wall opposite the cabin door.

"What depth do you sample to?" Josh asked. "Do you go all the way to the seafloor?"

"Sometimes. What's this all about? Why the twenty questions?"

Andrea touched Sullivan's shoulder. "We need your help. The whales are behaving strangely and we've seen lots of jellyfish. So you haven't noticed anything unusual in your water samples?"

"I told you, no."

"Question twenty-one. You sure your CTD has been calibrated properly?" Josh asked.

"Of course." Sullivan was clearly irritated. "What's next, a polygraph test?"

"Sorry, I'm just trying to understand. Is it possible the CTD isn't sensitive enough or doesn't work properly where oxygen concentration is very low?"

"Anything's possible, I guess."

"Can you corroborate your CTD results using another technique in the lab, like the Winkler titration method?"

"That takes time," Sullivan said.

Josh pointed at his sore leg. "I got nothing but time. Can you test a few water samples, especially several from the deep near the bottom?"

"You might find some interesting results to publish," Andrea said.

Sullivan's left heel tapped up and down shaking his leg. "Where did you see jellyfish?"

"Around thirteen hundred feet," she said.

"You saw them at depth, huh. Hhmm. We could lower your camera with the CTD and take a look."

"Hey, I like that idea," Josh said.

Andrea chewed her lower lip. "Josh and I will talk about this and get back to you."

"Suit yourself." Sullivan sauntered in the direction of the watertight door, stopped, and then turned and walked past them the other way down the hallway.

When Sullivan reached the far end, she slapped Josh's shoulder. "Hey, Matlock, it's not his fault."

He scowled. "I don't have patience for this anymore."

She guided him to his room. "You need to take it easy. And you haven't been granted day parole yet."

"Too late. I've already been sneaking around. I saw that dead whale."

Her voice softened. "Those whalers seem unstoppable."

"Pirates wouldn't leave a whale like that. The trauma to its head suggests a ship strike."

"Oh? Curt did mention something about military exercises happening nearby."

Josh raised his right knee stretching the hamstring. "If that's what's going on, then I'll bet that whale died from exposure to low frequency sonar. Navies use it to hunt subs. Any poor whale that swims too close will get its ears blown out."

She sighed and, with both hands, patted his chest. "Submarines, whalers, jellyfish. Let's not forget why we're here, okay? The priority is the crittercam and squid. I don't have much time left in my program."

He took a deep breath. “Why don’t we lower your crittercam with Sullivan’s CTD in the evening if we haven’t put it on a whale? This way it won’t interfere with your research.” Their eyes met. “Andrea, it’s your research that’s taking us somewhere important. I don’t know where yet, but I truly believe we must find out what’s happening in the deep.”

He seemed terribly worried. She hadn’t noticed before two faint creases on his forehead just above a small scar. She smiled reassuringly. “We better not lose the crittercam, that’s all I’m saying.”

THIRTEEN

After supper, and confirmation from the bridge the *Rubicola* was in position, Andrea joined a group gathered around the hydrographic winch, a drum the size of her cousin's Honda wrapped with steel cable. Two seamen were assembling a removable platform, three meters long with rope railings, which protruded out from the side of the ship next to the winch. The tall deckhand fed winch cable through a pulley hanging above the end of the narrow platform.

Sullivan and the guy from the lab carried their Conductivity, Temperature, and Depth probe to the platform. The CTD consisted of a variety of instruments sitting like a white bird in a titanium cage. A carousel of twelve gray cylinders for collecting water samples circled the sensors.

Perched high above the water like mutinous sailors sentenced to walk the plank, the deckhand and Durant attached the CTD and crittercam to the cable.

"You can never use too many zap straps," Andrea reminded Durant.

The deckhand leaned over and pushed the cable away from the side so the fragile equipment wouldn't bump against the hull. His left hand pointed downward and made small circles signaling the operator to lower the winch. One of the crew, a stocky brunette, stepped behind the controls and engaged the hydraulic motor. The drum slowly started turning and the crittercam slipped beneath the surface.

Choppy waves danced around the cable. Rationally the risk of losing the crittercam was far less when lowering it by cable compared to sticking it on a whale. Durant had tied it securely in several places and the cable's breaking strength was a couple thousand pounds according to the Bosun.

Black waves lapped against the side of the ship. Young giant squid could be looking at us right now. They might migrate to the surface at night, a conclusion derived from finding their beaks in albatross stomachs. Maybe we should've baited the crittercam to attract squid prowling at depth?

Andrea swung her legs over the side and dove cleanly through the waves. All terrestrial sounds like wind ceased instantly. Arms and legs stretched out wide like a starfish, she passed lanternfish and billions of other animals migrating up from the deep toward the surface. Steadily sinking alongside the crittercam, she didn't feel freezing cold or incredible pressure, only pure freedom and unspoiled wildness. Blue morphed gradually into darker blue and then finally to pitch black, yet she could see infinitely in every direction. Constellations of flashing and winking bioluminescence coalesced into wonderfully strange creatures. A jelly-like ribbon—a siphonophore—longer than a blue whale, with green, blue, white, and yellow lights in serial, glided endlessly between her legs. Bizarre fish, some eel-like, others quite round, with big black eyes, curved teeth often too long to fit inside their cavernous mouths, and glowing barbels waving above their heads or dangling under their chins, eagerly inspected the fresh meat happily descending from above. Numerous jellyfish, squid, octopi, and fish, either transparent or capable of producing their own light to match ambient levels, paraded past.

Below, mountain ranges more massive than the Himalayas and canyons deeper than the Grand Canyon provided topographic relief unlike anything existing on land. Tens of thousands of submerged mountains, mostly old volcanoes, jutted up thousands of meters off the bottom. Carpeting the seamounts, delicate suspension feeders like corals, sponges, anemones, and sea fans waved at her as they swept prey from nutrient-rich waters flowing upward from the deep. Vast schools of silvery amourheads gulped down small fish, squid, and shrimp. In swirling currents above the seamounts, flocks of seabirds bobbed above sharks chasing five hundred kilogram albacore tuna through the thick film of plankton.

Looming ahead, a fifty-meter-high stalagmite protruded from an expansive coral forest many hundreds of square kilometers in size. The abyssal plain rose to welcome her. Like a veteran parachuter on a windless day, she landed elegantly feet first in silty ooze. Winding tracks, holes, and miniature mounds provided evidence of bustling worms, clams, shrimp, and snails living in the chalky sediment created over millennia from volcanic ash, desert dust, and sporadic rain of dead plants and animals. Aggregations of sea urchins marched among clusters of brittle stars. Gelatinous sea cucumbers waving feathery appendages methodically filtered minute particles of food from the water.

Black plumes of super-heated water originating deep within the Earth's crust spewed from seafloor cracks. Feasting on volcanic gases, bacteria miraculously converted noxious chemicals like hydrogen sulphide and methane to sugars. Similar to terrestrial plants which convert the sun's energy to organic matter, these chemical-loving microbes form the base of deep sea food chains. White tube-dwelling worms, many as long as her, formed dense communities around the smoking chimneys. The tube forests provided shelter for clams, snails, shrimp, and fish. Andrea picked up several hairy white crabs and concluded they must indeed be blind because they had no eyes.

She strolled toward a vast brine lake. In places where cold methane seeped from the seafloor, tubeworms capable of living two hundred and fifty years sank their roots into the substrate searching for essential life-producing chemicals. She stepped carefully among crabs and worms feeding on methane along the shore of the submarine lake. Like Christ, she walked across the lake's surface, her feet bouncing off the highly saline water.

The seafloor abruptly dropped away; a deep trench plunged downward thousands of meters. She somersaulted off the cliff and fell between high rocky walls. Sea cucumbers drifting in the current floated above the bottom. Polychaete worms and giant single-celled protozoans the size of saucers sprinkled the seafloor. Startled, a flatfish emerged from the ooze and darted away—

Sundrop squeezed against her leg. Lights blinked in the distance. Hopefully they weren't ships butchering whales under cover of darkness.

They walked to the mess and filled two bowls with strawberry ice cream. They had a lifetime to wait—well, more like a very long ninety minutes; it would take forty-five minutes for the crittercam to reach the seafloor and a similar amount of time to come back up considering the equipment was descending at a rate of one foot per second.

They carried their ice cream to the bridge. Dimmed ceiling lights casting a yellow glow barely illuminated the darkened room. At times the officer who talked with a German accent flicked on a flashlight to see certain controls or to read. Something about being cloaked in darkness made everyone speak quietly, if at all.

Durant stood in front of the sounder. He grabbed the hand-held radio on the chart table. "Deck, bridge, what depth is the winch at?"

Andrea didn't like the eager tone in his voice. Walking briskly toward him, she jarred her hip against the unseen corner of a shelf.

"Eleven hundred and sixty feet," squawked a female voice over the radio.

Durant pointed at the sounder's screen. The flat outline of the seafloor suddenly rose almost straight up into a sharp pinnacle that reached through the water column halfway to the ship. He whispered to her, "We're creeping over a seamount. I sure hope the crittercam hasn't bumped into it." He called out to the Second Mate, "We're not holding station."

The Second Mate muttered in German and pushed several buttons. The ship vibrated.

Durant spoke into the radio. "Deck, bridge, stop the winch."

Andrea shoved her hands deep in her pockets and stepped away from the sounder. If the crittercam had drifted into the seamount it might have hit a rock and cracked the housing. The crittercam would instantly be crushed by the tremendous pressure. How difficult can it be to keep the ship in one place?

"What do you want to do?" Durant asked her.

She ran her hands through her hair. *Beside scream?* "Might as well keep going." If the crittercam were toast her program would be over anyway. "Please keep the ship away from any more obstacles."

The Second Mate somehow managed to obey her urgent command and steered the *Rubicola,* at a tortoise's pace, away from the seamount. The crittercam continued its long descent. She put Sundrop to bed and returned to the bridge around the time when the sampling equipment should be approaching the seafloor. Sullivan instructed Durant to stop the winch at two thousand two hundred and ninety feet, twenty-five feet from the bottom. One of the Niskin bottles opened by remote command and filled with ancient seawater. The grumbling winch started turning in the opposite direction pulling the equipment excruciatingly slowly back to the safety of the ship. Every two hundred feet another Niskin bottle popped open and collected a water sample.

The countdown started when twenty-eight feet of cable remained to be wrapped around the winch since the equipment would surface with eighteen feet of cable out. Andrea hurried with Sullivan and Durant down to the working deck.

"...twenty-one, twenty, nineteen..."

Cheers erupted from scientists and crew when the crittercam and CTD rose triumphantly out of the ocean.

"It lives to sample another day," Sullivan said, happily, to her.

Durant and the tall deckhand hauled the equipment onto the platform. Her entire body relaxed. The two men spent several minutes cutting zap-straps and unscrewing shackles.

Sullivan headed straight to the lab with his CTD to download data stored in the instruments and start analyzing water samples.

Andrea held the crittercam up to the boom lights. There appeared to be a slight dent on one side of the housing, but it seemed intact and there was no water inside. She said to Durant, "We'll meet you in the conference room in five minutes."

She jogged across the deck and down one level and pounded on Josh's door. The door flung open.

"We lost it," she cried out, her chest heaving heavy sobs.

Jubilation on his face immediately evaporated. "What!" His head drooped forward.

"It got dragged up a sea mountain and got stuck. They had to cut the cable."

"It hit bottom?" He stared at her in utter disbelief. "Those incompetent idiots!" His words echoed loudly down the hall.

Covering her mouth, she struggled not to laugh out loud.

He placed a hand on her shoulder. "I'm so sorry, Andrea. This is my fault." Bewildered he stepped back and sat heavily on the bunk.

She wiped her eyes. "We're meeting in the conference room. Can you sneak up there?"

Despondent, he grabbed a sweater off the top bunk. They walked silently down the hallway. He waited while she slipped into her room to check on Sundrop. Inside, she stood quietly watching cuteness cuddled on the top bunk. Listening to her breathing, she whispered, "Tiskin, please watch over Sundrop and protect her from harm and guide her safely through the night." She chuckled again at poor Josh and then frowned dejectedly when she joined him in the hall.

Mopey followed her into the conference room. Naeco and Susan were chatting near the television while Durant worked on the computer. The crittercam tote, smelling like old seawater, sat in the corner.

"You're a nasty, mean woman!" he cried out.

She laughed. He tried to grab her, but she stepped quickly around some chairs out of reach. "You looked like you found out Christmas got cancelled!"

"I'm ready," Durant said.

Josh dragged a chair out from under the table. "Where's Sullivan?"

"Busy in the lab," she said. "We'll compare notes after."

Durant turned off the lights. "We'll start at the bottom." He turned the television on and played with the mouse and computer.

The frozen gray image on screen burst to life—dense masses of jellyfish swirled around the crittercam. There was barely space for seawater.

"Where is this?" Josh asked.

Durant leaned closer to the computer screen. "Depth is two two five nine feet."

"There's only jellyfish here," Susan said.

"I don't know how anything else could live there," Josh said. "Where's this in relation to where Buffy dove?"

"Pretty much the same place," Andrea said.

"Sperm whales are going to stay far away from here," Josh said.

"I don't see any fish," Andrea said.

"This is why there were none in the trawl," Josh said.

Even though depth was decreasing by one foot every second, one would never know from watching the video. The jellyfish swarm remained thick for several minutes until it abruptly thinned where stronger currents swept individuals back and forth past the crittercam. A gray shadow materialized beyond the lights.

"This must be the seamount we drifted over," Durant said.

"Let's see if the crittercam hit it," Andrea said.

The crittercam moved steadily closer to vast sloping fields of rubble and gravel that covered the side of the underwater mountain. In places deep grooves in the sediment ran straight for hundreds of meters. Gnarled broken coral littered the moonscape; fragments had tumbled into irregular patches of yellow and orange sponges. Few fish swam into view.

Josh slammed his hand on the table. He stood and, arms crossed, leaned heavily against the wall.

"What's the matter?" Andrea asked.

He gestured at the television. "A deep sea trawler's already been here. This seamount's been obliterated."

"Way down here?" Durant asked.

The crittercam narrowly missed several boulders.

"There." Josh hobbled to the screen and pointed. "Between those rocks. See the torn chunks of net?"

Over a relatively flat pebbly area the metal cage scraped bottom, lifted off, and then came down hard tipping the equipment sideways. It then shot straight up; the seafloor rapidly melted away. Swirling marine snow slowed and numerous jellyfish reappeared until eleven hundred and twenty feet when they vanished for good.

"If I remember correctly the jelly layer began at thirteen hundred feet during Buffy's dive," Andrea said.

"I suspect they're vertically migrating. This video was taken in the evening," Susan said.

"Will they come to the surface?" Naeco asked.

"I don't know," Susan said.

Josh walked toward the door. "We need to know what Sullivan found out about the water here."

FOURTEEN

Josh and Andrea sat at the center of the long table in the same room where they had watched crittercam videos.

"...my father left my mother when she was pregnant with me," he said. "She raised me by herself, never remarried. I don't recall anyone in her life. I don't think she ever trusted men again."

Andrea quietly stared at nothing on the table.

"She died five years ago. I think she was pretty worn out. Life wasn't easy for her." He always felt a twinge of guilt when thinking or talking about his mother, like her life situation was somehow his fault. Being the only child, he had tried to stay in touch after moving to the coast and regularly sent money. "So tell me about your folks."

"Dad helps people with addictions," Andrea said. "Let's just say I got pretty good advice growing up. By grade ten all the girls in my class were pregnant except me and one other girl."

"You must've had some wicked parties."

She didn't laugh. "There's a lot of poverty and crime and high unemployment in our community. My parents really stressed education, but the quality of schooling was often pretty bad; it's hard to keep good teachers in such a remote place. I went to live with my uncle in Victoria during high school which helped prepare me for university. I always thought I'd go on in school before starting a family."

"So how does Sarah fit into the picture?"

"She's my daughter."

"I know that."

"I did an undergraduate degree and then started my Masters, but ended up rolling it into a PhD. I studied squid on the West Coast. I did most of my field work based at home, that was the main reason I took the project. Sarah was born about the same time I defended. I was twenty-seven."

"And you all moved to Texas and lived happily ever after."

"Well, some of us did."

"What happened?"

"Roy pushed me."

"Why would he do that?" Men move mountains to get close to women like Andrea, not push them away.

"I was afraid for Sarah. I don't want her to experience any kind of violence. So we left."

"Are you alright?"

"I am now. Physically it was no big deal..." Her amazing green eyes took a moment to study him. "We all have our crosses to bear, Josh. You're not alone. Sometimes we make bad decisions and the consequences suck. I hated Roy for what he did. At least you didn't mean for something terrible to happen which, in my books, makes your actions forgivable. But you need to forgive yourself."

"How long were you together?"

"About seven years." She pushed back cuticles on several fingers. "Don't you think your wife has forgiven you for what happened?"

He didn't answer.

"What if you had been killed instead? Would you forgive her?"

He scratched his cheek. "Probably."

"I bet she was a wonderful person. I'm sure she's already forgiven you."

Beyond stateroom bulkheads, Diane, alive and well, moved gracefully throughout their cedar split-level home. "She's an amazing woman."

"Now all you need to do is forgive yourself."

He shook his head. "I can't."

"It may take a long time. Do you think you can somehow at least accept what happened?"

"I haven't so far. I've just gotten more numb, that's all. Have you seriously forgiven your boyfriend?"

"Yes, that's how I eventually healed. Have you forgiven the driver who hit you?"

The possibility disgusted him. "Yah, we're best friends now. He eats dinner at our place every Sunday evening."

"Until you do you'll never be fully healed."

"So where's your boyfriend now?"

She examined chipped black nail polish on her fingertips. "Still there." She paused. "It's hard to leave. All my family and friends are there. I miss them so much, every day."

"Did you leave because of the job or him?"

"I thought we could have a better life elsewhere."

"Do you?"

She hesitated. "Yes and no. We live in a nice place. On the other hand some people are racist and Sarah is lonely sometimes."

Josh leaned back and casually gazed around the deckhead. "Have you thought about moving back?"

"There aren't many good jobs available. We visit quite often and I work closely with the fisheries biologist—"

Sullivan stepped into the conference room and closed the door quietly behind him. He sat near the entrance even though there were nine more chairs to choose from. He seemed either seasick or hung over and probably needed to be close to the head.

They moved to seats across from him.

"What did you see on camera?" Sullivan asked.

"Only jellyfish below eleven hundred feet," Josh said.

Sullivan didn't seem surprised. He leaned on his elbows, hands together like he was praying, and spoke in a low voice. "What I tell you stays in this room until I publish."

Andrea nodded. "Of course."

He oozed back in the chair. "As we discussed, we analyzed water samples collected every two hundred feet."

"How deep did you go?" Josh asked.

"Davy Jones' Locker around twenty-three hundred feet."

"So you analyzed twelve samples?" Josh asked.

"Something like that, yes. Keep in mind these results are very preliminary." Sullivan licked his lips. "Most variables were normal, but two...not even close." The thumb and finger on his left hand repeatedly pinched his lower lip. "Oxygen levels are quite low below one thousand feet. They're around one point four parts per million. This is quite unexpected."

"What is normal for here?" Andrea asked.

"Subsurface oxygen concentrations around two point five to three parts per million. Fish require concentrations greater than two parts per million."

Josh leaned forward, elbows on his knees, trying to understand what Sullivan was saying. "So there's a dead zone—"

"Hypoxic layer," Sullivan corrected him.

"There's a hypoxic layer from the seafloor, what did you say at twenty-three hundred feet, all the way up to a thousand feet. More than half the ocean is dead?" He suddenly felt light-headed.

Sullivan waved his hands like he wanted to push his words back to him. "Don't jump to conclusions—"

"What else did you find?" Josh demanded.

"The water is quite acidic."

"What does that mean?" Andrea asked.

"Normally pH for open ocean surface water is about eight point two. Our samples show seven point five." Sullivan was turning redder by the second, getting ready to explode. "There has always been a strong pH gradient with depth in the Galapagos region. But this is off the chart. The ocean hasn't been this acidic for hundreds of millions of years."

Josh stood, never taking his eyes off Sullivan. "Do you trust these results?"

Sullivan shrugged. “There’s no reason not to. We’ll do a much more complete analysis when we return State side though.”

Josh fought the urge to hyperventilate. Now he knew why Sullivan was sitting near the door. He, too, wanted to throw up…or run. The ocean was dying. Jellyfish were filling the depths and whales were diving shallow because that’s where their food lived, whatever remained, concentrated in a thin layer near the surface.

Without looking at either Andrea or Sullivan, he excused himself and limped out of the conference room.

Andrea quickly caught up to him in the passageway.

He kept walking. “I feel sick. I’ll see you later.”

She grabbed his arm.

He stopped and turned, struggling to maintain his composure. “What?” Her beautiful green eyes pierced his soul.

“I don’t know. I just know what you’re thinking.”

“You know what I’m thinking? We’re doomed, that’s what I’m thinking. Sperm whales, your beloved squid, plankton, you, me. It’s only a matter of time now. The world can’t live on jellyfish.”

“Don’t over-react. We don’t know that.”

“No.” He pointed a finger at her. “You’re in denial like everyone else. The ocean is the Earth’s heart. When it dies, life on Earth dies. This already happened several times in Earth’s history, the last time being fifty-six million years ago. The ocean runs out of oxygen and most species disappear. It’s over, Andrea. These changes are happening way too fast and species can’t adapt. None of our research matters. All we’re doing is rearranging deck chairs on the Titanic.”

“We can’t give up, especially now.”

“I’m done. I couldn’t save my wife and I couldn’t save those sperm whales and I sure can’t save the ocean.”

She pushed surprisingly hard against his chest causing him to step back into the bulkhead. Tears welled in her eyes. “I want Sundrop to have a good life. I’m not quitting on her. We can always do something.”

“Good luck.” He hobbled past her down the ladder, the railings holding most of his weight.

"Now you know how Indigenous Peoples feel!" she shouted from the top of the ladder.

He squeezed the railings with all his strength as anger seared behind his eyes. Saving the environment was a fool's game, always one step forward, two steps back. A few sperm whales survived the whaling ships. How much time did it really buy them? Until another ship picks them off? Or they get rammed by a tanker? Or they become so toxic from heavy metals and organochlorines they're nothing more than swimming tumors? Or they go deaf from all the noise in the ocean? Or they starve because their prey have either died or moved due to insufficient oxygen levels?

He pulled down on a pipe snaking above his head. Sperm whales were doomed anyway. Generally a species lasts a few million years before it goes extinct. It's just going to happen sooner rather than later. And within two or three billion years, as the sun continues to brighten, a runaway greenhouse effect will cause the temperature on Earth to soar and cook everything on the surface. The ocean will evaporate at which time all life will end.

He struggled through the watertight door lifting his sore knee with his hand. He slammed the stateroom door closed. Trooper hit the nail on the head years ago. We're here for a good time, not a long time. Might as well join the party. No use fighting it anymore.

He flopped down on the bunk. Circular brown knots dotted the wooden board supporting the mattress above. He examined the backs of his sunburned hands, not those hands that tenderly touched Diane's face when they kissed, but those that held the steering wheel when she died. His shoulders began aching so he lowered his trembling hands down by his side.

The ocean flooded over him, not clear, warm, sunlit waters, but dark, cold, deep waters. Using all his strength, he clung to Diane's enormous body, arms spread wide, fingers digging into her black leathery skin as she descended into the depths. Surface light faded and they sank in silent blackness. An unbearable coldness enveloped him. Down...down...down they fell, the ocean squeezing him in a suffocating bear hug.

At last Diane's giant body nosed into the seafloor several kilometers beneath the surface. Gray ooze billowed as she settled in soft mud. A mottled sleeper shark ripped chunks from her fluke. Swarming deep sea scavengers tore viciously at the fresh meat; some entered her mouth, others chewed their way through her thick skin—they festered in her body cavity and gnawed on her internal organs. She disintegrated under him as her blubber broke down and muscles fell away. Rotting organs turned into a semi-liquid mass trapped in a bag of skin which burst, the internal mass floating free. He clung to white bones, blobs of collagen sticking to his hands. Over time the skeleton gradually crumpled and he lay in sediment among the pile of bones, cold and terrified.

FIFTEEN

Josh woke shivering, his breathing shallow and hoarse. He had no idea the time or how long he had slept. Propped up on one elbow, he thought about the dream remembering every detail vividly. The unquestionable darkness that permeated the dream seeped into the very core of his being. Isolation and loneliness wracked his spirit. Face pressed into the pillow, he wept uncontrollably.

He stood and leaned over the sink. Puffy red eyes perched above tear-stained whiskers. Using a damp cloth, he washed his flushed face and wiped raw skin around the stitching. Turning his head side to side, he studied the outline of his whiskered jaw, the profile of his nose. For many seconds he and the boy in the mirror gazed at each other. When one blinked so did the other.

"You've lost everything," he whispered. "You gonna lose her too?"

Two pairs of smoky eyes stared unblinking. Take it easy, the boy in the mirror urged. There will be others.

Be a man for once in your life. He shook his head, growing more disappointed with himself by the minute.

He limped down the second deck passageway to Andrea's stateroom and stood outside her door. *Am I really doing what's right?* Going inside meant no turning back. Faint voices murmured within. He pressed an ear against the door. Although he couldn't tell what people inside were saying, one voice was deep, obviously male. Surprised, he stood paralyzed contemplating his next move. Then a seaman strolled around the corner. Feeling foolish, he hurried back to his stateroom.

He paced in a tight circle between the desk and bunk. Who could she be talking to? In rapid succession all good-looking male crew and science personnel flashed into his mind.

A soft knock directed his gaze toward the locked door. He didn't say anything, but quietly waited.

"It's me," said a small voice.

"Just a second." He hobbled to the door. "Hey, Sarah, how are you?" He smiled. "Do you want to come in?"

Her face brightened. She walked past carrying an armful of paper. He pulled the chair out from under the desk; Sarah dumped her load on the desk and squirmed onto the front of the seat. He lay down on the bunk. Neither one spoke.

"Is there something on your mind?" he finally asked.

"No." She gummed a clump of hair. "Mom told me you hurt yourself."

"Oh, it's nothing. I banged my head. Hey, do you wanna see the stitches?"

Her eyes widened. "Sure."

"Come closer then."

She wiggled off the chair and approached the bunk. He slid the baseball cap up.

"Eewww, gross." She stepped back.

"Nice, eh? There's nothing to worry about." He pulled the cap down.

"I brought you a magazine. Mom picked it out. Can I stay and color for a while?"

"Uh, sure." He quickly piled his clothes at one end of the top bunk. "How about up here?"

She conscientiously pushed the chair under the desk and climbed up the bunk ladder. He handed her the stack of construction paper and crayons. She stretched out on her stomach and started coloring, a fistful of crayons spread out beside her on the blanket.

He sprawled on the bottom bunk and flipped through the magazine. The main story featured African elephants. Six years ago on sabbatical he and Diane had taken a trip of a lifetime to Chobe National Park in Botswana and went on safari. At one time in his useless career he had seriously contemplated studying elephants because their life history was similar to sperm whales: matriarchal family groups, dispersing young males, bulls battling for breeding opportunities, and group protection against predators. The magazine story described research on elephants' amazing abilities to communicate over long distances using low frequency sounds people cannot hear.

A knock on the door corralled his wandering thoughts. "It's open," he called out.

Durant peeked into the stateroom and cautiously approached the bunk. "What'cha drawing, Sarah?"

"Just some whales."

"Can I see too?" Josh asked.

Sarah had colored most of the paper pale blue. Two gray boats surrounded several black shapes he assumed were whales. On the biggest boat a whale-like shape, with a spout or maybe teardrops around its head, frowned at him.

"We saw blows about a mile off starboard," Durant said. "Been picking up plenty of static too."

Josh tried to stifle a yawn. "What kind of hydrophone array are you using?"

"A directional one."

He had never used that type, but considered it for the new sailboat. His hydrophone received signals equally from all directions. Directional hydrophones have higher sensitivity to sounds from a particular direction and can be rotated to find the direction where signal strength is greatest.

Durant pointed at the deck. "It's lowered below the ship's hull to reduce any vibrations. Come have a look."

"Where are we?"

"About forty-five miles southeast from where we last saw them."

Josh stared straight ahead at his feet. Who was he kidding? There would be no new sailboat.

"I salvaged the GPS from your tag like you asked. Works fine now."

"Right, thanks for doing that," he mumbled.

Durant rubbed the back of his neck, nodded politely, and promptly left the room.

Josh massaged his knee. He had noticed Durant's thoughtful stare, his obvious disappointment, and fought to ignore it.

"Where do sperm whales come from?" whispered a small voice from above. Sarah's head hung over the side of the bunk.

He smiled at her black hair hanging straight down off her blotchy face. "You should ask your mom."

"Why?"

"Because I'm not qualified to give you the birds and bees talk."

"We did that in school."

"Then you already know. Two whales, one male, one female, who love each other get together..." He snickered at his own ridiculous anthropogenic rendition of sexual reproduction in the animal kingdom.

"I know where babies come from. Where do sperm whales come from? Like people used to be monkeys. What did sperm whales used to be?"

"To the best of our knowledge, *Pakicetus*."

"Who?"

He chuckled. "We need a time machine."

"I'm lying in one right now."

"Perfect. Will you come with me on a journey through time?"

Sarah squirmed around on the mattress. "Ready, Freddy."

Deep in thought Josh closed his eyes. "A long time ago there were no sperm whales or any cetaceans for that matter. Sarah, how old are you?"

"I'm seven and a half."

"You're seven point five, eh? Hhmm. Try to think how long a million years is. That's more than one hundred thousand times longer than you've been alive. That's a long time, isn't it? Pretty hard to wrap your mind around."

"It hurts my brain."

He chuckled. "You've heard of dinosaurs?"

"Yup. They're really big and people find rocks that used to be their bones."

"That's right. Dinosaurs were giant reptiles that perished sixty-five million years ago. No one knows why, but a meteor from outer space may have crashed into Mexico; the massive impact changed Earth's climate and dinosaurs couldn't adapt so they died."

"Those poor dinosaurs."

"It definitely wasn't a good time to be a dinosaur. Not only did dinosaurs that roamed around on land die, but also those that swam in the sea. But their extinction created room for other types of animals. Alright Sarah, let's try to picture the world fifty million years ago, long before humans existed, but after dinosaurs died. Continents like North America where you live aren't in the same places as they are now. Africa is separated from Europe and Asia by a warm, shallow body of water called the Tethys Sea, which stretches from Spain all the way to Indonesia and covers parts of Africa and Eurasia. You're standing on the shore of this vast sea. The air is warm and wet—very tropical. The blazing sun burns your skin so you pull a tube from your pack and spread sunscreen on your face and arms. Suddenly, nearby, you hear rustling in the vegetation." He lowered his voice to almost a whisper. "What is it? Prowling along the shore is a furry mammal, less than two meters long, with four skinny legs. It sort of looks like a cross between a dog and a small horse. What a strange looking animal! Goodness, it even has hooves. It lies down and rests its head on the ground listening for unsuspecting prey that it will ambush, kill, and eat. You're watching *Pakicetus*, a possible ancestor to all whales."

He paused. Sarah didn't say anything.

"I know you're thinking how can little *Pakicetus* be related to whales? In this strange animal's ear is a special bone called a bulla.

This bone allows *Pakicetus* to hear sounds in the ground. Whales also have this bone which allows them to hear sounds in water. Land animals don't have a bulla. Instead, we have an eardrum which lets us hear sound waves in air."

"But sperm whales don't look like Pachicetus."

"*Pakicetus.*"

"*Pakicetus…Pakicetus,*" she murmured.

"Alright, back into your time machine. Kazoom! A few million years have passed since you first met *Pakicetus.* You're standing in the same place. The air is hot and muggy. To cool off you wade into the warm waters of the Tethys Sea. Schools of fish tickle your ankles as they brush past. Oh no! You shouldn't be in the water. Sarah, get out! A four-meter-long crocodile is swimming straight at you!"

He raised his good leg and kicked the bed board of the bunk above evoking squeals from Sarah.

"Panicking you scramble up the bank and climb on a rock. Looking down you realize it's not a crocodile, although it resembles one. It has short thick legs, a long tail and snout, but it's covered with fur and has hooves rather than claws. *Ambulocetus* paddles around in the shallows occasionally plunging its head in the water to catch fish. It waddles on shore and rests its lower jaw on the ground listening for approaching prey. In its jaw are channels in the bone which carry sound vibrations from the ground to its ears. Hearing something, *Ambulocetus* waddles back into shallow water and submerges until it's barely visible. Soon out from the thick shore vegetation scampers a cute deer-like mammal totally oblivious to—"

"Stop! Stop!" Sarah cried.

Josh laughed. "What's the matter? Don't you want to hear what happens to the cuddly little deer with big brown eyes?"

"No." Giggling, she hung her head over the side of the bunk. "It's not going to be good, I can tell."

"Oh, no. It runs away and lives happily ever after."

"Hhmm, I don't believe you." Her head disappeared as she lay down on the bed.

He stood and started pacing and speaking faster. "You see, Sarah, all cetaceans evolved from a common land mammal after the dinosaurs died. Sometime between thirty-four and fifty-five million years ago some mammals found new opportunities, probably more food and less competition, in the sea than on land. Over millions of years these mammals gradually became more adapted to living in water until, at some point, they no longer needed to return to land for any reason—not to give birth or drink fresh water—"

Someone knocked on the door.

Is this Grand Central Station? He opened the door.

Andrea looked past him at Sarah lying on the bunk. Relieved, she smiled. "Hey, Sundrop." She motioned for him to step in the passageway.

He eased the door closed behind him. "Anything wrong?"

"Is Sarah bothering you? She wasn't supposed to stay long."

"Not at all. She's a terrific kid."

"She doesn't have a strong father figure in her life so—"

"I know. I like spending time with her. We're talking about whales."

"She mentions you a lot. I'm worried she might be growing attached to you. I just don't want her to start clinging to you and making you feel uncomfortable."

"No worries. I'm glad she came by. I'll take all the attention I can get."

Andrea grinned. "Good then." She turned to leave.

"Hey, thanks for the magazine. I didn't think you actually listen to anything I say."

She ignored him and kept walking.

Chuckling, he stepped back into his stateroom and rubbed his hands together. "Alright, Sarah, where were we? Oh, yes, as millions of years passed the ancestors of whales gradually became more whale-like. Eyes moved from the top of the head to the side. The external ear canal eventually closed off and the lower jaw became more important for hearing. Remember how *Ambulocetus* could hear using its jaw?" By now he was talking to the desk and his reflection in the mirror.

"Whales' jaws conduct sound waves to the ear through fat-filled canals. The nasal opening moved from the tip of the snout to the top of the head forming the blowhole. In toothed whales, teeth changed from grinding molars to a simpler peg shape for holding prey better. Baleen whales lost their teeth altogether and developed sieve plates of baleen. Front legs evolved into flippers. Whales no longer used their hind legs for walking so these eventually disappeared. They developed a tail for swimming. Whales also can grow much larger in water than they could on land because water can support a heavy body much better than leg bones can." He took a deep breath. Sarah was lying on her back, arms behind her head, eyes closed. "Sarah, you still awake?"

"I'm listening," she whispered without opening her eyes.

"Do you understand what I'm saying?"

"Some of it."

"So why did early whales split into toothed and baleen whales about thirty-four million years ago?"

She sat up, resting back on her elbows. "You're asking me?"

"Earth's climate changed dramatically when land masses began separating like when Australia moved away from Antarctica. This opened up the Southern Ocean and created a south circumpolar current that cooled Earth's climate and probably drastically changed the distribution of food in the ocean. Toothed and baleen whales may have evolved to take advantage of new food sources. Some whales became predators that developed the ability to echolocate to find prey whereas others became filter feeders. Within the toothed whale lineage, sperm whales came first, then the Ganges River dolphin, followed by beaked whales and ocean dolphins. There is evidence of whales with sperm whale characteristics twenty-five million years ago. By fifteen million years ago there were many species of sperm whales, but only three remain alive today: sperm whales, pygmy sperm whales, and dwarf sperm whales. Pygmy and dwarf sperm whales are smaller and evolved about eight million years ago. See how unique sperm whales are? They've been around about eight million years longer than any other toothed whale."

He abruptly stopped talking. He knew he was getting carried away when he said 'south circumpolar current' to a seven-year-old. "Here's a question for you, Sarah. What's the closest living relative to cetaceans? Remember cetaceans are descended from a hoofed ancestor."

Sarah was silent.

"I'll give you a hint. Whales are related to even-toed hoofed mammals like camels, cows, pigs, sheep, giraffes, antelopes, and hippopotamuses. Which one is most closely related to whales?"

"Camels?"

"Nope. Well, maybe to humpback whales." He snickered at his own joke. "Just kidding. The answer is hippos."

"Really?"

"I know, who would have thought? Cetaceans and hippos share the same common ancestor. Cetaceans split from a pig-like group of mammals called the anthracotheres of which the hippopotamus is the only surviving descendant. The rest died out about two and a half million years ago."

The top bunk was still. Sarah's steady breathing gradually intensified into snoring. Suddenly one eye opened slightly and she started giggling, very similar to the way her mother does. He loved hearing that particular laugh.

"You rascal." He messed her hair. "I thought for sure I bored you to sleep."

"I was listening the whole time. Let's go see the descendants of *Pakicetus* now."

"Wow, you sound like a scientist. Alright, Sarah, a descendant of monkeys, take me to the whales."

SIXTEEN

When Josh paused in the passageway to hook the stateroom door slightly ajar, Sarah scampered ahead through the watertight door and disappeared around the corner. He shuffled up the ladder and followed her outside on deck toward the helicopter at the stern. *What will Matthews do when he finds out there's been a jail break?* Andrea was nowhere in sight. Two seamen painting the base of the crane paid no attention to him. Three guys huddled around Randi next to the port side bulwarks.

Sharp, salty ocean smells and whiffs of coconut sunscreen pleasantly contrasted the stuffy odor inside the ship. Josh inhaled deeply, feeling invigorated. Squinting at diamonds of sunlight dancing across waves, his hand shielded his eyes as he searched for blows beyond a flock of seabirds bobbing like gray corks near the ship.

Five whales died for sure. Maybe five or six survived and regrouped. The bull was probably dead. In the past, charging sperm whales had a much greater chance of survival because wooden ships could be smashed sufficiently to sink them and bulls often escaped with only nasty headaches and splinters in their noses. But as steel replaced wooden hulls by the turn of the century, aggressive whales that rammed ships usually paid the ultimate price for their heroics. Whalers exploited the fight rather than flight behavior inherent to males and readied their exploding harpoons. No doubt the bull's fluke had already been rendered into tidy square steaks and stored in the blast freezer on one of the pirate whalers. The tailless carcass would be, by now, nestled in ooze at the bottom of the ocean. Maybe a biologist will find his bones in a trawl net one day.

"See any?" Sarah asked.

"Not yet." He continued searching for spouts along the horizon. "Sometimes in calm weather very little seawater pools in their blow-holes making blows tough to see. Have you seen them?"

Numerous tiny birds with white patches on their rumps swooped down near the ship; they didn't quite land, but dipped their little feet in and fluttered over the surface.

Sarah started giggling and tugged his arm. "Those birds are walking on the water!"

"They're storm petrels feeding on plankton in the surface film."

The birds fluttered near the *Rubicola* where waves concentrated plankton against the hull. He gave up trying to identify them; all three species in the Galapagos region had similar plumage.

Sarah thrust her arm out. "I see them!"

Near the horizon three pear-shaped spouts appeared, then disintegrated and vanished. Blows seemed angled rather than vertical, but sometimes rorqual blows were also oblique because the wind pushes them over.

Behind them, Andrea said, "What do two world famous whale researchers see?"

Josh stroked Sarah's hair. "The world's best marine biologist can barely see over the bulwarks."

Sarah suddenly grew by standing on the tips of her toes.

"But she sure can find whales," he said. "She's got eagle eyes."

"Durant made an interesting observation from the bridge." Andrea handed him binoculars.

"What am I looking for?"

"Sperm whales. You really did hit your head."

Under magnification blows periodically plumed into the air and backs of whales briefly emerged among waves. Eventually one blow blasted higher than others.

"I see him!" He adjusted the focus. The bull spouted several times. "I don't believe it!" He struggled not to get his hopes too high. They had traveled a considerable distance from where the attack occurred; this group could be another social unit or maybe another male had joined them. More than one bull might be roaming the Galapagos searching for receptive females.

"We need to find out if this is the herd we've been following," Andrea said.

"Are you planning to use the kayaks?"

She nodded.

"Take it real slow, alright? Who knows how they'll respond after what they've been through."

"Maybe they'll be more approachable." She bit her lower lip. "I'd feel better though if a zodiac stayed close, just in case."

Josh stood with Sarah off to the side while the deck buzzed with activity. Durant used the crane to lower the workboat. While crew did the same with the undamaged marshalling boat, the research team lowered one of the kayaks with the sling and tied it against the larger zodiac. Naeco mounted a camera on a tripod and filmed the group of sperm whales.

Josh and Sarah counted seven whales off the port quarter.

He knelt and gently held Sarah by her shoulders. "Can you do me a favor and run up to the bridge and see who's there? Don't say anything, just take a look and come back and tell me."

Sarah skipped across the deck and up the ladder.

He turned his gaze seaward waiting for the information his reconnaissance spy would provide. How will the group respond to trauma? Cultural knowledge will be permanently lost with those whales that died. What happens when an intricate social system is fragmented?

Would survivors scatter and regroup later or would some whales have trouble finding members of their social unit? Will they be more wary of humans and not allow us to approach near them again? What types of behaviors will wounded individuals exhibit and how will healthy members of the group respond—

"I'm back," Sarah said.

He glanced over his shoulder. "That was fast. Who did you see?"

"Guess."

"The Captain?"

Arms stretched above her head, she dangled from the bulwarks. "No, Curt and somebody else. I don't know his name."

"A tall, skinny fellow?"

"I think so."

"Will you be alright if I leave you here? I need to talk to someone."

"I'll go play with Randi."

He limped along the side past Andrea, Naeco, Sullivan, and several crew into the mudroom. The smell of sizzling bacon intensified as he passed the mess and unfortunately faded as he hobbled up the ladder to the fo'c'sle deck. He knocked on a door near the conference room.

"Come in," called out a gravelly voice.

He entered a sparsely furnished stateroom. Matthews, wearing black shorts and a crisp, white short-sleeve shirt, sat at a desk in the corner.

Never taking his eyes off him, Matthews lifted his hand off the phone's mouthpiece. "Honey, everything will be fine. You know the drill. Call the plumber, John Brown. Just pay whatever and stop worrying."

Near Matthew's desk were a filing cabinet and ample bookshelves, empty except for a white framed photograph of two attractive young women similar in age. Like in every stateroom, a tightly made-up bunk bed leaned against the bulkhead. Blank white walls surrounded two portholes, both closed even on such a beautiful day. It felt like a stateroom no one lived in. Josh remained standing even though two wooden chairs faced the desk.

"I have to go," Matthews said. "I'll call you tonight. Bye for now." He set the phone on the desk. "Goddamn sewer broke and flooded the basement. Stuff like this always happens when I'm at sea." He pulled open the bottom drawer in the desk and rummaged through its contents. "You should be in your stateroom."

"Your line was busy so I thought I'd come by and ask permission to go out in the zodiac one more time before I leave tomorrow."

"Permission denied."

Josh stiffened. "Even if we stay away from whaling ships?"

Matthews silently flipped through papers in a folder. Someone banged loudly on the door.

"Come in," Matthews said.

Sullivan leaned into the room. "Sorry, Captain, I didn't realize you're busy."

Matthews enthusiastically waved him in. "We're finished here."

Sullivan eagerly approached and stood beside Josh. "I have some interesting findings to report, Captain. Myself, Dr. Megin, and Dr. Templeton here have discovered significant changes to the ocean in this area: low oxygen levels and concentrations of jellyfish at depth, and the water is quite acidic."

Matthews closed the folder and rested his hands on it. "I never heard of this. Why is it happening?"

Sullivan shrugged. "I'm more familiar with dead zones in the Gulf of Mexico. Those are caused by farm fertilizers flowing into the Gulf from the Mississippi. Out here though, it's not so obvious. Generally water below three hundred feet slowly loses oxygen from decaying organic matter. Ocean currents are needed to mix deep and surface water to deliver oxygen to depth. My guess is by adding billions of tons of heat-trapping gases like carbon dioxide and methane into the atmosphere from burning fossil fuels like coal, oil, and gas we've messed up wind patterns and ocean currents. Water masses are more stratified and mix less."

Matthews steely gaze didn't waver.

"And adding carbon dioxide to seawater makes it more acidic."

"What's the problem with that?"

"Many organisms have calcareous shells and their ability to form body parts made out of calcium decreases as seawater becomes more acidic. This will eventually kill corals and certain types of plankton which form the base of marine food webs and provide half the world's oxygen."

"Every second breath I take comes from plankton?" Josh asked.

"They're small, but vitally important to just about everything," Sullivan said.

"So the ocean's changing because of heat and carbon dioxide in the atmosphere?" Matthews asked.

"I believe that's correct, Captain. The ocean and atmosphere are inextricably linked. What we do to one profoundly affects the other." Sullivan's bravado suddenly melted away like Himalayan glaciers. In a quiet voice he spoke directly to Matthews, "In my opinion, Captain, the ocean could be reverting back to conditions that existed hundreds of millions of years ago in the Precambrian…it's becoming more stagnant, acidic, with less oxygen, and the dominant life form is jellyfish instead of fish. Depending on the extent of these changes, it could profoundly affect much of humanity considering billions of people rely on the ocean for food."

"So what do you want?" Matthews asked.

"It would help to conduct more research to see how widespread this phenomenon is. Dr. Megin and Dr. Templeton should collect more deep sea video. You see, sir, once a system is pushed beyond a certain threshold it can flip to a new equilibrium which is much different from before—"

The shipboard telephone rang.

Sullivan added quickly, "It's possible the ocean has already flipped to an altered degraded state which is irreversible."

"Brad here." He partially turned and looked at the picture behind him. "Send him down." He lowered the phone. "I don't decide what science activities take place on this ship. I'll leave it up to you scientists to figure out whether your research is a higher priority than whatever else has been planned." He pointed at Josh. "I want you on that helicopter tomorrow. You have until then to sort this out." He pushed back from the desk and stood. "That'll be all, gentlemen. Good luck." He walked past them and opened the stateroom door.

Out of earshot at the far end of the passageway, Josh shook Sullivan's hand and thanked him. He walked directly to his stateroom and changed into a black wetsuit over which he wore gray nylon pants and a brown tee shirt. In ten minutes he was back on deck, a backpack slung over his shoulder.

He waved at Andrea and Naeco who were sitting on the pontoon in the workboat. "If there's room I'd like to come."

Andrea climbed up the ladder to the bulwarks.

"Captain's letting me go, but we better hurry before he changes his mind."

"I'm so glad." She kissed his cheek. "Welcome back, doctor."

He wished she had kissed him long and hard on the mouth. He struggled over the bulwarks. "You're not taking the kayak?"

"We should check them out with the zodiac. You never know."

Naeco started the engine and contacted the bridge. Josh knelt down beside the steering console and pretended to search his backpack, stuffed with a diving mask, snorkel, and fins. Andrea untied the boat and, on Naeco's command, pushed them away from the side. At low throttle they headed toward the sperm whales.

Standing beside the two women, he scanned the group trying to locate the bull. An unusually high spout soon gave away the whale's position.

I know you like zodiacs. Come on over, I dare you.

SEVENTEEN

The whales seemed unusually active. Several females stayed close to the male, sidefluking and spyhopping with regular frequency. Now Josh regretted not using the kayaks.

He gripped the binoculars tighter. "There are two bulls."

Lobtailing intermittently, a whale swam directly at the bull. The bull sidefluked and turned sharply to face the oncoming whale who was picking up speed. The massive beasts crashed head on. Immense flukes thrashed about, pounding each of the combatants. Seizing jaws, the two whales rolled over and over until a thunderous CRACK reverberated through the water column.

One of the males had an unusual mark on its nose, sometimes visible when it faced toward the zodiac. Could this be the bull that tried to ram the whaler? Slamming headfirst into a steel-hulled ship at thirty-five kilometers per hour would likely cause fatal injuries to even the whale with the hardest head. If this were the Hawaiian bull, the wound was definitely new.

"Naeco, could you cut the engine?" he asked.

The motor fell silent. They stood quietly, sharing the single pair of binoculars. Slowly the zodiac, pushed by the afternoon southeasterly wind, drifted into the group.

"These could be our whales," Andrea said. "The number's right, but I guess we won't know until they dive."

A tall spout plumed several hundred meters away. The whale disappeared until another exhalation blasted upward a minute later. Now the sperm whale was swimming toward the zodiac. Under magnification the immense leviathan loomed larger than life, filling the viewing lens. A badly swollen gash covered the broad nose.

Ten meters from the zodiac, the bull floated at the surface, moving sporadically, only the dorsal hump and a portion of his back visible. Foul air wheezed from the blowhole; rose-colored droplets rained down around his head.

"Oh, no," Josh murmured. "There's blood in the lungs..."

"That wound looks horribly infected," Naeco said.

Something seemed wrong with the whale, the way his head moved in a jerky, awkward manner.

Josh placed the binoculars on the console. "We need to get in contact with a veterinarian. I don't know much about trauma like this and how to treat it...if anything can be done." The *Rubicola* was at least two kilometers away. Kneeling, he pulled snorkeling gear from his backpack.

Andrea eyed him warily.

"Alright if I check this is the Hawaiian bull?" he asked.

"You okay? I mean, how's your leg?"

"Swimming's good physical therapy."

"Of course," she said, with a smirk.

He pulled a thin neoprene hoody over his head and donned the diving mask and snorkel. Lying across the pontoon, he submerged his face in the warm water. Salt burned through stitches on his forehead.

An immense black shape materialized in the hazy sunlit surface water. The square, barrel-shaped nose was one-third the length of the body. Smooth and rounded, the spermaceti organ protruded above and beyond the jaw. To his surprise the jawbone wasn't straight like on most whales; instead, the end curved sharply downward. The bone also appeared to be broken; it hung loosely, held only by a thick sheet of bloodied skin.

Josh peeled off the mask and offered it to Andrea. "I couldn't see the fluke. The angle's wrong."

She sat beside him on the pontoon. So she wouldn't slide overboard, he grasped her ankles when her head plunged under. Several times she lifted her head to inhale deep breaths, then promptly dunked her face back in.

Gasping, she hauled her upper torso into the boat. She pulled the mask off being careful not to tangle hair in the strap. "You definitely get a better idea of their size when you see them underwater."

He sat on the seat and pulled flippers over his feet. "Whales are like icebergs. What you see is only the tip of the iceberg."

"The jaw looks weird."

"It's a mess. I think it's broken...and deformed. Supposedly a small proportion of the population has deformed lower jaws—either they're twisted, or not the proper length, or were broken and didn't set properly."

"How will it eat?"

"Not sure. Deformed jaws don't seem to bother them though." He adjusted straps on the flippers one foot at a time. "Whales with lower-jaw abnormalities usually seem well fed, so teeth probably don't play a significant role in feeding. Squid found in sperm whale stomachs are often whole and show no teeth-marks. Young whales with no teeth seem to feed fine. I think they stun prey with sound waves so they probably don't really need teeth to hold food."

She handed him the mask. "Why do they have teeth at all then?"

"They might be a secondary sexual characteristic used by males when fighting. I'm gonna take a closer look."

He slid feet first over the pontoon being careful not to make a splash. *Man overboard.* Holding on to the pontoon with one hand, he glanced past water droplets on the mask at the *Rubicola* and imagined Matthews screaming and jumping around the bridge. He expected sirens and lights to start wailing and flashing as the ship raced to haul him out of the water.

The whale didn't seem to respond to his presence. He swam slowly, approaching from the side, carefully watching for any change in behavior. The bull remained relatively motionless, only his head swayed back and forth, the large eye tracking him. The fluke drooped downward, gently waving up and down. A chunk of one lobe was missing. Unpigmented white areas colored the lower jaw and genital region. Two eel-shaped lampreys were clamped on skin above the pectoral fin.

A couple meters from the bull's head, Josh stopped swimming. Numerous scars covered the prune-like skin on the massive nose, white etchings drawn on a black canvas depicting the whale's life-long struggles to feed and reproduce. Squid tentacles and arms had left circular scars and long scratches. Teeth from other male sperm whales had gouged thick parallel scars near the mouth. Conical teeth protruded from the whale's white lower jaw which hung loosely downward. A colony of stalked barnacles grew where the deformed jaw bone curled.

For the first time in his life he placed his hand on the tough, leathery skin behind the eye and rubbed in a circular motion. The grooved skin twitched under his fingers. Rolling back, the soulful eye tried to follow movements of his hand.

Josh could relate to the bull in a deep primordial way. They shared a common mammalian ancestor which evolved more than seventy million years ago, long after lobe-finned fishes crawled out of ancient seas and established an animal presence on land. Although they lived in different environments, they were similar in many ways, be it physical attributes such as certain body functions, cellular processes, and biochemical pathways or social attributes such as caring for young and protecting mates. Home for both was planet Earth and their survival depended on healthy oceans.

He pitied the bull, knowing how the remainder of his life will unfold, if he survives. A younger, stronger male had challenged and defeated him, thus ending his breeding opportunities. From this day forward the old bull will spend his remaining years in self-imposed isolation and not interact with other group members, the final act in a lifetime of gradual banishment. Born into his mother's boisterous social unit, the bull left when he matured and joined bachelor groups of other young males where socialization was minimal. During his breeding years, between his late twenties and early forties, he generally led a solitary existence except for those special mating periods spent with female family groups.

The movable lid flushed the surface of the eye. Is he conscious? Does he feel emotional pain? As an outcast will he feel lonely or afraid? We'll never know. Science can't answer everything, no matter how many of their skulls we slice and dice or CAT scan.

Suddenly the sperm whale's head jerked spastically to one side. Frantically Josh kicked away from the giant animal. A huge volume of minute particles of seawater, moisture from within the lungs, and blood burst skyward several meters. Loud sucking and bubbling noises followed as the bull drew tropical air deep into damaged lungs. The whale didn't bend his body to initiate a dive; instead, he slowly settled under the waves, little movement from the fluke or fins.

Josh twisted out of his lifejacket and flung it aside. "I'll be back in a flash!" He hyperventilated, jack-knifed at the waist, and dove after the bull.

EIGHTEEN

"Josh!" Andrea screamed. "Josh!" She desperately searched the surface where he had disappeared. Did the whale's mass suck him under? That's nutty. No, the fool deliberately swam after the massive whale. She automatically checked her watch. About fifteen seconds had passed. Josh's limp body, stunned by whale sounds, sank into oblivion. The sick whale swooped in and devoured him whole. Twenty-five seconds. Naeco's worried look didn't help.

Andrea pointed at the empty lifejacket. "Let's grab that." She needed to do something.

Naeco put the boat in gear and they puttered over to the floatation device.

Josh swam downward mostly using his arms to follow the sinking sperm whale. Several times he paused to pinch his nose and force air into his sinuses to alleviate pressure building in his inner ear. Descending too slowly, he reluctantly kicked his legs. His knee cracked and ached, but eventually he caught up to the bull and, suspended next to the whale's head, they sank together, two wild eyes locked on one giant eye.

Surface light dimmed. Cool ocean water leaked into his wetsuit. The perpetual stillness, punctuated by the rapid drumming of his heartbeat, quieted his frantic mind. Tiny bioluminescent organisms swirling around his head proved to be hypnotic. An uneasy calmness swept through him. His mind loosened its grip on reality—he was only vaguely aware of the ocean's embrace as water crushed against his shivering body. The seafloor beckoned to him.

Diane danced among fragmented thoughts. Seeing her for the first time at university in calculus class. Discussing assignments in genetics lab. Spilling pasta sauce on his yellow shirt on their first date. Going to movies on cheap night. Nervously meeting her parents. Huddling together watching lightning during rainstorms. Tasting those wonderful dinners she cooked for him. Refusing to give her more golf balls when she hit four in a row into the river on the eleventh hole at Southdale. Watching her reel in her first salmon, a beautiful twenty-three pounder. Proposing, and her instant joyous 'yes!' Lifting her veil to kiss her. Buying their first house and arguing what color the bathroom should be. Jumping up and down on the bed when she found out she was pregnant.

Twisted pieces of smoldering metal entombed her mangled body. Blood-filled eyes wide with horror looked at him knowing this would be the last time. She screamed. The terrifying noise jolted his mind from its trance-like state and fog in his head dissipated.

Convulsing, the bull belched high intensity sounds into the void. Then the whale fell silent. With several flicks of the fluke, the sperm whale swam into deeper water. Josh didn't follow; rather, he watched the body sink until vast emptiness swallowed the giant's outline. An all-consuming blackness, so dark and deep, engulfed him.

Have I died?

Forty-seven, forty-eight, forty-nine... Andrea silently counted off seconds and periodically confirmed them on her watch. With both hands she gently rubbed her lower back. *Tiskin, please fill Josh's heart with courage and his lungs with oxygen and his mind with serenity and give his muscles strength to keep swimming. Please take him under your wing and guide him home.*

Naeco quickly rummaged around the zodiac for a diving mask. Not finding one, she lay across the pontoon and plunged her head underwater hoping to see something...anything. Panting, she said to Andrea, "Call for help."

One minute. Andrea scanned the waves again and then her gaze settled on the *Rubicola*. She put the radio microphone near her mouth. *Please, Tiskin.* "Josh! Jooosh!"

"Wait!" Naeco smiled thinly. "He's joking with us." She leaned over the pontoon and searched around the water line and engine leg. Her smile faded as fear swept across her face.

Seventy-four seconds. Andrea knew what Naeco was thinking. By now any person would have drowned.

Josh didn't know if he were sinking, neutrally buoyant, or upside down. The urge to breathe intensified. Fighting to control waves of panic washing through his mind, he became increasingly aware he would soon drown. No visible light indicated the direction to the surface. He allowed several precious bubbles to escape his lips. Shivering violently, he pulled and kicked after the rising bubbles. Searing pain cut through his knee. His lungs burned, desperately aching for fresh air. He paced his ascent like sperm whales do and steadily chanted: *rage, rage against the dying of the light; rage, rage against the dying of the light.* How he yearned to see yellow, orange, and red colors again. Outstretched arms strained to pull closer the shimmering green light perpetually just out of reach above.

Suddenly his flippers struck something solid; a two-meter-long pectoral fin stretched out under his feet. The bull's eye steadied on him as he swam upward with Josh balanced on his fin. The mangled lower jaw snapped open. A harsh creaking noise, like the sound of a barn door moving on rusty hinges, pierced his body.

At last the ocean released him. His head broke through the surface and screaming lungs gulped down fresh air. Waves slapping into his face filled his mouth with salt water, causing him to choke. Gasping and coughing, he struggled to stay afloat by treading water.

Face down, arms and legs splayed out, he searched around for the bull, at first near the surface and then the abyssal depths. He saw nothing, only a deep, dark empty void. Loneliness consumed his soul. Tearing the snorkel from his lips, he screamed into the blue depths, muted guttural sounds bubbling from his wide-open mouth, arms and legs thrashing wildly at demons trying to pull him down. He screamed until every remaining molecule of strength had dissipated into the South Pacific.

Utterly exhausted and limp, he floated like a coconut, rising and falling with the low swell.

Faint splashing and staccato thuds indicated unseen sperm whales were smacking their flukes and breaching in the distance. Barely audible too were whistles, chirps, and squawks emitted by the group. Their singing grew louder as he drifted closer to the whales.

Several dark bodies gracefully slid through sunlit surface waters. One whale rolled beneath him, exposing its belly and flippers. The tactile mammals often touched and rubbed. Sometimes a fluke stroked another's side or jaws gently clasped in a kiss. Creaks and codas buzzed through the water. One whale seemed content to ignore all the bustling activity and slept head down just under the surface like a ghostly pillar.

Josh realized how much he missed the groups of twenty or so young male sperm whales he used to follow, sometimes for several days at a time. They didn't spend extended periods at the surface socializing like females. They certainly reacted to each other's presence, but they didn't form long-term associations. They probably aggregated because of food rather than for underlying social reasons. Did they disappear simply because there wasn't enough to eat?

A sperm whale hung vertically in the water column, her head protruding above the surface, blood flowing from her genitals. Violent contractions rippled across her abdomen. She contorted her body in a U-shape so her head and fluke poked through the waves. Repeatedly her back arched until she rolled on her side facing him. Through a cloud of blood a small fluke emerged from the genital slit. Her body contorted again, exposing half the length of the baby whale. With a final push she thrust the baby from one watery environment into another.

Placenta and body fluids drifted near him. The newborn whale, uniformly black with white markings around the lips, was about four meters long, wrinkled, its dorsal fin folded over and fluke curled. Mother rolled, snapping the umbilical cord. Shrill buzzing sounds filled the water when another whale appeared and jostled the calf. Instinctively the young whale, eyes open and fully alert, swam toward him, but Mother and the female hovering close intercepted and nudged the calf upward.

Josh lifted his head out of the water just in time to see the calf's first breath, hardly visible, puff from the nostril. Pure joy filled his heart. Swimming in a rocking motion, it blew every time its head thrust out of the water. Mother rubbed against it while it floated at the surface, inhaling and exhaling. Another adult, swimming on its back, joined the trio and vigorously shoved the calf with its head. Mother partially rolled, exposing two teats on either side of the vaginal opening. The calf moved parallel to her, head facing the same way, and seized a teat in the corner of its mouth. With its snout protruding above the surface, it suckled rich fatty milk as it would continue to do for the next two years.

Josh felt profoundly humble, like a special guest in a sacred place. The whales could kill him instantly, yet he didn't fear these peaceful animals, even after humans have slaughtered a quarter million of their kind. He silently prayed men in ships would never hunt this new life and squid would fill the deep ocean. He scanned the depths for signs of orcas or sharks. Somehow he will have to ensure this baby whale will live to be at least seventy years old.

When the calf stopped feeding and released the teat, foggy clouds formed around the nipple as milk continued to flow. The calf remained close to Mother and rubbed against different parts of her body, sometimes lying across her back, forming bonds that would last a lifetime.

The zodiac! He spun around. Andrea and Naeco stood some distance away looking in his direction. He extended both arms overhead and waved and then touched fingers to make an O-shape. They jumped up and down and hugged and waved.

Shivering uncontrollably, he adjusted the snorkel and started swimming using the front crawl stroke. Regular noises his breaths made from being pushed and drawn through the narrow tube set the rhythm of his swimming stroke. Beams of sunlight shimmered in the upper depths. Occasionally a sperm whale swam into view. Favoring his good leg, he imagined swimming in wide circles, round and round, never reaching Andrea. Periodically he stopped swimming to find her; invariably he was off course because the boat had drifted and waves had pushed his body. Plus the seafloor didn't have tiled lines to follow like the indoor pool at the university.

Whale sightings became less frequent as the group moved away. The patchy distribution of ocean life was never more apparent than now. Ten minutes ago a cacophony of sounds and tons of living biomass surrounded him. Now he made the loudest noises. Choppy waves occasionally broke over his head, sending droplets trickling down the snorkel. From time to time he exhaled forcefully blowing out saltwater accumulating in the tube. His body felt like lead and his arms and legs moved slowly. The zodiac's engine grumbled ahead in the distance.

"Should I whack him with the paddle?" Andrea asked.

Josh was now swimming parallel to the zodiac and only meters away; his face remained submerged and the regular splashing caused by his arms and legs continued.

"Maybe he's heading back to Canada," Naeco said.

"Josh, you can stop now!" Andrea hollered.

His head finally popped up and he treaded water. He slid the mask down under his chin and pulled the snorkel from his mouth.

"Get over here," Andrea said.

He spit out a mouthful of water. "I don't have the strength."

"Yes, you do. Dig deeper." She tossed the wet lifejacket at him.

Naeco steered the boat to him. As they drifted close he lunged at the pontoon and tried pulling himself up, but started sliding back in the water. Andrea grabbed under his arms and hauled him onto the pontoon. Tumbling into the zodiac, he lay where he fell struggling to catch his breath.

Practically jumping on him, she grasped his face in her hands. "Don't you ever do that again!" She hugged him furiously and whispered in his ear, "I'm so glad you're safe."

"Me too." He leaned against the pontoon and wrestled flippers off. "Thanks for watching out for me." Shivering in the afternoon breeze, he wrapped a towel around his shoulders. "Did you radio the *Rubicola?*"

"Yes," Andrea said, quickly. "You're in big whale doo-doo, mister."

"Ah, it was fun while it lasted."

Shaking her head, she said, "I can't believe you held your breath that long."

"I used to be a pretty good free diver."

"You never told me that."

He grinned meekly. "A man can't divulge all his secrets."

She playfully slapped his arm. "We should go. Since you're still alive I want to try the crittercam before supper. These whales don't seem too worried about us."

With the throttle low, Naeco piloted the zodiac away from the group and docked alongside the *Rubicola* behind the other boat.

NINETEEN

Josh slumped into the kayak's cockpit behind Andrea who was holding the long, bowed crittercam pole. Even though the paddle felt like lead piping, he immediately started paddling toward the whales because they could dive anytime. More importantly, he owed Andrea in a big way. The zodiac trailed off their port side with Naeco filming them. *Maybe they could make themselves useful and tow us to the whales?*

Fortunately a whale was swimming in typical undulating motion, apart from the rest of the group, but fairly close to the *Rubicola*. Deliberately and silently they approached her. She generally paid little attention until they were a boat length away when, abruptly, she raised her head out of the water and disappeared beneath the ripples.

Relishing the opportunity to rest, Josh stopped paddling to search for the whale. "You see the spermaceti organ that shapes their heads? It's proportionally much smaller in females than males. This suggests sexual selection may be occurring. Females might mate only with males who can produce sounds generated by a very large spermaceti organ. If that's true, large spermaceti organs in males will be selected for over time."

Andrea raised the pole to stretch her cramped arms. "Size matters with humans so you'd think it would also matter with sperm whales."

"Speaking of big males, why don't we slap the crittercam on the other bull? I'm sure he'll lead us to some squid. This one here seems tricky to follow."

"Have you seen him?"

"He's about four hundred meters away, ten degrees on the port bow."

Despite his throbbing knee, Josh paddled even harder now in pursuit of the only bull in the group. Unfortunately the bull was swimming with some purpose, not just milling about or sleeping, and his infrequent exhalations made tracking him difficult. Josh timed the blows and tried anticipating his movements and steered to intercept, but often the bull would subtly change course underwater. With persistence, however, they gradually gained on him, approaching like whaling ships do. Now twenty meters behind, Josh paddled vigorously and they gradually made headway. The bull spouted three times, each breath about fifteen seconds apart, and then dove shallow, showing no fluke.

Breathing hard, Josh said, "We'll have to attach the crittercam at full speed when he blows."

Andrea sat up straighter, holding the pole with bent arms.

He kept paddling as fast as he could. "Get ready." He counted each paddle stroke, one every second...*one hundred seventy, one seventy-one, one seventy-two...* "Okay, where is he?"

Powerful bubbling noises directed their gazes ahead and to the right. Josh jammed his right foot forward to turn the rudder and kayak. The boat teetered as paddle blades surged deep. Five meters ahead the first exhalation cut through the surface and exploded into a thunderous geyser. A loud sucking sound precluded the second spout. Broken waves sent white foam swirling over the bull's gray back.

They raced through a curtain of mist. Leaning to one side, Andrea raised the crittercam pole up high. The bull was much larger than Buffy. With the crittercam dangling above, the whale's back rose beautifully out of the water to meet it; she pulled down on the pole and slammed the suction cup onto the skin. The bull exhaled violently for a second time, partially rolled, and dove shallow showing several knuckles. The crittercam vanished.

Andrea let out a celebratory whoop. Nauseous and dizzy, Josh crumpled forward like competitive rowers do after long, grueling races.

"That was awesome!" She twisted in her seat holding a water bottle. "What a team!"

He gratefully chugged several mouthfuls. "You're a pro." He wiped his mouth. "We only had one chance and you took it. And, hey, just in time."

Two flukes, the zodiac, and the *Rubicola* drifting several kilometers away were the only exceptions to the blue blanket surrounding them. The zodiac stalked individual whales and then raced closer when flukes flared open so Naeco could take photographs. This would help identify the whales later and confirm whether this was indeed Buffy's group.

The last whale waved goodbye.

"We're late for dinner," Andrea said. "I hope the crittercam stays on overnight."

"We'll get it back, don't worry."

Josh paddled slowly toward the *Rubicola.* Andrea leaned back, resting the pole across her lap. Her left hand dangled over the side, tickling waves as they rolled past. Sometimes when the wind gusted just right he could smell almond sunscreen and apple cinnamon, maybe her shampoo. He'll be leaving tomorrow and possibly never see her again. Sure they'll correspond from time to time—probably mostly over email—since their research now overlaps somewhat, but back in the real world things usually become more professional and distant.

She stretched her arms over her head deliberately tormenting him. What an amazing woman. She should be on magazine covers.

The zodiac idled past, Naeco still filming. Josh sat straighter and tried to appear like a competent paddler. With a shout and a wave the zodiac sped on ahead to tie-up. They followed and the zodiac crew helped them unload. Andrea's firm butt, several steps above, enticed him up the side ladder.

Hobbling behind her on deck, he gently grabbed her arm. "I need to talk to you." He guided her to the side of the working deck near the freshly painted yellow crane. Numerous freckles sprinkled her nose and cheek bones. Like usual her delicate lips were remarkably moist even after being outside in the sun and wind all day. So incredibly kissable.

A seaman strolled outside from the mudroom. "Howdy, Andrea." Grinning, he wiggled a toothpick between his teeth. "Ready for a shuffleboard rematch?"

"Maybe later... okay, Alex?"

"Ah, come on. I'm on break now. Just one game."

"We're in the middle of something," Josh said. "Talk to her later."

Alex pulled the toothpick from his mouth while eyeing up Josh's two-meter frame. "I'm not talking to you."

Josh took a deep breath. Even a ship like the *Rubicola* wasn't big enough.

Andrea placed her hand on the idiot's shoulder. "How about after I finish supper?"

He smiled, showing off pretty-boy teeth. "I'll come looking for you in half an hour." The smile vanished when he made eye contact with Josh. He sauntered aimlessly across the deck.

Andrea seemed thoroughly amused and kept looking at Josh. Sweat trickled down the insides of his biceps. He tried to think of the right words to say, but nothing intelligent came to mind.

Finally she turned her attention seaward. "So what's on your mind, Dr. Josh? Seems like I might already have a date tonight."

"Alright if we meet later?" Procrastination had saved him countless times before.

In a business-like manner, she slowly counted several fingers on her left hand like she was weighing carefully every social commitment that evening. "I'll slot you in at eight-fifteen. You know where we live."

Josh simply nodded. Not hungry, he walked past the mess directly to his stateroom. He grabbed a towel and bar of soap, quickly showered, and returned to his room and locked the door. He changed into dry clothes and sat, eyes tightly closed, on the edge of the bunk trying to summon every ounce of courage he had. For he knew this evening he would need it all.

TWENTY

Josh slipped among long shadows on deck, out of sight behind the helicopter. The air was heavy and warm. He leaned against the cool skin of the aircraft. The ocean darkened as evening light faded. Silver clouds on the horizon turned brilliant orange, their edges ignited by the dropping fireball. For the first time he realized a spectacular sunset occurred every night, it's just sometimes you can't see it because of clouds. The perfect setting comforted him; it seemed to validate he was doing the right thing.

He reached under the collar of his tee shirt and fondled the oval silver locket and wedding ring hanging on a gold chain around his neck. Holding the locket in his palm, his fingers traced over its smooth corners. Soothing warmth settled through him. Inside was a tiny black and white picture—their two faces touching cheeks, grins stretching ear-to-ear. They had taken the picture in some photo booth in a Seattle shopping mall, one of those goofy things young couples do when in love.

He unclasped the chain, carefully slid the ring off, and slipped it on his wedding finger. He played with the ring, sliding it back and forth under the knuckle and spinning it. He remembered shopping with Diane for their wedding rings, discussing styles and prices. They joked how big the rock needed to be to alleviate any doubts her girlfriends had about his commitment and love for her. He moved the ring to his right hand where it would hopefully remain for the rest of his life.

He spoke quietly as if his wife were standing next to him. "Diane, I love you so much. I miss you terribly, every day, and wish you were here. I'm so sorry for what happened to you…to us."

He sniffled.

"I wish I could go back in time and change things, but I can't and I'm tired of punishing myself for what happened. I'd give anything to have died instead. I'm so sorry." Tears streamed down his face. The fist clutching the locket shook uncontrollably. "You haunt me, you just haunt me. I need you to forgive me so I can let go and move on with my life…and not keep ruining it. I'll never forget you and you'll be in my thoughts, always. I've been blessed in my life to have met two wonderful women, and it's not like I'll love you any less. I want to honor your spirit instead of being terrified by it. I want us to move forward together, you with me every day as my life unfolds. I need your strength to help me deal with challenges I'll face."

He took a deep breath. Darkness settled like a shadow over the ocean. "I'm letting you go now so both of us can be at peace." The locket trembled in his hand, their faces in the picture now difficult to discern in the faded light. He closed the locket and tenderly kissed it. "Diane, I'll cherish your memory forever."

He tossed the piece of jewelry off the stern, turquoise bioluminescence twinkling around the chain when it touched the surface. "Please forgive me, Diane." A wave splashed against the ship and her cool tears sprinkled his shoulders. Pacific winds tousled her hair. She blew him a kiss and walked away across a windswept Oregon beach.

Lingering behind the helicopter, he wiped his eyes. The wispy signature of the Milky Way and steady reflected light from satellites as they arced across the night sky momentarily fooled him into believing Hawaii and home were close by. But the unusual pattern of stars sparkling in clear patches caught him off guard. Constellations he didn't recognize, with names he didn't know, twinkled in the strange heavens. With his head crammed uncomfortably back, he searched hopelessly for the rock-steady North Star that always guided him.

The illuminated deck seemed deserted. He limped past the kayaks into the superstructure and cautiously stepped through the watertight door, taking care not to put too much weight on his sore knee. Washing his face and brushing his teeth made him feel superficially better. Knowing he was about to take action made his spirit feel better. He dumped the duffel bag on the top bunk, rifled through the pile of musty clothes, and changed into a reasonably clean pair of blue jeans and a green shirt hanging in the closet. He gargled mouthwash for an unusually long time.

Refreshed and more composed, he walked down the passageway to Andrea's stateroom and, without deliberating, rapped loudly on the door.

It immediately swung open. She stood in the doorway wearing blue pajama shorts and a gray tank top. Her green eyes were more stunning than sperm whale vocalizations.

"Uh, sorry I'm so late. If you're about to go to bed, I'll see you tomorrow."

She grabbed his arm. "Get in here."

The stateroom was a mirror image to his own except for the porthole above the desk. Only the reading lamp at the head of the bunk and a candle on the dresser cast light in the room. A circular shadow pulsed on the deckhead as the flame flickered in a pool of melted wax. The air, scented from the candle, smelled sweet and pleasant. Sarah, curled up with an oversized pillow, lay on the neatly made bunk quietly watching him.

"Oh, hey, Sarah." He sat beside her. "Did you see *Pakicetus* today?"

She giggled. "No, just his cousins."

"Do you know there's a new addition to the group? I saw a female give birth to a bouncing one-ton sperm whale bundle of joy."

Her mouth gaped open. "Really?!"

"Fifteen months ago it was only a twinkle in some bull's eye."

Someone knocked on the door. Sarah jumped off the bed and picked up a pink knapsack on the deck beside the closet.

Andrea knelt and hugged her. "Have fun at your sleepover. I'll see you in the morning."

His heart thumped in his chest. He barely remembered what freedom meant. He felt eighteen again.

In the passageway, Randi leaned forward and slapped her knees. "Ready, Sarah? We have two movies and a tub of ice cream."

Andrea gently closed the door and locked it. She hoped he wouldn't notice her nervousness. "Care for some wine? Red?"

"Sure, whatever you're having."

She took a bottle of Merlot from the closet, turned her back to him as she struggled with the stubborn cork, and practically emptied the bottle in two bulbous glasses.

"Sarah could've stayed," Josh said.

"You really mean that?" She smiled and handed him a glass.

"I'm serious, she's a great kid."

Sitting cross-legged on the floor, she took a sip and licked her lips. "We should celebrate."

He leaned against the bunk and raised his glass. "To the crittercam and our second picnic."

"And to you. You seem different somehow."

Wine swirled around in his glass. "I'm lucky to be alive."

"We all are."

"I nearly drowned and I should've died in the accident."

"Sshh, don't say that."

"You know..." He took a sip of wine. "After the accident I felt only guilt and fear. I don't want to make that mistake again. I want to live like you do with love and compassion."

"Good for you...and thank you."

He shook his head. "I'm not special. Every person is an unsung hero. We all have battles to fight every day, which most people face with considerable courage. How we deal with these battles defines our lives and who we are."

"Maybe these battles will be easier if we fight them together? You watch my back, I'll watch yours."

"I'll watch your back anytime."

"It's a deal then?" Pretending to spit in her palm, she sat up on her knees and held out her hand. He rested a clammy hand on hers. There was an unrelenting tenderness about him she craved. Someday she hoped Sundrop would find such a caring man who would worship her.

"I have a surprise for you." She placed her glass on the desk. "This is somewhat unorthodox, so please forgive me." She dragged the wooden chair over to the sink. "It'll take courage for you to do it." She motioned for him to sit down. "Take off your shirt if you dare."

He practically tore the buttons off and flung the shirt on the top bunk.

What a hunk. She found a brown towel in the closet and draped it over his lean chest and shoulders. She picked up a yellow box on the desk. "Compliments of the crew." She unwound the cord and plugged it in the outlet above the sink.

Electric clippers in one hand, she straddled his lap, her chest dangerously close to his face. She tenderly touched his cheeks, studying him—long lashes that protected inquisitive eyes, the cute dimple in the middle of his chin. She really liked the way he smelled. Slowly she lifted his baseball cap exposing wispy strands of disheveled thinning hair. He shifted subtly so she reassured him with a warm smile. His arms hung loosely by his sides.

"No more living on your heels," she whispered.

Gently holding his chin, she ran the razor over his scalp leaving only millimeters of hair. She trimmed around his ears and tidied his sideburns. To shave the back of his neck, she pulled his face into her shoulder; his arms tightened, embracing her warm, almost hot, body.

She turned his head from side to side surveying her masterpiece. She stepped back for a broader perspective and smiled, nodding her approval. He definitely looked younger, even more athletic, and damn fine.

She turned on the tap in the sink, felt the flow of water until it was just the right temperature, and eased his head back. She massaged a fragrant shampoo into his scalp. After rinsing the soap away, she pulled him up into a sitting position and draped a clean towel over his head. Straddling him once again, she rubbed the towel, her breasts nearly touching his face. He firmly locked his arms around her pulling her even closer.

The towel fell to the floor.

She wrapped her arms around his neck. "You have beautiful eyes," she whispered, kissing each lid softly, "a beautiful smile," and kissed him gently on the lips, "and a beautiful body," and kissed him on the chest. "You're a beautiful man inside and out."

"Thank you," he mumbled.

"You okay with this?"

"Best haircut I've ever had." Tenderly he pulled her face close. Their kiss was soft, gentle, and sweet.

With her legs still wrapped around his waist and arms around his neck, he tried to stand, but his knee buckled from the weight. She shrieked when he nearly dropped her. He recovered, wincing, and managed to kick the chair from underfoot.

"Very smooth, Tarzan," she said.

Kissing and touching tongues, they fell heavily onto the bunk. His sensual lips carefully tasted down her neck and then skipped to her exposed belly button where his whiskered cheeks delightfully tickled sensitive skin there. She moaned. It had been far too long since she's felt a man's touch. His warm hands slipped under her shirt and cupped her breasts. Her breathing quickened. The room started spinning. Roy stumbled toward her in a drunken rage. A calloused hand seized her jaw and throat.

"Stop!" She firmly grasped both his hands.

Roy pushed hard, snapping her head back, sending her reeling into the side of the couch.

Josh froze, looked up at her, and quickly pulled her shirt down to cover her bare tummy.

That look frightened her more than haunting memories of Roy. *He thinks I'm a crazy freak.* "I'm sorry, Josh." She wiped her forehead and felt her flushed cheeks. "I want to do this as much as you do, believe me."

"Hey, no worries, why ruin a romantic evening by having sex."

She smiled weakly. "Maybe we should slow down. We hardly know each other."

He grinned slyly. "We're getting to know each other right now."

She appreciated his attempts to keep things light. When he moved to stand up, she held on tightly to his shoulders. Nibbling on his earlobe, she whispered, "Please don't go. Stay with me tonight."

"Should I sleep on the top bunk?"

"Do you like being on top?"

"You're quite a tease." He grabbed her by the waist and tickled her until laughter turned to tears. They cuddled under the yellow sheet.

Against her cheek, his firm chest steadily rose and fell to the rhythm of his breathing. "I can hear your heart beating," she whispered.

"Is it fluttering?"

"Just a little."

He lightly kissed her hair. "If you suddenly don't hear anything, call Durant. He'll be ecstatic."

"I won't even ask."

The stateroom glowed softly from moonlight spilling through the porthole.

"You know, I was just thinking...we really are lucky to be alive," Andrea said. "Think about the history of Earth. People are living during a small window of life—a one-billion-year-long window, mind you—where all life, including us, is able to evolve in an incredibly lush environment. The four point six billion year history of our planet will show that most of the time life consisted only of single-celled organisms like bacteria—more complex forms have existed for only a small fraction of the total time Earth has existed. That's why we should celebrate the beauty of life around us because it is special, it won't happen again or last forever."

He twirled long strands of her hair around his finger. "I know what the meaning of life is."

She rolled on her back. "Do tell, O Enlightened One."

"It's love, plain and simple...and forgiveness."

"Family too."

"When I realized I might drown, do you know what I thought about?"

"Me, no doubt?"

"Sure, and my family, friends...whales. Know why? Because they're what I love. And a life without love is meaningless. If you love someone it means accepting them for who they are, their inherent frailties, and understanding they will fail you at times. With love comes forgiveness and it's these two principles that give meaning to life."

Forgiveness. Such a complicated word. She squeezed him tightly; it felt so good, a perfect fit, two interlocking pieces at the center of a complicated puzzle. She cried softly, but this time she didn't feel self-conscious, only happy, peaceful and, for a very dear moment, safe.

TWENTY-ONE

Muffled shouts from the deck above wafted into the stateroom. Josh stirred, his face nestled comfortably against Andrea's back. Her essence sweetly engulfed him—the warmth of her body, the fragrance of her skin. He watched her back for several minutes as he had promised last night; her gently curving shoulders, the rounded peak formed by her shoulder blade. Softly he kissed a freckle between the two blades.

Quietly he turned on his side. Beams of sunlight streaming through the porthole indicated they had probably missed breakfast. Often footsteps reverberated in the passageway.

He climbed stiffly out of bed. Unable to see the deck through the porthole due to the position of the stateroom, he listened to the sounds of a busy ship—faint shouting mixed in with methodical splashing as the ship's bow surged through rolling swells. The *Rubicola* seemed alive this morning.

He leaned over the sink and studied his neatly shaven head in the mirror. Andrea was right—he did look better with short hair. His left hand rubbed over bristly hairs. The new and improved Josh Templeton. Until now he hadn't realized how much he let himself go after Diane died. Quite amazing Andrea found him attractive at all.

He sat on the edge of the mattress beside her. She seemed so fragile, almost childlike, yet ironically harbored such incredible strength inside. He still couldn't believe they had spent the night together. He felt like a freshman in university, but this time he wanted to stay, not bolt for the door.

Overpowered by the urge to touch her, he caressed her forehead. She got pretty upset last night, seemed almost scared. She might carry a ton of baggage from her past relationship. Who doesn't? Mom never recovered after dad left. What will happen after this trip? Andrea has an established career in Texas and Sarah will have good friends there and go to school. Long-distant relationships only last so long—

Someone pounded on the door.

Josh jumped up and considered hiding in the head. He touched her shoulder. "Sarah's here."

"You there, Andrea?" Durant called out from the passageway.

"Huh?" She sat up, instantly awake. "Good morning."

"We got the crittercam."

She grinned widely. "Right on! I'll meet you in the conference room in ten minutes." Wearing only panties and a tee shirt she strutted over to the closet. "The crittercam came off yesterday evening."

"Oh, really? That's too bad."

Facing away from him, she pulled the shirt over her head. "The suction cup just isn't working out. It was already dark so we couldn't look for it. But the ship followed it through the night." She slid gorgeous legs into a tight pair of jeans. Thunderbird tattooed on the small of her back embraced her with its outstretched wings reaching from her spine all the way around her sides. Its head was turned profile, beak agape, the round, white eye watching him. Shirtless, she walked to him, hands behind her back fastening the bra strap. She kissed him firmly on the mouth. "I'll meet you there after I powder my nose."

Andrea, Sundrop, Josh, Durant, Naeco, Susan, and Randi once again huddled around the television in the conference room. Sullivan promised to join them later after he finished speaking on the satellite phone with several colleagues.

The television flickered dull light throughout the room. The bull sperm whale swam alone amidst constant clicking sounds. The ocean gradually faded from blue to black. Andrea stole a glance at Josh. He must have felt so lonely diving in such vast nothingness.

One thousand feet came and went without the crittercam seeing much of anything except the whale's rippled skin and shimmering white plankton. Occasionally a solitary red umbrella-shaped jellyfish without tentacles floated past. Absent was the infinite horde from Buffy's dive.

The bull's sonar started firing rapidly. A neutrally buoyant shadow materialized hovering in the water column with its head and arms angled downward.

Andrea leaned forward, both hands covering her mouth. "I don't believe it." Depth on the screen read one thousand two hundred and thirty-six feet.

"What is that?" Durant asked.

The bull headed straight for the purple-red dark matter. Reflective eyes bigger than hubcaps, the largest eyes in the animal kingdom and the second largest ever to exist on Earth, watched without blinking. A pair of fins waved at the tail end of the three-meter-long mantle which expanded drawing seawater inside to bathe the gills.

Seawater blasted through a hose-like funnel below the head and the thirteen-meter-long giant squid, with two muscular tentacles outstretched, quickly jetted away. The bull gave chase, picking up speed—the depth counter spun rapidly past fourteen hundred feet.

The squid vanished into jellyfish. The bull didn't slow down; he, too, plunged straight into the jelly wall. Balls of plasma bombarded the crittercam. The giant squid, hiding amongst the jellyfish, abruptly emerged in front of the bull. The whale barreled straight into the squid's flailing arms; serrated suckers viciously slashed skin around his head. A snapping parrot-like beak protruded from the buccal cavity.

The crittercam violently twisted sideways and spun upward. The bull and giant squid disappeared. The crittercam bobbled between jellyfish like a pinball during its gradual ascent to the surface.

Andrea jumped up in front of her team. "We saw a living *Architeuthis*! This is the first time one has been found in tropical waters." She clasped her hands together. "Yes!"

"Where are they normally?" Durant asked.

She purposely breathed deeply several times to settle her nerves. "They're thought to breed in the subtropics and then migrate to higher latitudes to feed. A blue shark caught off Africa in the Atlantic near the equator had a four meter giant squid in its stomach. And someone found a juvenile in a lancet fish off Chile. They might be more broadly distributed then we realize. We know so little about them."

"Don't they live much deeper?" Josh asked.

"Yes, I believe so."

"Do you think this one was injured or sick?"

She shrugged. "It seemed to move with vigor."

"How far away was the other jellyfish swarm you saw?" Susan asked.

"About fifty kilometers," Andrea said.

The door opened and light spilled into the darkened room. Sullivan entered and pulled out a chair at the opposite end of the table.

"Do you want to see the video, Sullivan?" she asked. "It's amazing."

His chunky fingers drummed along the table's edge.

"Is everything okay?"

He took his time looking for a moment at each person. "I just spoke with a colleague on the *Forager*. I asked her a couple days ago to analyze some of their water samples..."

A tsunami of fear suddenly swept away wonderful feelings about giant squid.

"Unfortunately they found similar results," he said, quietly. "Low oxygen levels below seven hundred feet and surface pH around seven point nine."

"Where were samples collected?" Josh asked.

"Guam."

"So this isn't a local phenomenon."

"Apparently not."

Mortified, Josh's face turned ashen. "This is happening around Hawaii too." He buried his face in his hands.

Fear smothered her. Andrea placed her hands on her hips and summoned Tiskin. He wrapped broad, strong wings around her and lifted her up. She walked deliberately around the long table touching her friends' shoulders as she passed. "My grandfather often told me stories about how my people hunted salmon, fur seals, and gray whales. We took only what we needed for survival, nothing more. When Europeans arrived everything changed because they commercialized hunting. This led to my people's destruction because we killed animals for profit and local food sources were soon wiped out. But now with the human population in the billions and modern technology readily available, we are a super species with the ability to impact not just local areas, but the entire planet including the deep ocean. We need to do something immediately."

The room was strangely quiet. Heads down, people stared at the floor like a junior high class being scolded for misbehaving and everyone was afraid to look the teacher in the eye.

"Come on," she said. "I see a room full of smart people who are experts in their fields. Let's put our heads together and think of solutions."

Sullivan leaned back in his chair. "This is a complex issue probably on a global scale."

"Forget it, nothing can be done," Josh muttered.

Andrea leaned on the table beside Susan and glared at him. "We have to do something. Our survival depends on intact marine ecosystems. If carbon dioxide in the atmosphere is threatening ocean life, then it is a threat to us, our families, and our children. We must think of ways to stop it."

Sullivan shrugged. "At the end of the day we need to change government policies. That's the only way things will ever change."

"How?" Josh asked, sarcastically.

"Governments need to entice industry and the public to cut carbon dioxide emissions. I'm not an economist, but I'm sure there are ways.

Governments need to protect the environment like they do their precious economies."

"Sullivan's right," Susan said. "People working in government must clearly understand the issues. This means voters must be informed and concerned so they elect the right people. We need to get our message out to the general public."

"That's precisely why we should publish this research quickly."

"Sullivan, the public doesn't read scientific journals," Josh said. "Most people get their information from the internet or newspapers or the news on TV and this information is either inaccurate or biased or journalists unfairly present both sides of a particular issue which just leaves people confused and undecided."

"Why is telling both sides of a story unfair?" Randi asked.

"It's called journalistic balance," Josh said. "There might be a hundred experts who all agree on something, but journalists always want to present an opposing argument for the sake of appearing to have a well-rounded story so they search for one crackpot who will refute what all the experts say. The problem is readers don't know it's a hundred against one or what the true credentials of the 'one' are or their motives. Anyway"— he rubbed his eyes —"most people simply don't care. No one wants to cramp their lifestyle."

"That's not true," Naeco said. "I have lots of friends who are worried about the environment."

"Your friends are unfortunately a minority," Josh said. "There's a big disconnect between people and Nature, now more than ever. Few people know where their food comes from and how important it is to have clean air and water and fertile soil. We believe we're Nature's master and technology will solve all our problems."

"Okay, so how do we get this important message out to the public?" Andrea asked.

"I'll tell my friends," Sundrop said.

Andrea kissed the top of her head. "I think that's a wonderful idea."

"We certainly can't leave children out of this," Susan said. "The ocean's fate is in their hands."

"We could make a video from the crittercam footage," Naeco said. "Isn't a picture worth a thousand words? Show clips of sperm whales, jellyfish, giant squid..." She glanced slyly at Andrea. "And someone with a sexy voice can narrate it."

"You'd do a terrific job," Andrea said.

"We can send copies to television networks and hopefully it will make the news," Susan said.

"What about nature channels and environmental shows?" Durant asked.

"I can write articles and send pictures to newspapers and magazines," Susan said.

"I'll do a talk at school," Sundrop said.

Andrea stood beside the television in front of the group. "I really like what I'm hearing. Josh, will you and Sullivan take the lead in writing research papers and informing the scientific community?"

Sullivan nodded.

"Naeco, can you edit video?"

"For sure."

"Will you put together a crittercam video that shows all the glorious highlights?"

Beaming, Naeco said, "Absolutely. This is a dream job."

"Okay. Sarah will tell her school and Susan and I will fire off some articles. Together we'll bombard North American voters so they're informed and, hopefully, they'll become more engaged at the political level."

"It's a good start," Sullivan said, nodding his head in approval.

"It's only the start," Andrea said.

Carrying his luggage and a container normally used for storing food, Josh emerged from the mudroom into a brisk breeze flowing over the working deck. The *Rubicola* was cruising at a good clip, probably around ten knots. Many people stood near the bulwarks pointing out at the water and taking pictures. Bow waves created by the ship formed a temporary playground for playful bottlenose dolphins. Gray bodies shimmered under the surface as the muscular mammals easily kept pace with the ship. Dolphins surrounded them, probably at least one hundred, the biggest super pod he had ever seen.

Dan stepped down out of the helicopter and climbed on a ladder under the rotor blades. Realizing he still had a few more minutes before blast off, Josh propped his belongings against the bulwarks and waved at Andrea and Sarah who were waiting by the trawl winches. He hoisted Sarah up and held her close and, together, they climbed the ladder to the fo'c'sle deck and walked around the bridge past the electric windlass that lowered the anchors. Holding on tightly to the flagpole under the fluttering Stars and Stripes, they stood above two immense black anchors hanging by thick chain cable. Dolphins streaked like torpedoes under the *Rubicola's* bow. Sarah quivered in his arms from all the excitement.

Dan waved after completing the pre-flight inspection. Josh hugged Andrea and Sarah one last time, but he deliberately didn't say good bye; he had learned from his mother and Diane to hate this social custom. Better to keep conversations casual and bury any feelings. He had worked with many different researchers throughout his career—colleagues, students, and volunteers—and often for longer periods of time; however, he definitely would miss this group the most.

The *Rubicola* slipped out from underneath and the helicopter dropped astern of the research ship. In her wash, frothy white-tipped waves propagated in an ever-widening V-shaped pattern. Countless dolphins leapt over the moving hills of water, forever playful, blissfully ignorant of the devastation heading their way.

Dan cracked his knuckles; Josh knew the signal and held on tight. The helicopter banked hard and swooped down across the *Rubicola's* busy deck. What Josh saw reaffirmed what he already knew; humans and sperm whales were actually quite similar. Below, a group of people moved as a cohesive unit with a similar sense of purpose. Clusters formed where individuals socialized and strengthened bonds. Naeco and Durant photographed several dolphins swarming along the starboard side. They exchanged information through conversation and made subtle physical contact—at one point Durant put his hand on Naeco's shoulder. In another cluster adults transferred culture to the young. Andrea and Randi stood near the crane by Sarah training the next-generation marine biologist. Andrea waved and made the SCUBA gesture for 'I'm okay'.

The *Rubicola* disappeared behind as the helicopter turned toward the Galapagos Islands.

TWENTY-TWO

Josh tugged the shoulder belt to stop it from digging into his armpit. "I trust we have plenty of fuel?"

"Stuffed to the gills," Dan said. "I'll make the call when we need to high tail outta there."

The helicopter climbed to five hundred meters and altered course from the scheduled flight plan taking them in a southeasterly direction away from the Galapagos Islands out into the Pacific.

Arching his back and twisting, Josh dug around in his back pocket for a piece of paper. "A destroyer relayed this to the First Mate yesterday at sixteen hundred hours. Zero one degrees, fifty-seven minutes, fifty-seven point three one seconds south, ninety-two, seventeen, eleven point six four west."

Dan keyed the coordinates into the GPS mounted on the control panel. "That's seventy-eight miles from here. Might as well sit back, relax, and enjoy the flight." He stretched back and shoved his left hand under his leather belt. He barely touched the joystick with the other hand—his version of autopilot—and the helicopter seemed to basically fly on its own.

The steady clatter dulled to a muffled thumping. Josh swept binoculars back and forth searching for whales and ships.

"So are you and that fox an item, the scientist taking all the pictures?" Dan asked.

Blue and white ripples vanished. Andrea appeared, nude, arms draped around his neck, gorgeous black hair not quite covering her firm breasts. Josh soaked up the view for as long as possible. "Hard to say, probably not."

"Too bad for you."

"She's more like a wolf than a fox."

Wind jostled the helicopter and they suddenly dropped sharply. He instinctively grabbed the handle above the door.

"You two look good together. What's the matter?"

Dan hadn't even flinched so Josh figured he shouldn't worry either. He relaxed his grip. "We barely know each other. And she lives in Texas."

"So? Go to Texas."

"It's not that simple."

"You got a wife and kids?"

"No." Under different circumstances he would have laughed at the question.

"What's the problem? Worried about your job? They're a dime a dozen, a woman like that is one in a million."

"Are you married?"

"Yep, my third wife." Dan looked away out the side window. "Buried the first in Vietnam, cancer took the second. Joan's still kicking…" He chuckled. "Far as I know."

They penetrated some low cloud cover and the brilliant view vanished as cotton wisps streaked by. Josh wondered why some people seemed to be better at surviving than him.

"If I had a chance with a woman like that, I'd do anything," Dan said.

"Andrea would think you're desperate."

"So? Real love is desperate."

Something appeared on the horizon. Josh wedged his elbows against his knees to steady the binoculars. "Thanks for the advice, Casanova."

They descended two hundred meters.

"Mai is the love of my life." Dan's eyes narrowed. "Don't tell Joan. We met in Vung Tau near the end of the Vietnam War. I stayed, left my country for her and our son. If I can leave a country, you can leave a job."

The ship seemed larger than the *Rubicola.*

"So what happened?"

"One day she found a land mine."

"Oh, I'm really sorry, Dan."

"We had six great years together. I wouldn't trade it for anything."

Josh couldn't help wonder if Dan hadn't met Mai maybe she would still be alive.

Fresh green paint covering the super trawler's hull matched the water quite well; she seemed to melt into the ocean surrounding her. Not a derelict local boat, rectangular steel doors hung on both sides of the *Ocean Predator's* stern. Black rubber rollers and thick chain lay in neat rows near the tilt stern. Many men wearing rubber overalls stepped over fishing net covering the deck. A section of net dangled from the crane; several people surrounding the net pinnacle struggled to remove chunks of limestone coral, some pieces as tall as them.

Josh found his camera under the seat. "Coral that size must be thousands of years old."

Fishermen generally ignored the helicopter hovering above. He took many pictures. Groups of two carried coral to the stern and heaved it overboard. Several others shoveled piles of fish scattered across the deck over the side.

"What are they fishing for?" Dan asked.

"This isn't fishing, it's mining," Josh muttered. "The only way a ship this size can pay for itself is to plunder and move on."

When they finally arrived at the coordinates, the helicopter climbed to seven hundred meters and flew in a wide circle so Josh could search in all directions.

"Down there!" He pointed to the northeast. The helicopter started descending. The white dot swelled into a sleek modern ship. "Our white knight."

"She's fast," Dan said. "Looks like a coast guard cutter."

"Good eye. She used to be. Now she patrols marine protected areas in the Galapagos."

They buzzed the bridge on the thirty-meter-long ship. Painted on the white hull next to the black letters 'SOLace' were five vertical green, red, and yellow stripes.

Dan spoke into the microphone, "*SOLace,* Maynard. Any sign of pirates?"

"Negative. We have a vessel on radar twenty-two nautical miles, bearing one five seven.

"Roger dodger. We'll take a look-see."

"Maynard? Isn't he the guy who killed Blackbeard?" Josh asked.

"We're gonna take down some pirates, aren't we?"

They leveled off at two hundred meters. Swells below blurred as they sped past at one hundred and fifty kilometers per hour. A dark speck soon emerged at the horizon.

Josh kept binoculars glued to his face. "I think we found one." A hazy cloud hung ominously above the ship. He grabbed the radio. "*SOLace,* Maynard. We've located the whaling ship *MV Runto* at"—he leaned close to the GPS—"zero two degrees, forty-two minutes, forty-three point two seven seconds south, ninety-two degrees, twenty-eight minutes, five point zero four seconds west, bearing three five nine, over."

Two blows erupted far in front of the whaling ship.

"Cut them off," he said.

The helicopter banked toward its new target. Two broad, bluish backs surfaced in synchrony, one slightly behind. Geysers blasted from paired blow holes; misty pillars drifted above relatively small, curved dorsal fins.

"*SOLace,* they're pursuing blue whales, a cow calf pair."

Dan pushed the joystick hard to one side. "Payback time."

The helicopter reeled around and, skimming over waves, headed away from the whales directly toward the ship. As the rusting hull loomed ahead, they climbed steadily to bridge height. Dan seemed strangely relaxed even though they were flying on a collision course with a maze of metal scaffolding on top of the bridge.

"Better hang on," he said, casually.

"Look out!" Josh squeezed the sides of his seat. "Pull up!"

Crruunch

The helicopter's nose snapped downward, flinging them forward as far as their safety belts would allow. They pitched to one side before the helicopter shot upward at a sharp angle above the ship.

Josh craned his head around to see what the skis had hit. A chunk of metal crashed down on top of the bridge.

"Sooo looong radar," Dan sang out.

"That wasn't part of the plan!" Hyperventilating, Josh rubbed his face with sweaty hands. "I'll never make it to Texas."

The *SOLace* arrived like a bat out of hell and didn't slow, barreling straight toward the port side of the *Runto*. At the last minute she turned parallel to the whaler and unleashed a torrent of seawater from a water cannon that cut a swathe from stern to bow, knocking over people and equipment.

"They sure know how to make an entrance," Josh said, gleefully.

The speedy *SOLace* maneuvered half her length ahead of the freshly washed *Runto* and then started to gradually turn, forcing the whaling ship to steer away from the blue whales. The *SOLace* then abruptly slowed, deliberately, allowing the pirates to run. With perfect timing crew lowered a black zodiac; within seconds they were pounding toward the *Runto*, figures in dark clothing almost invisible against the pontoons, waving their arms and shouting.

"Sure they're not Navy Seals?" Dan asked.

"They're heroes. Without them there wouldn't be any blue whales."

The zodiac maneuvered against the starboard side of the whaling vessel's bow. Two people stood and hurled objects up onto her deck.

"That's our cue." Josh reached behind for the special container sitting on the seat.

The helicopter descended above the crowd shouting from the foredeck at the activists. When they were hovering over the bridge, he tried to open the door, but it wouldn't budge.

"The window," Dan said.

Josh pulled the window down. Warm air blasted his body. Noise from the rotor blades was deafening. He yanked the lid off and shoved the container outside; down fell the tracking device from his satellite tag suspended inside a tough epoxy shell covered with adhesive. It landed somewhere on top of the bridge behind the smashed radar.

"You can run, but you can't hide," Dan hollered.

"Hopefully it survived the impact." Josh pushed the window closed.

The helicopter banked away from the ship and gained altitude. The zodiac also turned and headed at full speed toward the whales to protect them and take photographs. The *SOLace* quickly accelerated and resumed chase. A trail of black exhaust from the *Runto's* stack washed over her deck.

"They're almost in international waters," Josh said. *That's it, SOLace, chase the bad guys straight out of town.*

Both ships were running with engines wide open and appeared to have similar top speeds because the *SOLace* could only slowly gain on the *Runto.* They flew over the whaler and Josh took many photographs. Fortunately no pirates seemed to be poking around on top of the bridge where the tracking device had landed. After ten minutes the *SOLace* slowed and the gap between the two ships gradually widened. The white vessel eventually veered to starboard and started turning around.

"Maynard, *SOLace,*" said a gruff voice over the radio, "we won't pursue further. We'll alert other ships in our fleet about the *MV Runto.* See you at our Santa Cruz office."

"Roger, you saved those blue whales. Keep up the good fight," Josh said.

Dan brought them down low over the *SOLace.* Several people on deck waved as they flew over.

They continued flying north toward the Galapagos Islands. Below, the zodiac raced in the opposite direction at thirty knots, suggesting the whales had already dived. The afternoon sun beat warmly against the helicopter's shell. Cotton ball cumulus clouds billowed along the horizon. The magnificent blue ocean spilled endlessly in every direction.

Dan casually tapped the fuel gauge. "Not sure if we have enough fuel to make it back. I kinda lost track during all that excitement."

Josh paid little attention, absently rubbing stubble on his chin. Humans have incorrectly named this planet, Earth, he decided; rather, planet Water would be more appropriate. He marveled at the ocean's miraculous beauty; she is the source of all life on Earth and life is utterly dependent on her for survival.

"Maybe we'll make an emergency landing on the *Rubicola,*" Dan said. "You can tell the wolf you're moving to Texas!"

Somewhere far below the wolf was packing her equipment as the *Rubicola* steamed to a different area to start a new research project. Andrea's definitely right...the world needs to know what's happening in the deep. Even brave eco-warriors at the front lines in a war to save the whales probably weren't aware of the dangers lurking below for the same whales they risk their lives to protect. Sarah and the baby sperm whale deserve to live on a vibrant planet where water and air are clean and pure. What Andrea wants to do—make a video, write papers and letters—is admirable but, who's kidding who, it won't make any difference. People don't recognize subtle.

If they hadn't shown up today, those blue whales would be dead. The *Runto's* sister ship will probably kill them tomorrow anyway. And if not tomorrow, then next week or next month or next year. Weariness seeped from his bones; he slumped in the seat. We're nothing more than predatory pimps who have turned pure, lovely, respectable Mother Earth into a whore, using her body for profit, poisoning her in our blind pursuit of selfish pleasures.

And there was absolutely nothing he could do about it. His own research and writing and talking had produced nothing of significant consequence. His destiny—his soul reason for being—always eluded him. Is his destiny to do nothing meaningful with his life, only to watch helplessly as the planet dies and human misery increases exponentially? He envied those fortunate people with clear life paths, free to move confidently with a sense of purpose, their choices obvious.

Whump

The helicopter shuddered. Blood and feathered chunks splattered across cockpit glass.

Dan seized the joystick with both hands. "A bird hit the prop."

Josh's stomach tightened as they abruptly dropped in altitude. He wondered what species had disintegrated in the rotor blades.

"Wouldn't that be funny?" Dan said. "After all the bullets I've avoided, it's Tweety Bird who finally takes me out."

Red fluid streaked toward the edge of the window. Ironic how one little bird's death could profoundly impact their lives. Maybe death forces us to consider our own mortality? Or it makes us more aware of the life that was? Josh figured he will probably die a forgotten old man. Would he be better off than Diane whose untimely death was a senseless tragedy?

He sat a little straighter. Who says you have to wait for the Grim Reaper to take you when you're old, or at some random point in time? What about a carefully planned death designed for maximum impact? If done right he could influence more people in one moment than in a lifetime.

The bubble of helplessness surrounding him popped. His destiny was suddenly crystal clear. His life…no, rather his death will have meaning. He will die so many can live. A life for life.

He settled back in the seat and closed his eyes. A small smile formed. For once he enjoyed dreaming about the future—one he will shape—not a dystopian one, but instead a renaissance in humankind's evolution when a drastically reduced population, governed by democratic institutions which oversee sustainable steady-state economies, lives in harmony with Nature.

TWENTY-THREE

Andrea leaned over the side of the drifting seven-meter-long panga. Powerful lamps clamped at various places on the skiff illuminated the upper depths. Beyond the halo of light, the towering rocky cape, Cabo Virgenes, loomed silently cloaked in darkness.

It felt good to be busy again. At least it was better to be thinking about Dr. Jekyll while conducting a squid survey in the Sea of Cortez instead of moping around the house. Their relationship, if you could call it that, had ended before it started. They hadn't spoken for three months, ever since their awful date during spring break in Vancouver at Stanley Park. How she resented his casual and unemotional demeanor, his 'I-couldn't-care-less-about-anything' attitude. Sundrop deserved more from men. When she freaked out on the *Rubicola,* she knew she had lost him. She considered herself lucky it ended quickly and they didn't have time to get to know one another or she would've fallen hard.

Luis, a stout, muscular man in his late forties with dark brooding eyes and black hair combed straight back, cranked the handle on the plastic reel, paused to rest, and then vigorously turned it again.

Andrea called to Naeco who was rummaging through a tote full of SCUBA gear at the bow. "We finally caught one."

"How long did it take?"

She looked at her watch. "One hundred and three minutes."

"It used to be seconds," Luis Santos Inez said. Now he strained to turn the handle. "It's heavy." Suddenly his left hand started spinning, making rapid circles. "Mierda, lo perdí!"

The florescent chrome jig shot out of the water. Andrea stepped back, her arms raised out front to shield her face. She grabbed the fishing line and examined the fleshy blob still attached to the jig. All that remained was a black chitinous beak wrapped in whitish musculature the size of a tennis ball.

"The hunter becomes the hunted." She worked the jig's numerous spikes out of the rubbery flesh and dropped the remains in a plastic bag. "Hooked squid are defenseless and often cannibalized by others in the school."

"What are you going to do with that?" Naeco asked.

"The buccal cavity?" Andrea held the bag up to the lights. "We'll examine it to confirm the species and size. This is definitely a Humboldt squid though."

Luis tossed the jig overboard and let the line spin off the reel down to seventy meters. Humboldt squid rise to this depth at night searching for food. During the day they remain in deeper water where low oxygen levels deter potential predators.

Something tugged the line. "Esta picando." He yanked hard to drive spikes into the squid's arms. "They swarm now." He started hauling the line up again.

A large squid surfaced against the side of the boat. Struggling to jet away, it sprayed streams of seawater through its short hose-like funnel into the air soaking Luis's yellow, checkered shirt. The skin pulsated like a strobe light flickering between maroon and white colors.

In one fluid motion Luis yanked the squid over the side smearing a trail of black ink against the silver fiberglass. Andrea pounced on the muscular mass lying in the bottom of the boat, several sucker cup-riddled arms still stuck against the side. They lifted it onto a portable wooden table.

"Careful, don't touch its eye," she said.

Luis moved his left thumb away from the round, black eye.

In a note pad she recorded lengths of the body and mantle. It was almost the same size as Sundrop. No hectocotylus. She wrote in the Sex column an 'I' for 'Immature'. Luis slid the blob on a scale. Eighteen point three kilograms, she scribbled. Since it had no tag to identify that it had previously been caught, she sewed a red plastic one through the rubbery mantle. Her goal was to tag one hundred squid. That meant sixty-seven more to go. She recorded the tag's number next to the squid's biological information. Whoever caught this squid in the future and returned the tag to her would receive fifty dollars for his trouble.

They dumped the squid overboard and it swam away under the boat.

"Los diablos rojos," Luis muttered with a shudder.

Several squid darted around the skiff chasing silvery flashes. Tonight prey was mackerel.

Andrea joined Naeco at the bow. They sat beside their respective tubs and quickly changed into SCUBA gear. Luis resumed jigging near the stern, his arm jerking up and down in a deliberate spastic motion. Andrea noticed him watching them. When she wiggled her slender legs into the tight-fitting wetsuit his discrete ogling turned into blatant gawking.

This could've been all yours, Dr. Josh Templeton. Seductively licking her lips, she stood, arched her back, and slowly pulled the zipper up between her breasts. Bending over provided Luis with full view of her toned buttocks. His arms went limp, hanging down by his sides. Soon he stopped jigging altogether and stared shamelessly at her.

The show ended when she dug her mask out of the tub and adjusted the snorkel strap. She wore a black wetsuit with green stripes on the rented floatation vest. A glow stick was strapped to the single tank on her back. "Ready when you are, Naeco."

"I'll be right with you."

Andrea carried her mask and flippers to the back of the panga. She spit in the mask, wiped saliva around the inside of the lens, and dunked it in the warm water. This would keep the lens from fogging up during the dive. Gingerly she pulled the mask over her hoody. Distant blobs of light on dark water resembled stars on a clear night sky. Tonight, like on most calm nights during the summer, a few pangas—all that remained from a once vibrant fishery—spread out along the eastern shore of Mexico's Baja California to lure squid to the surface with their powerful lights.

"All clear," Luis mumbled. The jig flashed about four meters down. One squid, at first tempted, swam near it, but then streaked away after a more appetizing fish. He coiled the remaining line on the reel.

Andrea pumped air into the floatation vest and turned on the headlamp. She called to Naeco, "I'll be waiting out there." Ignoring the helping hand Luis offered, she tumbled backward off the stern.

Splash

Startled squid and mackerel darted away. Bobbing behind the skiff, she put the snorkel in her mouth and swam in a wide circle. Squid jetted near, flashing white to pink and back to white in a fraction of a second.

She hollered to Naeco who teetered on the side of the panga, "There's a bit of current here."

A smaller squid swam directly up at her out of the darkness. Two tentacles snapped forward; their club-like ends smacked her leg. Kicking her flippers scared it back into the shadows.

"One just whacked me," she said to Naeco who was swimming toward her. Andrea dipped her head under. "Sometimes these red devils act fairly aggressively. When you only live a year or two and need to grow up quickly, you need to eat a lot."

"I hope we're not dessert," Naeco said.

"We should stick close and not go too deep. Sometimes I wonder if fishing agitates them and makes them unusually savage." She called to Luis, "We'll check back in fifteen minutes."

He waved.

Facing each other, they allowed air to escape their vests and settled under the surface. Andrea inverted first and swam downward. At a depth of twenty-three feet she stopped and gestured to Naeco the 'okay' signal. A puddle of white from lights on the boat shimmered above their heads. Periodically they checked their glowing gauges to make sure they were floating at relatively the same depth. They had sunk a little and were now twenty-eight feet below the surface.

She poked Naeco and pointed. A dull green light approached; something was disturbing the plankton causing the miniscule plants to glow. Out of the blackness emerged two large squid feverishly pulsating. Propelled by forcefully expelling streams of seawater, the squid maneuvered effortlessly around them, their positions in the water column controlled by the pair of fins undulating at the tail end of the mantle. Relaxed arms loosely trailed in a streamlined manner. Naeco rotated to follow them, the camera flashing repeatedly.

One squid stopped and hovered. Abruptly its long body contracted and arms flared open like hyperactive petals on some kind of grotesque alien flower. The squid shot directly at the camera and rammed it against Naeco's mask. Writhing arms with toothed sucker cups groped at her face and head. She tried pushing the squid away with one hand while holding on tightly to the camera.

Andrea swam closer and punched the squid with her dive light. She stiffened. A sharp holler bubbled into her regulator. Fire seared her leg. She smashed her light against the squid wrapped around her thigh until she was forced to equalize to relieve crushing pressure building in her inner ear. The squid was pulling her deeper! Frantically she kicked her legs. She clawed the knife from the sheath strapped to her calf and stabbed the squid again and again, the blade striking it in the head and eyes. In a cloud of ink the squid released her and vanished.

She fought to slow her rapid, shallow breathing in the suffocating blackness. She couldn't see Naeco anywhere. The depth gauge read sixty-nine feet. Relieved to still be within the safe depth range for recreational diving, she swam toward the surface, bubbles streaming from her regulator, the flashlight flailing in every direction searching for more attackers. One squid swam close, hovered, but then jetted out of sight.

Her head broke the surface. She ripped the regulator from her mouth. "NAECO!"

"Andrea! Thank God!" Naeco, twenty meters away, started swimming in her direction.

"Get out of the water!" Andrea shouted.

They swam toward the panga where strong arms waited to haul them to safety. Gasping, they clung to the side of the boat.

"Are you hurt?" She examined Naeco's face around her mask for lacerations.

"I don't think so. Thankfully the camera was between me and the squid. What happened to you?"

"The other one pulled me down." Trembling, she nearly dropped her weight belt when passing it to Luis. "Really hope I didn't rupture my ear drum." She tilted her head and pressed a finger against her throbbing ear.

Luis grabbed their arms and pulled them into the panga. "You're bleeding," he said to her.

Surprised, she poked a finger through the hole in the wetsuit on her leg where the squid's sharp beak had chewed through the neoprene. She shrugged. Just another field souvenir. "It's only a scratch, I'll live."

"We go home," Luis said, stepping over the seat to the outboard motor.

Exhausted, they sat at the front and slowly peeled off their wetsuits.

Andrea could now relate to the mighty sperm whale after grappling underwater with a huge squid. She touched Naeco's arm. "Do you hear anything?"

Naeco stopped changing. The occasional murmur from fishermen on a nearby panga drifted across the water. The wind gusted from different directions. The Sea of Cortez seduced them with her nighttime whispers. "Not really."

"That's the problem, it's dead quiet now. Nobody fishes here anymore. Squid used to be an important source of income for people from Santa Rosalia and across the Gulf at Guaymas. Many turned to commercial fishing after the copper mines closed." Andrea shivered uncontrollably under the damp beach towel draped over her shoulders. "And this was an important feeding area for sperm whales. Before, sometimes all you could hear was their blows."

"I've heard this story before," Naeco said. Dark waters revealed no signs of giant mammals. "Maybe they'll come back."

Luis waited by the engine, watching them, nervously twisting the throttle.

Andrea's cell phone, buried in the knapsack, started ringing. Who would be calling now? A sense of dread smothered her. *Sundrop*! "Hello?"

"Where are you? Are you driving?"

"I'm on a boat. What's going on, Laura?"

"Are you sitting down?"

Her stomach tightened. "Yes, why are you calling?" *Please, Tiskin.*

"I'm sorry. It's about Josh."

TWENTY-FOUR

Her hair still wet, Andrea stood over her laptop on the kitchen table in their rented house and googled the newspaper *Ottawa Chronicle*. Following her sister's instructions, she clicked on the title, "Protester collapses at Parliament Hill". She forced herself to look at the photograph above the news article. Paramedics and protesters surrounded an elderly man who was lying on his back on a grassy field in front of the Parliament Buildings. The man's head had rolled to one side, stringy short brown hair matted against a hollow, tanned cheek. Gray pants and a blue golf shirt loosely covered his gaunt body. Her chest heaved with relief. Laura was mistaken. Probably a crazy homeless person.

A white sign with a wooden handle lay picture-perfect next to the motionless man. LIFE ON EARTH WITHOUT A HEALTHY OCEAN. A thick arrow pointed downward at the person holding the sign. Chills crawled up her spine. No way could this sick man be Josh.

Protester Collapses at Parliament Hill

By Cindy Fletcher, Ottawa Chronicle

OTTAWA — A protester collapsed at Parliament Hill yesterday amid a group of supporters and tourists.

> Paramedics arrived quickly only to be turned away by the protester before they could administer treatment. The protester refused to be taken to the hospital. The protester is Dr. Joshua Templeton, a marine ecologist who has recently become a frequent visitor to the Parliament Buildings. He is in the fifth week of a hunger strike—

Her hand covered her mouth. Five weeks! She glanced again at the picture above the article.

> —fifth week of a hunger strike to raise awareness about the state of the ocean. Dr. Templeton repeatedly has said countries, economies, and people cannot survive without a healthy ocean just like a person cannot survive without food.
>
> The Minister of the Environment, the Honorable Marc Tolberg, has stated he is willing to meet with Dr. Templeton on the condition he stop the hunger strike. So far Dr. Templeton has declined the invitation.
>
> Dr. Burgess, a physician from Queens Grace Hospital, urges Dr. Templeton to resume eating immediately. "Dr. Templeton is risking his life by not eating for so long. I understand he has only consumed water during the past thirty days. In the advanced stage of starvation like we unfortunately have in this situation, the body cannibalizes itself, devouring its own muscle tissues to keep critical organs like the brain alive. Without immediate ingestion of vitamins, minerals, and proteins it is possible Dr. Templeton could suffer a heart attack or succumb to infection. This would be tragic and totally preventable."
>
> Protesters at Parliament Hill—

Yellow curtains framing the patio fluttered as gusts of warm evening air flowed through the wide open door. Andrea pulled the sliding patio door closed. How long had Josh been planning this stunt? Even when they talked on the phone at Christmas after the Galapagos trip he had acted strangely distant. Why didn't she see it? The passionate man she had fallen in love with disappeared once he flew away from the *Rubicola*. Why didn't he tell her?

Bitter anger turned to compassion. She yearned to see him right away. Using the internet she found a cluster of hotels within walking distance to Parliament Hill and called six places, but none had a Josh Templeton on their guest list. He must have started the hunger strike the moment she left for Mexico. A coincidence?

While packing she called Naeco and explained why they must unfortunately postpone the squid survey. Next she phoned her dad to discuss why Sundrop should remain with him on the West Coast for at least another week.

Two days later she flew to Ottawa through Chicago, arriving at 9:35 pm. After a short cab ride she stood at the front desk of the Waldbank Hotel. She booked a room for two nights, drank half a carafe of the house red in the cozy lounge downstairs, and finally fell asleep sometime after 2:00 am while channel surfing.

The telephone rang. Andrea groped sleepily for the receiver on the bedside table.

"Good morning," said an automated female voice. "Thank you for choosing the Wal—"

She tossed the phone on the comforter at her feet. She had forgotten about the 8:30 am wake-up call. It felt like the middle of the night.

She opened brown drapes covering the window above the air conditioner. Morning rush-hour traffic, four stories below, flowed steadily in one direction down Albert Street. Since the weather was overcast and cool, she dressed in blue jeans, a loose-fitting red shirt, and comfortable running shoes. Friendly front desk staff provided a map of downtown and circled locations of the nearest coffee shops and restaurants.

Chai tea latte in hand, she crossed Wellington Street in front of Parliament Hill and joined numerous camera-toting tourists strolling past a pyramid-shaped fountain along a wide walkway that split the manicured grounds. She walked toward the Center Block, a massive rectangular sandstone, stone, and marble building whose main entrance was at the base of the ninety-two-meter-high Peace Tower with its four-faced clock. Well-dressed politicians drunk with power, their faces contorted in perpetual smirks, strode purposefully between buildings where they concocted legislation that invariably hurt Indigenous Peoples. No one could pay her enough money to take a tour of the Parliament Buildings and watch Canada's finest bicker in the House of Commons while one in two Indigenous children lived in abject poverty.

Bells on the Peace Tower chimed. She bee-lined toward a sizable crowd consisting of the young, elderly, and many more in their twenties and thirties; it wasn't only hippies carrying placards with statements like SAVE THE OCEAN and THIS IS THE OCEAN ON ACID. Unfortunately no commanding figure seemed to stand out and people wandered about somewhat aimlessly.

"I'm looking for Josh Templeton," she asked a guy with sunglasses and curly brown hair who was gulping down a tube steak.

He swallowed a mouthful and swiped his cheek with the back of his hand. "I haven't seen him for a couple days."

She thanked him and kept walking. She asked a group of students sitting on the grass the same question.

One guy with better hair than her jumped up. "He usually comes in the afternoon. You looking to join the movement?"

She faked a smile. "Did you see Josh yesterday?"

"Nope. I think the hunger strike thing's getting him down."

Shielding her eyes with her hand, she looked in the direction of her hotel. "Is he staying downtown?"

"Not sure." He nodded toward a pretty brunette talking with two young guys. "Haley might know. I've seen them come together sometimes."

The tall, twenty-something woman had brown eyes, a flawless complexion, and effortlessly wore a long yellow skirt and white blouse.

"Hi, I'm Andrea, Josh's friend. I hope to see him today."

"Me too."

Andrea lowered her voice. "Do you have his number?"

Suspicious, Haley's eyes moved quickly from Andrea's face to her feet.

"Can you call Josh and let me speak to him?"

Haley took her cell phone from a backpack lying on the grass, walked a short distance, and turned away. After a minute, she said, relieved, "He's probably on his way here."

Until Andrea could see and touch him, she wouldn't stop worrying. "Where's he staying?"

"He doesn't want anyone to know, sorry."

"Josh and I are colleagues. We research sperm whales and squid together." She hoped he had mentioned something like this to her.

Haley silently chewed her pouty lower lip.

Andrea wondered if they were sleeping together. "Why don't you come with me?"

She called Josh again. Still no answer. By now Andrea was almost frantic.

They hurried several blocks to Haley's gray station wagon and drove out of downtown over a bridge into a residential area with a mixture of older character and modern homes narrowly spaced along wide streets with treed boulevards. Haley had first met Josh at university; he taught several of her courses. She had been working in Ottawa for over a year, not far from the Parliament Buildings. An ardent environmentalist, their paths crossed again when she heard about the protests. Josh no longer wanted to stay at a hotel and spread word he was looking for cheaper, long-term accommodation. Her aunt happened to have an empty suite in her house. Andrea told Haley about their Galapagos research. Haley seemed like a good person with her heart in the right place.

They parked on a quiet street in front of a white two story house and followed a stone path, through a gate, around to the backyard. A clothes line hung from the kitchen window, above raised garden beds, to the corner of a white garage at the end of a long, cracking driveway. They climbed stone steps to the back door.

Haley knocked timidly and waited. "I guess he's still out."

Andrea reached around her and pounded on the wooden door. "Do you have a key?"

Haley hesitated.

"He might be inside and need our help."

She rummaged through her backpack and produced a single key. She unlocked the door and stepped into the foyer. "Josh...hello?"

Andrea walked past her into a showroom kitchen with stainless steel appliances and oak cabinetry. The only sign of anyone using the kitchen was a single glass of water on the table. A musty odor lingered.

A toilet flushed in another part of the suite. "Hey, Haley," a raspy, yet familiar, voice called from the hallway. Pale and stooped, Josh shuffled into the kitchen. "Andrea!" He teetered in the doorway like a buck gazing into truck headlights.

She rushed to him. "Please sit down." She could only feel bones in his arms. They certainly weren't the same strong arms that held her firmly on the *Rubicola* and made her feel so wonderfully safe. He reminded her of Uncle Louie after his awful long fight with leukemia.

Haley pulled over a chair from the kitchen table. Using Andrea for support, Josh gently lowered himself onto the seat.

She said to Haley, "I'd like to speak to Josh alone, if you don't mind."

The back door closed. Andrea smiled compassionately at him. "I've seen all those people at Parliament Hill. You're a hero. It's time to pass the torch and come home."

Leaning forward, his bony forearms rested on bulbous knees. His bloated midsection sagged downward under his tee shirt and growled constantly.

"You're playing a very dangerous game with your health. Let us take you to the hospital. You need a doctor."

"I'm doing this for Sarah," he murmured.

No you're not, this is all about you, she wanted to say. "If you really want to help Sundrop then be a part of her life. That's what she really needs."

He didn't look up. "Her life will be better after I do this."

"Do what? What exactly are you doing?" She knelt and grasped his skeletal hand. Her voice softened. "Our lives are better when you're with us. We miss you so much. Stop this, please."

He pushed off her shoulder, stood, and stepped away.

She kept pressing. "Remember Les Miserables? Those kids who planned the revolution got slaughtered. They didn't accomplish anything. But Jean Valjean changed many lives by subtly helping those who needed it. We can change lives too, one by one. It just takes time…a lifetime."

Starting to wobble, he leaned against the counter, his back to her. "I haven't been able to make a difference until now."

"Get healthy and we can spend the rest of our lives fighting this fight if you want. I promise."

He turned and gazed at her for a long moment. "I'm not leaving Ottawa."

At first she didn't understand. Then the significance of his words hit harder than Roy's fists. Tears filled her eyes.

"This is my destiny. You must understand—"

"Forget your destiny!" she cried out. "They'll bury you here. Nothing will change, Josh. A month after…" she couldn't say the words… "the world will continue to chug along as it's always done. Nothing will change except Sundrop's heart will be broken."

"You're wrong."

Silently she pleaded with him.

"Don't mourn me. Move on, find a nice guy—"

"What?! Find a nice guy?" A rage she had felt only once before sprang forth. "Is that all you can say to me?!"

A corpse with bloodshot eyes stared pathetically at her.

Every muscle in her body clenched. How she wanted to scream at this fool who was deliberately destroying his own gorgeous body. And for what? She walked somberly in a line among Josh's family and friends past the open casket. It horrified her to think this would be her last memory of him. She should never have come.

"Do you really want to die here...with Haley?" She shook her head in disbelief. "You've gone mad."

His voice was hoarse and weak. "You're amazing, Andrea. I—"

"Answer the question!"

He exhaled heavily. "Thanks for coming, it means a lot to me, really."

She barely heard him, her head was spinning. She was wasting precious time here. She smiled thinly and delicately kissed his pallid cheek. He smelled sharp, not sweet like the man she had snuggled with on the *Rubicola*. "Good bye, Josh." Her hand brushed against his pointy elbow.

She walked slowly out the door and down the stairs overcompensating for wanting to get away as quickly as possible. She didn't dare look back as she stepped from the mausoleum into the rain-drenched land of the living.

When Andrea disappeared around the corner of the house Josh's knees buckled and he slumped forward on all fours hurting both wrists on the tile floor. His labored breathing sounded unfamiliar, like a sick, wild animal. No tears flowed; he didn't have the energy to weep.

He struggled to stand and staggered to the table where several times every day he had sat, glass in hand, head back, cheeks bursting with the elixir of life. Oh, how he savored every delicious drop that slid down his constricted throat.

Once more he held the glass of water. He gritted his teeth and winced. His churning stomach felt twisted in knots, every joint ached, never-ending migraines jack hammered holes through his shriveled Swiss cheese brain. And now she's here torturing him, tearing apart his weak heart.

I can't keep dying like this.

He dropped the glass in the sink, chipping it, sending a handful of water splashing onto the counter. Without water he would last, at most, three days. Tomorrow he will stay on the Hill until he dies. Soon the world will know what he gave his life for. Hopefully a few from the hundreds who have protested beside him will find the courage to pick up his sign and champion his cause forward.

Diane glided across the beach and kissed him. She took his hand and led him into the dying room. Andrea tugged his other arm and motioned toward the door where sunlight spilled through stained glass into the foyer. He stood motionless with both arms straight out, like a crucified criminal, looking right then left, right, left.... He had no idea how much time passed while in a stupor with two beautiful women competing for his attention. When they dissolved like honey in a cup of hot tea, he stumbled over to the colorful futon under the draped picture window and collapsed.

Fantastic animals and arthropods that had existed, evolved, and then went extinct throughout Earth's history slithered, crawled, walked, hopped, flew, and swam over him. African primates jumped down from trees and walked upright across the savannah, their hands free at last to build, create, and carry weapons. Consciousness settled into their rapidly expanding brains. Wandering out of Africa and throughout Europe and Asia, several groups of hairy hominids like the Neanderthals, with their sturdy, strong limbs and large eyes, tried unsuccessfully to adapt to different habitats and climates and eventually died off, outcompeted by modern humans.

Crouching on a rocky bare patch, he plucked several waxy leaves from sparse low shrubbery and meticulously chewed each one. In the distance, tawny rolling hills swallowed overgrown crumbling remains of a decaying city. This day he will curl up under a gnarled tree and gratefully fall asleep never to awaken. He is the last surviving human being, nowhere for that bundle of incredible genetic material honed by millions of years of adaptation to go except back to the soil.

TWENTY-FIVE

Josh started the engine and pushed the throttle forward. The *Catchalot* darted ahead, her bow rising high out of the water and then lowering as the boat picked up speed. Warm wind blasted his face. The hull cut through choppy waves. Occasionally seawater sprayed over the bow.

Suddenly silver flashed at the surface bouncing off tops of waves. Gliding on enlarged pectoral fins spread out like wings, several flying fish sailed into the pontoons when the boat slowed. One fish landed in the *Catchalot,* its deeply forked tail vibrating in a sideways motion as it tried to gain height to get back in the water. Using the bailer, he gently scooped up the fish and dumped it overboard.

Lono stood on the stern ramp holding a long rod, its tip high in the air bobbing vigorously. "Caught one!"

"Get me another tag!" Josh hollered.

Something splashed at the surface near the zodiac. Lono yanked the struggling fish to the stern. Not bothering to use the net, he grabbed the line and heaved his prize up on deck.

The zodiac slammed against the *Go For Broke.* Josh tossed the bow and stern lines over the bulwarks. Lono jammed the rod into the holder, hurried across the deck to wrap the ropes around a cleat, and then jogged back to his fish.

Josh leapt over the side and ran into the wheelhouse. A silent ocean blared through the hydrophones. The sounder showed the seafloor and a shallow scattering layer at four hundred and eighty feet. The familiar arch-shaped blip was gone.

He walked briskly through the galley on deck where a slender body flopped at Lono's feet. On the fish's blunt, nearly square head a frowning mouth riddled with small teeth gulped desperately for oxygen. A sail-like dorsal fin extended the length of the body and ended at a deeply forked caudal fin, which hinted at a capability for speed. Vibrant metallic colors seemed to flow off the mahi-mahi as seawater pooled on deck. Blotches of iridescent greens and blues covered its back and sides. The golden underside had several blackened lesions.

"Lono, where's the whale?"

"Don't know." He placed a foot on the writhing fish. "It dove and took off."

"He didn't start echolocating?"

"I didn't hear anything." He pointed a screwdriver in a southeasterly direction. "It went that way, bearing one three nine." Through the mahi-mahi's eye he jabbed the sharp instrument. Instantly, like a switch had been flicked, beautiful colors sparkling on the skin faded to a uniform silver color. Bright red blood flowed from the eye socket over the operculum. Triumphantly Lono held up the dead mahi-mahi impaled on the end of the screwdriver. "Probably a fifteen pounder." He slapped the drab, twitching fish on the sorting table and tore the hook from its mouth. By now the fish was almost the same color as the aluminum.

For a moment Josh glared at Lono's bloodshot eyes. Diane gazed back at him, red tears streaming down her cheeks. Shaking his head, he climbed up to the flybridge, an observation platform above the wheelhouse. Standing between two patio chairs, holding down the cap on his head, the full force of the wind gusting against his torso, he searched near and distant waters for blows since sperm whales can move three kilometers during a dive. Like usual the afternoon winds were building; curling whitecaps frothed on lumpy gray water. Unfortunately witches tits like these might make him seasick. Dusky clouds, several morphing into shapes resembling whales, scuttled across the somber sky making it difficult to discern where water ended and sky began. The colorless world mirrored a black and white photograph with shades of gray providing the only contrast.

Was that a blow? Hard to tell with so many breaking waves. Tears fought the wind to keep his eyes from drying out.

He slumped down on deck against the side. The only conceivable way they could have lost track of the whale is he dove shallow, didn't start echolocating, and swam like crazy away from them. But that's ridiculous. Sperm whales don't behave like that.

He reached under the collar of his tee shirt and touched the locket. "I have no one to help me," he whispered, rage simmering within.

Below, Lono wandered out on deck and smoked a cigarette while urinating over the side. Nearby a taut white rope, one end tied to a cleat, disappeared into foam-topped waves rolling past the *Catchalot.* The sea anchor, a small parachute, slowed the drifting *Go For Broke* and kept her bow pointed into the waves.

Josh climbed down the ladder, walked over to the open hatch near the sorting table, and climbed down into the engine room. Head bowed in reverence to low metal beams, he walked along a stainless steel pathway that led from the base of the ladder around the Caterpillar engine, a piece of machinery the size of a car. There was Lono, kneeling, holding a flashlight, one arm deep inside the engine.

"Checking the belts?" Josh knew there shouldn't be anything wrong. A chart hanging on the bulkhead indicated it had only been one hundred and eighty hours since the engine's last detailed inspection, which occurred every five hundred hours.

Lono wiped his hands with a greasy cloth. "I hope it'll start again."

"You and your dad do a good job maintaining it."

"I'm done here." Lono moved toward the ladder. "I'll make some grub."

Josh followed Lono into the house. Lono casually opened the door on the cast iron oil stove and, by turning a knob inside, adjusted the heat down. On either side of the stove stood a miniature sink and beer fridge; above the counter hung wooden cupboards that held a garage sale's assortment of dishes.

His teeth clenched, Josh leaned against the bulkhead and crossed his arms. "You got a stash of Maui Wowie on board?"

"What?"

"You were supposed to be tracking the whale, not smoking pot and fishing."

Lono filled a glass with orange juice from the fridge. Taped to the door, last year's Miss September mouthed a kiss at him. "It took off. Nuthin I could do."

"I've been searching years for that whale."

"Relax, man, the ocean's full of them. I'll find you another." He lifted a green cushion off one of the benches around the table and rummaged through the pile of dry goods stored inside. "I saw two a couple weeks ago from the beach."

Josh shook his head in exasperation. "Those were humpbacks. That," he pointed over his shoulder, "was a sperm whale, remember? The largest living toothed whale on the planet and one of few breeding males." He breathed deeply fighting to control his anger. "Lono, I need your help out here. Do your job and absolutely no drugs."

Lono chose a jar of salted peanuts and replaced the seat cover. "It's my boat. I do what I want."

Josh stepped closer. "No, this is Peter Tanaka's boat. His sweat paid for the *Go For Broke,* not yours. I've known your dad as long as you have. And you know who's paying for this boat right now? Me. So that gives me the right to voice my concerns and expect certain behavior, especially from the Captain who should be setting an example. This is a university research boat, not a fishing boat, and we do things differently than maybe what you're used to."

"Know what I'm used to?" Lono tossed a handful of peanuts into his mouth. "Fishing eight hundred traps a day and making a shit pile of money for two months work. Exploring cool spots from Nihos Island to Kure Atoll. This is boring." He coughed mashed peanuts into his hand. "I can't believe I'm working for a tree hugger. You killed our fishery by micro-managing the shit out of it. You blame us for everything—no lobsters, starving Monk seals." He tried pushing past Josh to get to the wheelhouse.

Josh spoke more quietly. "Lono, you're a smart guy with a bright future. Don't mess it up."

"You're just like my old man, a pain in the ass."

"Please stay focused. We must find that whale."

Sitting on the flybridge, Josh tried eating dinner—farmed tilapia with garlic bread and pre-washed salad—but most of the mushy fish remained untouched on his plate. Still no sign of the whale, nothing detected visually or by the hydrophones that can detect vocalizations seven kilometers away.

He carried his dishes inside and washed them in the sink. While Lono played solitaire at the galley table, Josh found a tin can in the garbage, washed it, and covered the top with foil, leaving a small hole for cigarette butts to pass through.

He filled a mug with hot water from the kettle on the oil stove. "Lono, I made an ashtray for your butts. Can you please use it instead of throwing them overboard? Seabirds like albatross eat the butts because they think they're food. They also feed them to their chicks."

"Yah, sure," Lono muttered.

"Thanks, I'll leave it outside the door." While the tea bag flavored the water, Josh silently studied the curvaceous twenty-four-year-old Hawaiian woman on the fridge door. She had sperm whales to thank for her beautiful ethnic features: wavy black hair, light brown skin, and white cheerful smile. As Hawaii developed into an important whaling port in the nineteenth century, many whalers eventually settled on the islands and married local Polynesian women, forever altering the racial composition of the population.

The bull…where did he go? Will he come back?

"Up for a quick game?" Lono asked, shuffling the deck of cards.

Josh turned. "Thanks, no. I'm gonna wait in the *Catchalot*."

"Taking her for a spin?"

"For some reason the whale seemed to like the zodiac. Maybe he'll show up tonight."

The curtain of night descended rapidly on the ocean when clouds drifted in front of the moon. Only the *Go For Broke* provided an oasis of light in the desert of darkness as she swayed at the center of a glowing circle cast by the navigation lights. High up on the mast two round working lights glowed red, a signal to other vessel traffic the boat was not under command. The hum of the generator could be heard at times over night winds.

Josh spent his first night in the *Catchalot* four years ago when Mars was unusually close to Earth and visible through binoculars. He and Diane had lain for hours on the hard deck watching the red planet and other celestial bodies. They were so vivid compared to what they could normally see in the city where light pollution hides distant, fainter objects. Last year a spectacular meteor shower had tempted him away from the smelly fo'c'sle for two nights.

Instead of looking up at the heavens, he lay sprawled on the pontoon watching green and yellow pinprick lights shimmering under the surface. Lanternfish, which have light-producing organs along the sides of their slender bodies, vertically migrated from depths of several hundred meters to the surface at night.

Suddenly the drops of light vanished. He swept the flashlight over the surface searching for the fish, but none darted through the yellow beam. He switched the light off and waited, his heart thudding louder as each second passed. A flick of the flashlight's on/off switch revealed the tagging gear nearby. With every muscle tensed, he barely endured the calm before the storm.

When the sperm whale blew, his heart nearly exploded. The flashlight's beam stabbed at darkness in the direction of rushing air. Shaking the flashlight failed to strengthen the dull bulb and reveal the sixteen-meter-long leviathan lurking nearby.

A spout blasted somewhere behind the *Go For Broke,* probably one or two hundred meters away. The next breath seemed louder so he taped the flashlight halfway down the pole. Surface waters being displaced sounded like a ship approaching. He dropped tag six three zero one in the dispenser and turned off the flashlight and waited, crouching, for blobs of color burned in his vision to fade as his eyes grew accustomed to the darkness.

A swath of shimmering phosphorescent plankton approached directly at the *Catchalot.* His head suddenly snapped back and bounced off the pontoon when the zodiac lurched sideways. Dazed, Josh rose to his knees and raised the pole over the pontoon. Shiny, wrinkled black skin gleamed in the light. The great beast floated motionless against the zodiac, the body extending seemingly to infinity in both directions. He stepped carefully to the stern and, next to the outboard, leaned over the pontoon. Somewhere nearby the nostril flared open and showered him with a mist of putrid droplets.

He extended the pole to half its full length and held the tag above the crease along the top of the head where the nose and trunk met. Only when the flashlight beam revealed the middle of the back did he lower it.

"Take me to some females," he whispered, pushing down firmly on the pole to embed the satellite tag. Quickly he hauled the pole back in the boat. The sperm whale barely moved, remaining almost touching the pontoon. He freed the flashlight and pointed the beam back and forth along the glistening back of the motionless animal. He reached out to touch the skin, but stopped after deciding it wouldn't be appropriate. Being a researcher he should maintain his distance and objectivity. Humans had interfered enough in the lives of sperm whales.

Josh sat on the deck and leaned back against the pontoon. Strange how this whale almost wanted to be tagged. Explosive expirations startled him for a while until he got used to the predictable sounds. Eventually not much moved beyond the pontoon except endless water. Maybe the whale fell asleep? Between thunderous breaths the giant animal created little sound. Occasionally the *Catchalot* bumped against something solid.

TWENTY-SIX

Josh rolled uncomfortably on his side, one spaghetti leg dangling awkwardly off the futon. Cottony brush strokes clumping near the horizon reminded him of massive icebergs in the Amundsen Sea near Antarctica. High altitude winds dispersed the white vapor trail behind an airplane moving silently in a northeasterly direction.

He peeked over the pontoon. The wind had finally died down having blown itself out last night. The chop had dissipated; only smooth swells making their way toward distant shores rolled under the *Catchalot.* A slender dorsal fin on a scarred gray back sliced through the surface near the bow. The Risso's dolphin puffed several times before diving under the *Go For Broke* and disappearing.

Unbearably famished, Josh pulled the toolbox out from under the seat and found a knife among assorted tools. He braced the coconut between his legs and cut through the thin, smooth outer husk and chopped away at the fibrous mesocarp until the dark brown, hard shell that protected the seed appeared. Using a screwdriver he hammered a channel through one of three germinating pores. A swollen tongue tried to moisten cracked lips. Holding the coconut above his head, he poured delicious milk into his dry mouth. It took several attempts to swallow the saliva paste stuck in his throat. He placed the stone in a plastic bag and, with several swift blows from a hammer, broke it into numerous pieces. He stepped to the bow with the bag of coconut chunks; his starving body sank easily between the pontoons.

He bit into the white flesh, nibbling carefully, savoring its sweet delicious taste. Where did the seed originate and where would it have gone if he hadn't intercepted it? Where did the whale come from and where will he go? For the sake of the species he must survive and reproduce. The next piece still had the hard shell attached to the kernel. What a remarkable fruit. No wonder the seed of the coconut palm is such a terrific colonizer of new islands. The hard outer layer protects the vulnerable inner seed from seawater or desiccation. The embryo can lie dormant, barely alive, until conditions are conducive to life like when the coconut washes up on a beach. When this happens the once impenetrable outer coating starts to deteriorate and the seed inside begins to grow. The coconut tasted extraordinarily fresh, distinctive. He hungrily devoured piece after piece appreciating more than ever the remarkable bounty of the ocean.

Bang bang

He struggled to lift his head. The neighbors? He peeked through the drapes at several cars parked under street lights along the dark street. Someone at the door? Lead limbs sinking into the futon made standing impossible. Chronic fatigue pushed down on his eyelids. The refrigerator in the kitchen sang its siren song to him. Calmly he accepted he won't be answering the door let alone going to Parliament Hill. Thankfully the coffin where he lay was relatively comfortable.

Beautiful Andrea emerged from the fog and hovered over him. He reached for her. *Take me to Parliament Hill.*

"Thank you, Tiskin," she whispered.

Haley and two burly First Nation men stood at the entrance to the living room.

"Please relax," Andrea said. "We're taking you somewhere safe to get well."

"Parliament buildings," he mumbled.

The mountain-of-a-man picked him up like a baby. "We admire what you're doing, Mr. Templeton." He carried him through the kitchen and out the wide-open back door. The night air was cool and damp. The other man jogged ahead and opened the sliding door on a van parked on the driveway. All the rear seats had been removed. They gently lowered him down on his back on an aluminum camping cot.

Andrea knelt beside him. "You won't be coming back. Do you understand? Is there anything you need?"

"Parliament..."

"Where's your wallet and ID?"

"Leave me," he murmured.

She turned to the men who were speaking quietly on the front lawn. "Go with Haley into the bedroom and find his wallet and any other personal items and bring some clothes." She unscrewed the lid on a thermos. "Here, eat some fish soup." She gently poured several spoonfuls into his mouth.

He could barely swallow the delicious broth, but it didn't seem to matter as his body instantly absorbed the nourishment. He raised his head like a bird begging for more.

"That's enough for now. Your stomach's shrunk so you shouldn't eat too much right away."

One of the men reappeared holding a stuffed garbage bag. "We got a jacket with a wallet and passport and clothes that were on the bed and in the closet."

"Okay. Haley will send us anything else."

The linemen climbed in the front seats. The van slowly backed down the driveway.

Andrea sat beside him and rarely spoke. Glowing dashboard lights softly illuminated her graceful profile. Occasionally she stroked his forehead sending shivers down his neck. The van slowed sometimes, stopped altogether once in a while—presumably city driving—and then sped up and moved smoothly at a relatively constant speed. At one point she said quietly, "I have no right to interfere. Will you ever forgive me?"

"Not for as long as I live..."

"Hopefully not for many, many years then." She leaned against the back of the front passenger seat and stretched her legs out.

Josh figured he must have suffered a stroke because the men chattered in a strange language he never heard before. Classic rock played on the radio. Endless kilometers slipped past unnoticed in the night. He became fidgety, craving more soup but, for some reason, he thought it best to remain quiet. He didn't ask where they were going. It didn't really matter.

Sprawling over the side of a sagging rubber life raft, he stabbed with a crude spear at mahi-mahi bumping where the barnacle-encrusted bottom protruded from the weight of his toothpick legs. Adrift for weeks, the scorching sun had baked his skin brown and leathery. Boils caused by constant exposure to salt water covered his feet and legs. Leaping fourteen kilogram mahi-mahi landing on their sides splashed seawater into the raft. He jabbed again at the colorful mirages streaking past in the clear blue. Too weak to hold on, the spear slipped from his grip and, like a falling leaf on an autumn day, silently sank shrinking to the size of a pin. It turned black and steadily grew larger. He seized the sides of the flimsy raft. The sperm whale surfaced beneath, lifting the raft; thunder without lightning bellowed and torrential rainfall washed away the merciless sun. Wearing a black wet suit, Andrea raced down the whale's back and leapt fearlessly into the water tackling a monster mahi-mahi. Grinning smugly, she climbed on the whale's pectoral fin and tossed the thrashing fish in the raft. He pounced, severing the fish's spine with a knife. The raw flesh tasted somewhat like tuna. Eyeballs cracked when he bit into them squirting fluid against the back of his throat. He slurped up fatty globs surrounding the spinal cord. Partially digested flying fish in the mahi-mahi's stomach were a bonus treat—

The van slowed and the road became bumpy. Small rocks crunched under the wheels; several ricocheted with a clang off the undercarriage. Gravel, he presumed. How will he explain his sudden disappearance? Who cares? No one will notice. He had no family. *Maybe I won't have to pay income tax for the rest of my life.*

Tree branches brushed against the van as it crawled uphill with high beams on along a narrow winding road toward several lights flickering through the forest. Out the vehicle's rear windows, pitch-black swallowed the road and trees behind.

The van braked directly in front of the house. Andrea jogged up wooden stairs to a poorly lit screen-covered porch. Moths battered against the dim bulb hanging above the front door. Mosquitoes buzzed around her head.

Patiently waiting, William stood from the couch on the porch and, cane in hand, shuffled toward her. Deep creases riddled an ancient face. Gold-rimmed bifocal glasses sunk into puffy cheeks. A white goatee surrounded a mouth containing few teeth. He wore his long, white hair in a style similar to Andrea's—pulled back in a ponytail.

She opened the rickety metal door. They hugged.

Supporting each arm, the men carried Josh, his feet barely touching the creaky stairs.

William nodded at him. "Kwey, William nidijinikàz."

Josh babbled incoherently through the kitchen and down the hall. The plywood floor groaned under the weight of the men. A skinny black cat Andrea didn't recognize rubbed against her leg before jumping into the living room.

She was surprised they took Josh to Wilfred's bedroom instead of the empty room upstairs. They lay him on a metal-framed double bed covered by a heavy, gray hand-knit blanket. Above, a dream catcher hanging from the ceiling twirled like a mobile. The room was sparsely furnished with simple wooden furniture: a small dresser supporting a mirror, a chair on which stood a coal oil lamp, and a table with a pitcher of water and wash basin. The closet had no door; inside a brown jacket and matching pants hung from wire hangers. A pair of leather high-top shoes lay on the wooden floor beneath the clothes. A heart-wrenching sadness lingered in the musty air.

William fluffed a white pillow and stuffed it under Josh's head. "As your body weakens, your spirit grows stronger." He lifted Josh's feet to smooth the blanket underneath. "What's the creator saying to you now?"

"More soup," Josh mumbled.

To no one in particular, William asked, "How much soup did he have?"

"Very little," Andrea said.

"Give him more."

She hurried outside to the van and found the thermos under the seat. She filled the thermos cup halfway and, sitting on the bed, spoon-fed Josh. It was truly wonderful he craved more. He wanted to live! She stroked his cheek, feeling much more at ease now. Although he may never appreciate it, she had given him the most important gift, what she treasured most.

"Where am I?" he whispered when William left the room.

"You're safe here."

"Where's here?"

"Kitigan Zibi." She wiped the corners of his mouth with her thumb.

He didn't understand.

"It's an Algonquin Nation community in Quebec about two hours north of Ottawa."

William returned with a wooden tray carrying an abalone shell, two brown eagle feathers, and a tightly wound bundle of some sort of plant material the size of a banana. One of the men closed the door and held the tray. Standing in the middle of the room, William struck a match and held the flame against the bundle in the shell. Wisps of smoke curled upward. Chanting, he fanned the smoke with a feather. The odor of burnt sage filled the room. The warm, soothing smoke temporarily purified the stale air of sadness.

He leaned close to Josh. "Do you believe your strength will return?"

Josh nodded.

"Good, then it will." He sprinkled ash from the shell on the floor in the doorway.

For five days Josh ate only fish soup, with portions becoming progressively bigger every day. It was the perfect food, he eventually concluded—delicious, packed full of nutrients, and easy to digest. Far less appealing was the bitter tea-like beverage William sometimes urged him to drink. Josh suffered intense stomach cramps; however, they expected this considering how foreign solid food had become to his emaciated body. A nasty bout of diarrhea—his first bowel movement in sixteen days—alleviated some concern about how well his colon and intestines were functioning.

Satellite television in the living room blared continuously every day, loud enough to be heard in most rooms. His disappearance made for juicy tabloid news and proved to be highly effective—maybe more than his death would have—at bringing attention to his cause. Many news channels discussed the protests at Parliament Hill and anthropogenic dangers to the ocean. But mostly they endlessly speculated about his abrupt disappearance. Conspiracy theories grew in number and ridiculousness: the Canadian government killed him; American corporations kidnapped him; or (his favorite) he was an alien who got fed up with silly Earth and decided to return home.

Andrea remained faithfully by his side until she departed for the West Coast. She was noncommittal about when they would see each other again considering she had been separated from Sarah for over a month. William happily assumed responsibility for his care and soon a fishy diet expanded to include mashed fruits and vegetables. The kindly old man often stayed for meals since they ate the same types of food. He had a lifetime of fascinating stories to entertain Josh with and they quickly became good friends.

On day eleven, Josh ventured for the first time outside further than the couch on the porch. A mature forest insulated the house from the rest of the world. The house itself was a scar on a beautiful face—an unimaginative rectangle with pale yellow walls and brown roof. The screen porch, where he spent most afternoons, extended the entire length along the front of the house.

He walked downhill along the gravel road among towering pine trees. Cheerful songs from many unseen birds sang above a distant gurgling stream. After a minute or two he started breathing hard so he stopped, fearful of the uphill grind back to the house. Bent over, hands on his knees, he rested to catch his breath. He wondered how this 'pine forest island in an ocean of humanity' had managed to escape the gnashing teeth of chain saws. Although wonderful on one level, he believed tiny Nature pockets like this one were essentially dangerous because they created an illusion that people were adequately protecting biodiversity. Loss of biodiversity on a global scale from activities such as logging, fishing, hunting, agriculture, and urban development had occurred frenetically since the nineteen-fifties. Sarah and the baby sperm whale will, unfortunately, witness during their lifetimes the disappearance of rainforests, coral reefs, and most species.

He ambled around to the back of the house and rested on weed-filled grass in a sunny spot near a rusting antique tractor. The warm sun was a welcome change from the shady, cool house. He spied the small curtained window to his room among five others on the peeling, yellow wall. Why were windows on houses square and portholes on boats round? Somehow round windows seemed more elegant. Whose room was he staying in? There, time had essentially stopped. The rest of the house, although plain, was much more modern. William never mentioned anyone. The room seemed strangely old-fashioned, yet quite clean—it wasn't neglected—similar in some ways to his gracious host who appeared to live alone with several outdoor cats that came and went as they pleased.

The West Coast... Josh did the math in his head. Must be three hours behind. Andrea and Sarah were probably just getting up. Maybe they'll be spending the day at the beach. He wondered how often she talks to Roy. Does he have any idea what he lost? *You didn't, you big dummy.*

William appeared carrying two intricately carved walking sticks. "Kichi-minogìjgad na. Come walk with me?" He offered one stick to him.

Although fairly comfortable, Josh couldn't refuse William anything so he followed his friend past a fire pit circled with stones, and a partially collapsed wooden shed, to a trail leading into the forest. A startled robin hopping along the path dropped a caterpillar and flew into the trees.

William frequently stopped walking; either he needed to rest or out of consideration for Josh. He lovingly patted the trunk of a tall, thin tree growing next to the trail. "Forests used to cover our territory. They sheltered animals we hunted for survival. Newcomers cleared our forests like they cleared the grasslands and killed the buffalo. We still suffer from this loss as do our brothers on the plains. All First Peoples know"—he tapped his chest with his knuckles—"how it feels to lose the resources we need for survival, to lose our way of life, our identity." He squinted at something off the trail. "We live far from the ocean, but it is great and powerful and part of the circle of life. We must treat it with respect, no different from that wolf."

"Where!?"

William pointed a crooked finger. "That's a relative of mine. So is this tree. I'm surrounded by my ancestors. I'm never alone. They will help me if I ask."

They followed the trail to a stream and walked along the grassy bank to where the stream slowed and widened into a weedy pond. A thin layer of green scum covered the surface in places.

William knelt and, using both hands, picked up a black boulder. "You are this rock." Stumbling forward without his walking stick, he heaved it into the pond creating a big splash a meter from shore. "You make a wave, yes, but it takes most of your energy, it's imprecise and disruptive, which most people don't like. Better to be a pebble." He gathered a handful and tossed them one by one in different directions, some near, others far. "Gather many pebbles and make ripples in many places, be strategic and persistent, never let them forget."

Josh pointed at his own temple. "There's a big rock in here."

Facing him, William placed arthritic hands squarely on his shoulders. "Soon the world will know the pain all First Peoples have experienced when we lose the natural capital we need for survival." He swept his arm in a horizontal semi-circle. "This is a special place with great healing power, but it, too, has become sick."

On the way back to the house, William pointed at several rabbits, a hawk circling above, some beetles and spiders, all his ancestors. At times he stepped off the trail to dig something from the ground or peel bark off a tree.

Struggling to tie closed a pouch hanging from his belt, he said, "The night Andrea brought you here...she feared she was already too late."

Beams of sunlight filtering through the canopy ignited intricate silky orbs suspended above the forest floor. Leaves rustled, birds sang for potential mates, insect wings buzzed. Some kind of weasel, a mink or marten, raced over a rotting log and jumped into the underbrush. Eyes closed, Josh breathed deeply the fresh forest air. If only he could stop time and hold this moment forever. There was absolutely nothing that would suggest billions of people existed beyond their pine forest sanctuary.

"I don't want to live in the future that's coming," he finally said. "I yearn for another unspoiled Earth. This is where I belong."

"So do we. That's why we stand steadfast with you in your crusade." In a surprising clear voice, William sang, "Don't it always seem to go that you don't know what you've got till it's gone—" His jack-o-lantern smile faded and eyes steadied.

Josh joined in and together they sang, "They paved paradise and put up a parking lot."

Days passed delightfully slowly, Josh adjusting easily to life in the Bubble, as he called it. His body weight and strength were gradually increasing, and walking up and down the road evolved into jogging and occasionally sprinting. He surpassed William in eating ability and regularly devoured meat and cheese and wonderful dishes of quinoa, beans, lentils, and eggs. His withered muscles demanded protein and William made sure there was plenty to go around.

On his thirty-fifth birthday Josh jogged most of the way to the pond. Since the sun was high in the sky and air sufficiently warm, he removed his sweats and tee shirt. He marveled how his body had transformed during the past couple months. Noodle legs dangled from pelvic bones poking through skin. He twisted around to check out his flat butt, the first major muscle group to disappear as he starved.

Swimming using the breast stroke allowed him to sneak up on painted turtles sunning themselves on rocks and logs. Today he remained extra vigilant for snapping turtles. He easily caught a poor frog with three hind legs, a limb deformity likely caused by some form of water pollution. He wondered whether artificially high nutrient levels in the water from fertilizers could be promoting excessive algal growth which, in turn, may be harmful to frogs. Sitting on a rock, he scooped a handful of pond water. Minute critters scurried about; like the Titan Atlas he held an entire world in his hands. Remarkable how this very water will eventually find its way to the ocean and some molecules will slosh around in sperm whale blow holes.

Two deer patiently chewing their cuds generously shared a matted grassy area with him. As William had instructed, he pressed his soaking wet body against Mother Earth to invite in the healing properties of soil. Birds flitted in and out of immense pine trees swaying in the summer breeze. Dragonflies performed aerial acrobatics while chasing mosquitoes. The cleansing water, warm sun, calm air, and abundant wildlife filled his soul with a new-found sense of peace and vitality.

A *frawnk* sound drew his attention across the pond where a great blue heron descended through the trees, circled, and then landed among tall grasses. It strode purposely until settling on a prime fishing spot where it stood motionless for several minutes waiting to strike at young pike or bass. The bird's graceful long legs, grayish-blue plumage on its back, and slender curvy neck somehow reminded him of Diane. He smiled, remembering how they once enjoyed an afternoon eating ice cream and watching a nesting colony of herons at a park in Victoria.

The heron hopped a couple of steps and took flight. A gray blur jumped over a fallen tree and disappeared in the grass. Josh quickly rose to his knees. It was too big to be a dog. The wolf, silvery gray and nearly black along the back and tail, emerged near the water's edge, head low, nose to the ground. A gray face with sharp, yellow eyes turned in his direction. No sign of the rest of the pack. He could hear the wolf lapping pond water and grass blades rustling behind it. A fuzzy, white pup with lanky legs and oversized paws jumped on her back and nipped at her ears. She lay down and nuzzled the pup, sometimes gently biting its legs. His fear dissipated as Mother and pup seemed to be alone and playfully snuggled and drank water. It seemed they all had come to the pond for the same reason.

He sat cross-legged like Andrea and cleaned his teeth with a stiff piece of grass. He hadn't spoken to her for days. She was probably already back in Texas settling into the summer routine. *She saved your life, man. She values your life more than you do.* The pup bounced up and down chasing something. He squinted. Maybe a butterfly. He recalled Sarah ecstatically jumping around when the whales surfaced. Does she know what Roy did? Are they close? He stretched back on his elbows and tilted his face up enjoying the hot sun on his body. Over time he had learned not to think too much about his old man.

The wolves vanished. He stood and gazed about the grassy clearing. The deer were gone too. He seemed to be alone. The brook flowing from the pond bubbled and gurgled. He physically ached for her. He trusted no one more. *Make yourself worthy of her.*

"Helllooo there, Josh."

Adrenaline crackled through his body like a million pinpricks. "Over here!" Quickly he wrestled sweat pants on. Like solar radiation, joy penetrated every cell in his body.

Andrea, wearing shorts and a snug white tee shirt, walked into the clearing. She raised her arms. "Surprise!" She ran over. "Happy birthday old fella."

He hugged her firmly, lifting her off the ground. "I'm so glad you're back." He buried his face in her neck.

Without hesitation they kissed, tongues exploring mouths. Together they sank down on the warm grass.

She abruptly stood straddling him and reached for his hand. "Get up."

Frantically he searched for a pack of snarling wolves. About five meters away a black bear was standing upright on his hind legs sniffing the air. "I hate Nature," he mumbled. Quietly he slipped on shoes without socks.

In a low voice, Andrea said, "I just have to run faster than you. Hopefully you're still weak."

"Not much meat here. You're pretty tasty though."

Side-by-side they backed away from the bear all the while looking down in a submissive non-threatening manner. Andrea spoke calmly to the bear about various kinds of berries his West Coast cousins like to eat. Fortunately the bear seemed more interested in drinking than eating.

Once in the forest and out of sight from the bear, she tried to trip him and then ran ahead along the trail. He sprinted after her for a short distance until laughing too hard forced him to walk.

She wrapped her arm around his waist. "Such a beautiful place. Blacky seems to like it too."

Feeling flushed, he pressed a fingertip at random spots on his pink arms and shoulders. He had burned quite a bit this afternoon. "Hopefully we can go back tomorrow."

The smell of dinner cooking on the barbeque wafted along the trail. Andrea stopped behind a tree near the shed. Sarah was skipping around waving a plastic stick that produced soapy bubbles.

"Your birthday present," Andrea said.

He smiled and kissed her cheek. "I can't think of anything better."

Rainbow-brushed spheres floated haphazardly around the yard popping where ever they touched grass. Sarah crept up behind William while he adjusted the temperature on the barbeque and blew a string of bubbles into the back of his head. Giggling, she ran to the tractor and tried turning the rusty steering wheel.

Josh hesitated, wondering whether he should ask. "So how do you know William? Why did you bring me *here*?"

"He didn't tell you?"

"No, I meant to ask him…something about it didn't feel right."

Andrea held his arm tightly, never taking her eyes off Sarah. "My grandfather and William were good friends. I came for a visit when I was a teenager."

"Whose room am I in?"

"Wilfred's…William's son."

"What happened?"

She hugged him. With a cheek pressed against his chest, she said, "One day Wilfred vanished from this place. Nobody's seen or heard from him since."

"How old was he?"

"Eleven, I think. Now he'd be about the same age as my dad."

Josh wondered whether a bear or wolves had eaten him and all the incriminating evidence.

"Wilfred's disappearance has consumed most of William's life," Andrea whispered. "He'll never stop searching and waiting. Poor man."

Josh swallowed hard. Sympathy for everyone who had prematurely lost someone special overwhelmed his heart. How could he, even for a split second, have deliberately wanted to vanish from Sarah's life? *What a selfish, reckless fool I am.*

Grasping Andrea's hand, he walked with her into the yard. Sarah jumped off the tractor and ran to them. All three embraced, arm in arm.

Josh strolled over to the barbeque and shook William's hand. "Thank you, my friend, for treating me like family."

William simply nodded and flipped the mushrooms on the grill.

EPILOGUE

"My name is Sarah Megin and I would like to talk to you about changes I've seen throughout my life. I am considered to be an elder now because the years have taught me wisdom and patience."

"Please speak up," someone called out.

Illuminated by ceiling lights, she stood at center stage, both hands out front rigidly holding several pieces of paper. She glanced nervously at the audience. A long pause followed as she searched through the notes.

"Sixty years ago a group of scientists tried to raise awareness about the impacts of climate change on the ocean. Unfortunately few people listened to their warnings and now the ocean and Earth are gravely ill. Happiness I once knew as a child has been replaced by sadness and fear."

She turned the page over. A light gust nearly blew the paper from her hands.

"The ocean is warmer now than when I was a girl. Most cold water corals in British Columbia have died. There are no living tropical coral reefs in the Caribbean anymore and only about ten percent of reefs in the Indian Ocean and Australia are healthy and not bleached white and dying. Coral reefs are to the ocean what rainforests are to land; they provide invaluable habitat for many species, most of which are important to people."

"The ocean is more acidic too and this has also contributed to killing most of the world's coral reefs. As well, those animals and plants with hard body parts like scallops, mollusks, lobsters, crabs, marine snails, and certain types of plankton are now rare. They were important food for many species."

"Otters got all the crabs," an old man shouted.

"Changing ocean currents have altered distributions of phytoplankton communities and decreased primary production. Distributions and abundances of many fish have also changed, creating havoc in most fisheries. We have seen mass mortalities in bottom communities along the West Coast because water layers are mixing less, causing less oxygen to be delivered down deep. Ocean currents tremendously influence climate because they act like conveyor belts that redistribute heat around the world. I'm sure you all know the Gulf Stream no longer brings warm water and weather to many European countries. The French are now colder than ever."

Several people snickered.

"Weather is much more extreme now. Where I live heavy rains are common, but relentless droughts and fires in the American Southwest and Canada's interior have severely hurt North American food production." She took a deep breath. "Nearly all ice in Polar Regions has melted and there hasn't been summer ice for many years. Polar ecosystems are far less productive today because ice is important for algae and krill and these are the basic food for most animals. Ice used to be important habitat for seabirds and mammals like penguins and polar bears. Shipping, oil and gas extraction, and commercial fishing in the Arctic have devastated a once-pristine environment. As ice caps and glaciers in Greenland and Antarctica have melted, and seawater expands as it warms, sea level has risen forcing about one billion people, most of them poor, away from low-lying coastal areas. Critical habitats such as corals, mangroves, sea grasses, salt marshes, and oyster beds have drowned and most nesting sea turtle beaches are no longer usable."

"Climate change isn't the only culprit. It combined with overfishing, pollution, eutrophic..."

She had struggled with this word when practicing earlier.

"Eutrophication and increased ultraviolet light have severely impaired the ocean's ability to support life, which is why global fisheries have collapsed and marine biodiversity is at its lowest level in seventy million years."

"Our decisions and actions in the last two hundred years have created the sixth great extinction event in Earth's history. By killing the ocean, hundreds of millions of people no longer have enough food. Our quality of life has deteriorated and unemployment is high, and this has created social unrest and supported the rise of violent extreme ideo...ideo...logical groups. There are many more conflicts between nations as they battle for scarce resources. This is why I chose not to marry and have children—because I didn't want my children to suffer in this world we are destroying."

"Poor baby!" Auntie Mary sang out.

"Sixty years ago we were at a crossroads and we chose what seemed at the time to be the easy road. Ironically, it turned out to be the hard road and now all humanity is paying dearly for those short-sighted decisions. If you had the opportunity to go back in time and change something, what would you do differently?"

She lifted the bottom of her blue dress and curtsied the way Randi had taught her. The crowd, mostly cousins and friends, stood and clapped loudly. She jumped proudly off the stage.

Andrea gave her a warm hug. "You read it perfectly."

"Now we just have to dress you up like an old lady and no one will know the difference," Josh said.

Josh left Andrea and Sarah to talk with family and wandered outside the school's gymnasium with Andrea's father, a sinewy man with wire straight, black hair and deeply set brown eyes. Stepping around pot holes filled with rainwater, they strolled along a gravel road past a grassy field with a paved basketball court. It had been drizzling on and off for three days, ever since Josh arrived. He crossed his fingers tomorrow would be sunny.

Frank stopped and picked a handful of yellow salmonberries growing on thorny bushes along the side of the road. "You two are doing a wonderful thing. I'm proud of both of you."

"You raised an incredible woman."

"Andrea's always been special. The second she was born I knew there must be a good reason." Deep creases zigzagged out from corners of his eyes when he smiled. "She used to have a toy microscope and loved to look at all the critters in drops of seawater. She would always let them go by washing the slides in the Cove."

They walked past a white bungalow with a red cross in the window. Across the road the wall of vegetation thinned to reveal a sheltered bay at the heart of the community. The road merged with another at a rickety cedar wharf just wide enough for one of the few vehicles in the village to drive down to meet the water taxis or float plane.

Part way along the wharf they leaned against the rough wooden railing. Fishing boats of all sizes and shapes tightly filled fingers in half the bay. Several wrecks lay on their sides on the beach. Across the bay near the grocery store a gang of naked squealing children were jumping off a platform with a slide.

"Sarah's right." Frank gestured at the boats tied against one another. "They never used to be here, especially in the summer. They'd be out fishing salmon and halibut, feeding their families. Now you have to go all the way to Alaska to catch a salmon. There's nothing here anymore except mackerel and squid." He pointed at a break in the trees where distant Coast Mountains peeked through. "I haven't seen snow on those mountains for twenty years. You see, not one has a white top." His gaze dropped beneath the wharf to the gravel shore fringing the bay. "And I hardly recognize our beaches. Josh, you wouldn't believe it. Littlenecks have been pushed aside by a bunch of other clams and even they have to fight all the crabs and worms and seaweed that have shown up." Frowning, he turned to face him. "Change can be good or bad, but the changes we see around here all seem bad and only hurt us."

"I sympathize, Frank. That's why we're trying to get the word out. The conference we're going to next week is pretty big with an international audience."

Frank turned his back to the bay. "Don't mind me, I'm just a rambling old man."

"Hardly." Josh placed a reassuring hand on his shoulder. "Your people are intimately connected to Nature. You see these changes and recognize their importance. Others have no idea. Indigenous Peoples should use whatever legal powers they have to protect the environment, for all our sakes."

"Maybe this is our destiny now. Somebody has to step up."

"You're a wise elder just like Sarah."

Frank grinned, his white teeth sparkling. "She's such a cutie. How's she holding up? Tomorrow's a big day."

The Cove was a special place of spiritual significance for Andrea and her people. During low tide one could walk into the Cove by skirting rocky headlands on either side. During high tide the Cove could only be reached by boat or winding trail through dense rainforest behind. Andrea loved coming here when she was a girl, first with her dad and grandfather, then with Laura or simply by herself. The Cove naturally became one of Sundrop's favorite places too.

Stagnant North Pacific waters sparkled under the late morning sun. As the tide gently receded, golden rockweed lay down and smothered exposed cobble, and clusters of purple ochre sea stars huddled to avoid desiccation. Last night the tide had reached mid beach, evident by the wavy line of kelp and woody debris deposited across the brown sand. Sun-bleached white horse clam shells the size of dinner plates speckled the beach. Today the summer breeze struggled to reach into the Cove; the group gathered near the water's edge found the warm, muggy air stifling.

Andrea stood facing Josh, holding his hands. Her slender white evening dress showed off her athletic figure. On her head sat a woven garland of delicate white flowers she had picked yesterday afternoon in a marsh near the village. Today she was almost unrecognizable; her cousin Martha, a professional hair stylist, had liberated her ponytail. After growing for nearly two years, her hair now brushed the small of her back, completely covering Thunderbird. Layers of foundation, mascara, and eyeliner smothered her natural look.

The white pants and long sleeve shirt Josh wore glowed brilliantly in the sun. A teal sash complimented the all-white ensemble. The corsage pinned near his heart was a cluster of small flowers with green petals and yellow centers cut from a male Jojoba plant growing in California. He had explained how this desert plant saved sperm whales from extinction when people discovered the waxy oil in its fruit could replace sperm oil.

He was dangerously handsome today, like when he first stepped off the helicopter on the *Rubicola*. It took seven months to gain back the nineteen kilograms he had lost during the hunger strike. Ironically he looked younger—softer somehow—even though several more creases had appeared on his forehead and around his eyes. She figured all the tension he used to drag around had finally disappeared.

Standing next to her, a radiant Sundrop wearing a pretty red dress carefully held empty ring boxes. Immediate family, plenty of cousins, and Peter stood in a semi-circle around them.

A slight, energetic balding man with a pink nose, not from the sun but from his love for spirits, had agreed to perform the ceremony for a small fee and the promise of a free seafood dinner. Father Dempsey patiently waited for an answer.

"I definitely do," Josh said, looking into Andrea's eyes.

"And do you, Andrea Dawn Megin, take this man, Josh Scott Templeton, to be your lawfully wedded husband?"

"Hmm, well I guess I should since we're all here..." She paused. "Of course I do." She chuckled at his sheepish expression.

"By the power vested in me I pronounce you wife and husband." Father Dempsey nodded to her. "You may now kiss the groom."

"Just a personal touch," she whispered to Josh.

They threw their arms around each other and kissed. Firmly holding her, he bent low and then stumbled forward.

She screeched.

He recovered and pulled her upright again. "Oh, my knee."

"Yah, right. You did that on purpose."

He picked up Sundrop and kissed her cheek. "I can't wait to come to your wedding."

She scrunched her nose. "Boys are yucky."

"Yuckier than fish eyeballs?"

"Yep!"

They hugged and mingled with their guests. Frank opened several coolers filled with jugs of homemade punch. The real celebration wouldn't start until evening in the school gym where the entire community will feast on farmed salmon and shellfish.

Andrea led Josh over driftwood piled in the high intertidal, through a shady tunnel in salal bushes, and along a worn path she knew by heart that eventually emerged on the rocky headland that separated the Cove from the main beach fronting the village. High above, near the top of an old cedar tree, an abandoned bald eagle's nest still reminded the community something sinister was happening to the ocean. Mates for life, the pair of bald eagles had watched over the Cove for sixteen years until their sudden disappearance last year, about the same time when humpback whale sightings dropped precipitously. Villagers believed she starved and he died of a broken heart.

They waved at family and friends below who cheered heartily. Front beach stretched for a kilometer and a half. Out in the channel where winds blow in from the open ocean, a massive gray propeller on a tall wind turbine silently rotated. Sometimes light flashed on roofs of peeling, dilapidated houses as newly installed solar panels reflected the sun's rays.

"Welcome to the future," Josh said.

"We're almost completely off the grid," Andrea said, proudly. "We'll be carbon neutral by this time next year."

"Thanks to you."

"We're developing real expertise in our community about renewable energy. We see many terrific business opportunities."

She stepped closer to the edge of the rock pile and looked down at the green pool shimmering several meters below. One day, she had promised herself many years ago, she would finally make this jump. On one extraordinary day...

"I need to wash this crap off my face," she said.

"White and water can be very revealing, you know."

She shrugged. "We're all family here."

"You might give Peter a jammer."

She laughed. "Poor man. Three weeks with us on the *Blue Wanderer*... I don't know." She pulled him close. "Are you ready Mr. Megin-Templeton to take the plunge with me?"

He held her hands. "Your call changed my life. I can't thank you enough."

"You should thank the bull, not me."

"I want you to know how much I love you. I can't imagine what my life would've been like if I hadn't met you."

"Josh, I—"

He touched a finger to her lips. "Please listen... alright? Let me say this. You mean everything to me. I promise you, today, I won't take you for granted. I'll never forget how important you are. I'll spend the rest of my life loving you with all my heart. I'll worship you for all our days together. And I'll never forget what I've said today, I promise."

Tears filled her eyes. "You better not." She almost started crying. "Josh, you're the man I dreamed of spending my life with." She tenderly stroked his cheek. "I love you."

He gently brushed a few strands of hair away from her eyes. "I'm ready to take the plunge now, Mrs. Templeton-Megin."

They kicked off their sandals.

"One, two, three!"

With eyes wide open, they stepped off the rocky ledge together into a dying world where unknown dangers and pain lurk, where joy is still attainable if one so believes, where unimaginable beauty abounds, and where time is limited.

www.ingramcontent.com/pod-product-compliance
Ingram Content Group UK Ltd.
Pitfield, Milton Keynes, MK11 3LW, UK
UKHW041630190726
13854UKWH00006B/2409

9 781773 705811